A Wicked Proposition

She drew back from him, staring up into his face. He was gazing intently at her, his eyes sparking with passion, his mouth wet from her kiss.

"That was even better than I'd thought it might be," she admitted.

"So you've been imagining this?" His voice was ragged.

"Yes, of course," she replied.

"And how was it?" he asked.

It was tremendous.

"You know how it was." She took a deep breath. Reminding her, as she inhaled, that his fingers were still on her breast.

"It was." He paused. "What do you propose we do about it?"

She lifted her chin, meeting his gaze forthrightly. "I propose that we have an affair."

By Megan Frampton

MEGAN FRAMPTON

NEVER A BRIDE

A DUKE'S DAUGHTERS NOVEL

AVONBOOKS

An Imprint of HarperCollinsPublishers

NEVER A BRIDE. Copyright © 2019 by Megan Frampton. All rights reserved. Printed in the United States of America. No part of this book may be used or reproduced in any manner whatsoever without written permission except in the case of brief quotations embodied in critical articles and reviews. For information, address HarperCollins Publishers, 195 Broadway, New York, NY 10007.

First Avon Books mass market printing: May 2019

Print Edition ISBN: 978-0-06-286740-7
Digital Edition ISBN: 978-0-06-286741-4

Cover illustration by Gregg Gulbronson
Cover photographs by Shirley Green

Avon, Avon & logo, and Avon Books & logo are registered trademarks of HarperCollins Publishers in the United States of America and other countries.

HarperCollins is a registered trademark of HarperCollins Publishers in the United States of America and other countries.

FIRST EDITION

19 20 21 22 23   QGM   10 9 8 7 6 5 4 3 2 1

*To all the exuberantly tall men
in the Frampton Admiration Queue.
Thank you for the inspiration.*

NEVER A BRIDE

Report from Africa

The HMS Albert, steam-sloop, Captain Griffith Davies, captured a valuable slaver, based in Brazil, off the coast of Monrovia on February 17 of this year. The slaver attempted to evade its captors through nefarious deception, but the brave and courageous sailors aboard the man-of-war noticed the ship's suspicious activity and boarded after exchanging a volley of shots. None of the British crew was wounded, although two of the slaver's sailors were slightly wounded. Captain Davies and his crew liberated the men on board and brought the ship's captain and crew to the Brazilian authorities in Monrovia for judgment. It remains to be seen if the British authorities will reprimand Captain Davies as he did not follow proper procedure.

Chapter 1

April 4, 1851
London, The Mermaid's Arms, a not-so-respectable
pub on the dock serving mediocre porter.

$\mathscr{I}$ think we should get some more ale," Griffith
said to his first mate, Clark, as he downed the
rest of his drink. *"That's* proper procedure," he
snorted ruefully.

Proper procedure in this pub meant that he would
get more beer. But proper procedure, at least according to Her Majesty's government, meant
that innocent people would likely die, caught in
the conflict between nations. Proper procedure
meant that women and children would live in a
ship's hold for months, with meager provisions
and unsanitary living circumstances.

So he'd acted improperly, according to the naval authorities. It smarted, being told he'd done
wrong. But he had acted entirely properly when
it came to Griffith's own law, which demanded

that people be free to live as they wish, not kept in captivity.

It was one of the many reasons, and the most altruistic, that he'd run off to sea when he was sixteen—he'd seen the inequity of his family's situation, that they were blessed with wealth and land and power, and the families that worked for them were entirely dependent on their largesse. He would not stand by and benefit merely because of the lucky circumstance of his birth. Especially if he could do something about other people's unlucky circumstances. That he would eventually have to claim his duties because of his lineage was a truth he refused to acknowledge.

Also there was the fact that he and his parents had not agreed on anything. They wanted him to follow in the footsteps of all the Davies sons before him, which meant getting the best education and then forgetting entirely about it since it wasn't seemly to appear too intelligent.

Not that Griffith believed himself to be too intelligent—school had been difficult for him. He wanted to be outside all the time, moving his body rather than sitting in a wooden chair for hours.

Although after several months at sea, this chair in the pub felt quite comfortable.

"Clark?" he said again. "Another drink?"

Clark did not answer. Likely because Clark had already had enough and was currently sleeping on the table.

"More!" Griffith called as he downed the rest of his drink. One of the barmaids nodded.

"Excellent service, don't you think?" Griffith asked Clark. "Very proper procedure," he couldn't help but add in a low aside.

Clark snored softly in reply. Not even appreciating Griffith's wit.

Griffith shrugged, adjusting Clark's head so he was lying more comfortably. That was one of the secrets behind being a well-respected captain: making certain your crew was taken care of.

He'd taken such good care of Clark that his mate was getting some well-deserved rest. Albeit in a pub, his nose pressed against a wooden table.

He didn't see the point of being sober either if he was on land, but unfortunately it took a lot for him to get drunk, since he was so large—he towered over everyone on his crew and couldn't get comfortable below deck. His jackets always felt a bit snug too, since it seemed tailors did not actually believe that a person's shoulders could be as wide as Griffith's.

The curse of the Davies family.

The barmaid placed another glass on the worn wooden table in front of him. "You need one for your friend here?" she asked.

Griffith shook his head no and tossed a few coins to her, which she caught handily. "Thank you," he said as he took a long draught. The porter was fair to middling at best, but it was *beer*, so that made it all right.

They usually ran out of beer aboard the ship sometime around the second month of the voyage, and this most recent voyage had been over ten months. Too long without alcohol. Or a woman, to be honest.

He did feel slightly fuzzy around the edges, which was good. It also had the benefit of disguising the quality of the alcohol. And the lack of female companionship.

He might've attempted some sort of discourse with one of the barmaids, but several ships had docked in London this week, it seemed, so the pub was full to bursting, and the women were scurrying about with no time for flirtation.

And, while he'd engaged in anonymous couplings in the past, he found the idea distasteful now. He wanted something more, although he had no hope of finding more for the short time they were ashore. So he'd resigned himself to looking—discreetly, so as not to cause distress—and consoling himself with beer and sleeping in a bed long enough for him to stretch his entire body out.

That was heaven for him. Even if it was a solitary heaven.

Plus there was Clark to consider—it would be downright rude to leave his first mate here alone.

Even if Clark was currently unconscious, so perhaps not the best company.

"It's you and me, love," he said to the glass, which was already nearly empty.

He, Clark, and his crew had made shore only that morning, and after filing the ship's paperwork with the authorities, he had told his crew to do whatever they wanted until he sent word they were needed. He presumed they were scattered around London, doing exactly what he was doing, give or take a few ales and women.

Or, like Clark here, getting some well-deserved rest.

He took the last pull from his glass as he saw the door to the pub open. His mouth dropped open as he saw who had walked in—not that he knew the lady, how could he? Just that she looked like a glorious angel, a vibrant, dark-haired woman wearing a dark cloak of excellent quality. The glimpse he got of her face indicated she was truly stunning. And was entirely out of place in this dingy dockside pub.

"I wish you were awake for this," Griffith murmured in Clark's direction. "And I'm reconsidering my stance on anonymous couplings. Although she is clearly a lady, so that would not be possible." Too bad, he thought. For him, not for her. He didn't think a lady would wish to have anything to do with someone like him.

Even though, theoretically at least, he was a gentleman.

The female wore an enormous bonnet, making her have to turn her head to glance around her, a newspaper tucked under one arm, while in the other she was brandishing a—a tiny sword? A poker for the fire?

Oh. A *hat pin*. Of course. Because young, beautiful ladies often ventured into disreputable establishments carrying only a newspaper and an accessory.

"The fool," he muttered, shaking his head as he watched her movements. He felt his body tighten in an unconscious protective position. He wished he weren't so determined to rescue anybody who seemed they might need help, but that was what had propelled him thus far, so he supposed it wouldn't stop just because he was off duty. He shrugged, taking another drink as he accepted his own inability to stay uninvolved.

She held the hat pin in front of her, clearly apprehensive. As she should be. The only women in the pub worked here, and they were definitely not ladies. The noise had been growing steadily in the short time he'd been inside. There had even been a few scuffles, although there hadn't been any full-fledged fights. At least not yet. She glanced around, her gaze, from what Griffith could see of it, intent. As though she were looking for someone or something. She picked her way over to the bar, a few tables away from where Griffith sat and Clark slept.

Griffith rose slowly from his chair, now relieved he hadn't had more to drink. This lady had no idea what she was walking into, or she would have at least brought a Derringer pistol.

"Pardon me," he heard her say to one of the barmaids in what was obviously a cultured accent, as though her clothing didn't give her status away. She wasn't able to finish her sentence, however, mostly because the barmaid she'd inquired of was too busy handing out the ales at the other end of the bar.

The noise in the room began to subside, as the occupants heard and saw the newest arrival. A lady in this disreputable bar would rouse the most determined sailor from his ale. Griffith grimaced as he heard the low hum of talk that wasn't the rowdy conviviality of a few moments earlier. This conversation held a tone of suspicion and interest, both of which portended trouble for her. After all, she was clearly an interloper trespassing on their domain.

Damn it. It seemed likely he would have to interfere.

"Who's this, then?" The voice came from behind Griffith, and he turned, seeing the man wobble up to his feet, a predatory tone in his voice.

It wasn't one of Griffith's shipmen, unfortunately. If it were, he could command him to sit back down. To ignore one of Griffith's direct commands meant immediate dismissal.

"I am looking for someone," the lady said, raising her chin—and her hat pin—as she turned away from the bar to face the man.

The man walked toward the bar, a lewd grin on his face. "Looking for me I'd say. How about we grab a drink and get to know each other? I've always wanted to have a la—" But he stopped speaking as she raised her arm and stuck the hat pin into the man's chest, making him yelp as he took a few steps backward.

Well. He had to applaud her response time, even if her response itself was bound to cause even more trouble than just appearing in the pub in the first place.

"I am looking for someone," she repeated, punctuating each word with a poke as the man grimaced. "And I suspect it is not you."

Griffith's body tensed as he anticipated how the man, and his companions, would react. She didn't belong here, and they would protect their environment with force, if necessary. Even against a lady.

Sure enough, the man's table companions rose, their postures clearly indicating violence. There were far too many of them to take out just with a chair. He'd have to try diplomacy. He rose from his seat.

And if diplomacy failed, he'd upend a few tables.

"Now, gentlemen," Griffith began, walking toward the scene as he held his hands out in a placating manner, "there's no need to make a fuss, the lady—"

The man grabbed the hat pin and pushed it back toward her, even as she struggled to keep it pinned in him. It must have hurt, Griffith had to admit.

"Stay out of it," the man interrupted without glancing at Griffith.

"I cannot," Griffith said, stepping up and grasping the pin, yanking it out from the man's hand. "I will see to the young lady. There is no need for you to bother yourself any longer." Sometimes there was a benefit to forever championing the underdog in a lopsided fight. Now he could get a better look, see if she was as beautiful as he thought.

The man opened his mouth as though to argue, then looked up—and up—at Griffith's height and obvious strength and apparently thought better of it. He nodded at his companions, all of whom lowered themselves slowly back down into their seats.

Griffith exhaled. It wasn't that he was dreading a fight, but it would be a shame to waste some of his precious free time busting sailors' heads. There was beer to drink after all.

"And who are you?" she asked, turning her gaze to Griffith. Unlike the man, she didn't seem intimidated at all by his size. That was a surprise; most people at least blinked twice when they saw him. Plus, he had just rescued her from an unpleasant situation. The very least he could expect would be some gratitude.

None appeared to be forthcoming.

She was as beautiful as he'd suspected; her dark hair was swept up underneath her hat, a few enticing strands falling down around her face. Her eyes were dark also, with delicate eyebrows that were raised in question. Her nose was perfect, and her mouth—her lips were full and red, and she had a mole to the right of her mouth that seemed—to Griffith, at least—a visual marker for where his own mouth should start kissing her.

"I am your stalwart savior," he said. He gestured toward the table. "Would you care to sit down and have a cup of this pub's finest ale? Which, admittedly, isn't very good. But I promise, the company is superb," he added with a rakish grin.

She glanced toward the table, and Clark, and looked back, a wry expression on her face. "I'm not certain I should, if that is what happens after having some ale. Or is it that you are such a dull conversationalist that he's fallen asleep rather than talk to you?" Her expression was teasing, and he admired how full of aplomb she was, given that she was clearly completely out of her element here. And yet was still holding her own.

"I am an excellent conversationalist. When I am not rescuing damsels in distress—" he began.

"I was not in distress," she interrupted. "Merely impeded by a ruffian in pursuit of my goal. Not the first time that has happened," she added in a rueful tone.

He wanted to know more about that, but he suspected she wasn't the type of lady to reveal her secrets all at once.

"I was doing just fine without you," she continued, crossing her arms over her chest.

In fact, he suspected she would reveal none of her secrets. Which only piqued his curiosity more.

"As I said, pre-ruffian, I am looking for someone," she said, glancing around the pub again, a frown on her lovely face. "Perhaps you can help me find him?"

"I would be happy to." Griffith took his hat off, sweeping low into a bow, as genteel and respectable as he'd been taught so many years ago. "Captain Griffith Davies at your service. What is the gentleman's name?"

Her expression was puzzled, and then it cleared as she whacked him hard on the arm, her mouth opening into a wide smile. He was definitely not expecting that reaction. "You're Lord Viscount Whateverhisname! You're the person I'm after!"

Griffith hadn't heard anyone reference his title in so long he nearly opened his mouth to deny it. Then realized he couldn't, because it was true.

"I am." He sounded as surprised as she looked. "What business do you have with me?" He tried not to sound dismissive, but it was unlikely she wanted him for any good reason. He'd left his title when he'd run off to sea, and he was damned glad not to be that person any longer.

The lady didn't reply, just grabbed his arm and began to walk him toward the door. Or tried to walk him toward the door; when he wanted to, Griffith could be an immovable object.

She turned and pointed at his chest with the hat pin. "Don't make me use this," she said half-jokingly.

"You need to tell me what you want first," Griffith replied, folding his arms over his chest. "And I am sorry to tell you, but a hat pin, no matter how skillfully wielded, is not going to persuade me."

"It's important."

She spoke in an urgent tone, and he couldn't help but believe her, even though he still had no idea what she wanted. Besides, he was entirely intrigued, so he was willing to accommodate whatever she wished.

He softened his expression. "Important, is it? Why didn't you say so? Lead on, Lady Hat Pin."

She nodded, and when she tugged on him now,

he walked with her toward the door. Because why not? It would be an adventure.

They both halted when the door suddenly sprung open.

A phalanx of men poured in, all wearing the garb of the Royal Navy Police.

Griffith did not think they were here for the ale. He positioned himself in front of the lady in an unconscious need to protect her. Was she wanted by the authorities? Was that why she was here, attempting to hide out?

In which case, perhaps he might want to know why she was looking for him in particular. And if that was one of her secrets.

Today was far more interesting than he'd suspected it would be.

"Captain Davies!" one of the policemen said, sweeping his gaze over the pub's occupants. "We need to locate Captain Davies."

"You wish to speak to me?" Griffith said, his tone skeptical. Because while he suspected they weren't here to drink, he hadn't thought they might want him. But perhaps this was the day when everyone came to this pub looking for the former viscount/ current ship captain.

Maybe Queen Victoria herself would show up eventually. And he'd have a word with her about ensuring there was enough beer on board her ships. Not to mention discussing what proper procedure should be.

Two of the men went to either side of him, taking his arms. They did not want him for a polite conversation, then, unless they were determined to have his full attention. For that he could have told them a full pitcher of beer, a large soft chair, and the company of a beautiful, spirited lady could have done just as well.

He glanced from one to the other, considering whether he should shake them off. He could do it, but it would likely just be postponing the inevitable. And he'd hate to wake up Clark, just for something like this.

The man who'd spoken pushed through to step in front of Griffith, his face blanching as he looked up. "You're Captain Davies?"

Griffith bowed, at least as much as he was able to, given that his arms were being held. "At your service. What's this about?"

"You're being arrested by the authority of Her Majesty's Royal Navy. If you'll come with me?"

"As though I have a choice," Griffith muttered. His improper procedure must have drawn the ire of Her Majesty's Navy. He'd like to have a word with Her Majesty even more. It was unfortunate the queen wasn't waltzing into disreputable pubs brandishing hat pins.

He glanced toward the lady who had done just that, nodding in her direction. "We'll have to schedule another time to speak, my lady. As you can see, I am somewhat busy at the moment." He winked as she glanced from him to the officers and back again, a frustrated expression on her face.

"DAMN IT," DELLA fumed as she watched the police escort the gentleman away. She didn't doubt but that he could overcome the policemen—he was certainly muscular enough, and she'd sensed his confidence when he'd stood up for her at the pub. Not that he'd *rescued* her, she hastily amended; he had merely hastened the inevitable conclusion. She had been doing fine by herself. Reminded, she tucked her hat pin back into her pocket, but kept her hand on it in case she needed it.

As she watched the group recede from her view, a part of her wished he would do something to escape. It would certainly be exciting to watch.

The most aggravating part was that he *was* the person she was hunting for: Griffith Davies, Viscount Stanbury, the mysterious nobleman who had turned his back on his aristocratic family and gone to sea. It wasn't his viscountcy she was after; no proper aristocrat would deign to speak to her anyway because of her scandal.

And she was grateful for that, she assured herself.

It was that he was the captain of record for the ship her friend Sarah's husband had been aboard before going missing. He was the only lead they had on where to find Mr. Wattings. And unlike Della, Sarah actually loved her husband, the father of her child.

Della was just relieved that the father of her child had not married her despite his promises, and that he had run away when the couple had run out of money. She would never be swayed by a charming blackguard again. She'd long ago resolved never to get involved, much less married, to anyone again. There was too much risk.

Besides, she didn't lack for family and companionship—Sarah and Della's sisters, whom she'd been reunited with in London after running away to a tiny town called Haltwhistle. Her sister Ida had come to fetch her, and Della had agreed to return, even though Society was certain to blackball her on account of Nora, her illegitimate child.

Haltwhistle was also where she'd met Sarah and her daughter, Emily. *Her family*, even though they weren't related by blood. Sarah also knew just what it felt like to be on her own with a small child.

Sarah had rescued Della when she'd been at her lowest—no money, no food, and holding Nora, who was six months old and crying constantly, in her arms.

Della had never doubted her ability to survive, but in Haltwhistle, abandoned by Mr. Baxter, she'd begun to feel hopeless.

Until Sarah had given her food and a warm

place to sleep. Eventually, Della had shared her story, while Sarah had shared hers.

They'd forged a bond of motherhood, lost love, and a determination to thrive, despite their birth families. Della would do anything for Sarah, and her friend would do anything for her.

So, if Della could possibly find a way to return Mr. Wattings to his wife, she would. And if it meant she had to storm the Navy Police headquarters to speak with Captain Enormous, she would do that also.

She just needed more than a hat pin.

"SARAH!" DELLA CALLED as she burst into the hallway of the small but serviceable London house she shared with her friend, their daughters, and the assortment of people and animal rescues Della and Sarah had already acquired in their short time back in the city Della had grown up in.

The house wasn't close to the luxury she'd been accustomed to when she had lived with her parents, but it had the distinct advantage of not housing either the duke or duchess. Neither of whom wanted to see her. Perhaps the only thing they had in common now.

The house—purchased with help from Della's brothers-in-law, all of whom were besotted with her sisters—was comfortable, from the mismatched chairs in the dining room to the worn rug in the hallway. Neither she nor Sarah had to worry that their daughters would ruin the furniture by playing. The furniture was already well used, and it made for an altogether more relaxing abode.

It wasn't in the most fashionable area of town, of course, but it was convenient to the shops and wherever else the ladies chose to walk. Their neighbors were friendly, but busy, and none of them had raised an eyebrow at seeing the variety of occupants.

That was definitely a refreshing change from what she and Sarah would have expected if they lived in a more fashionable area. Della because of her reputation, and Sarah because of the color of her skin.

Della ran into the dining room, narrowly avoiding a few pairs of discarded shoes, carrying the morning paper. Sarah was seated at the long wooden table, a piece of toast on a plate beside her.

"What is it that has you in such a state?" her friend asked, raising a dark brow. "You bolted as soon as the paper arrived."

Della went to the other side of the table where Sarah sat, laying the paper in front of her and pointing at the news item.

"That's the name of your husband's captain. It isn't the same ship, of course"—*that one capsized, with most of the crew still unaccounted for*, not that she needed to remind Sarah of that—"but the captain is here. In town." She didn't tell Sarah just how impossibly large and handsome he was.

That was not pertinent to the story.

Della put her hand on Sarah's shoulder and squeezed. "He's never been so close, he certainly hasn't answered all those letters we've sent. This is the best opportunity we might ever have to being able to find out for certain." She took a breath. "In fact, I went and found this Griffin person, though I didn't get a chance to ask him about Mr. Wattings's whereabouts."

"Griffith Davies, Viscount Stanbury," Sarah corrected in a soft, faltering voice as she stared down at the paper.

"Viscount Whateverhisnameis," Della said firmly. *Captain Enormous.* "The point is I saw him. And I'll do whatever it takes to speak with him, to find out what happened to Henry."

When she was able to talk her way past the Navy Police desk officer. And persuade the rakish captain to hold off on flirting so he could actually assist her.

Only a minor impediment.

"Della," Sarah began, her voice even softer. She stared up at Della, her eyes wide. "I'd nearly given up hope. If you can find out what happened, that would be . . ." she continued, her gaze unfocused, and then she swayed in her chair and slumped to the side, avoiding falling completely out of her chair because of Della's hand on her shoulder.

Of course Della should have anticipated that Sarah would be overwhelmed by the shock.

She took Sarah's deadweight into her arms, gently sliding her onto the carpet. It had happened before, so it wasn't a complete surprise, but Della felt her heart thudding in her chest. If anything were to happen to Sarah . . .

"Damn it, Della," she said to herself, "you are far too abrupt." Not many people were as resilient as Della was, a fact she frequently forgot.

She settled Sarah on the floor, then rang the bell on the table before plucking Sarah's napkin from the floor and fanning her friend with it.

"You rang, my lady?" Mrs. Borens said a few minutes later as she entered the room. "Oh my lord, Mrs. Wattings," she said, bustling over to kneel at Sarah's feet.

Sarah uttered a moan, and Della leaned into her friend's face, watching anxiously as Sarah's eyes fluttered open.

"Sarah? Are you all right?" Della asked. Her heart was beating so hard and so fast it felt as though it might just emerge from her chest. "I didn't mean to upset you with the news, I just—" She shook her head. "I just got excited."

"You always do," Sarah replied with a slight tilt to her mouth.

Della exhaled and leaned back on her heels,

relief coursing through her at her friend's familiar joking tone. Mrs. Borens patted Sarah's ankle,
took the napkin from Della's hand, and folded it
instinctively.

"It will be too upsetting for you to come with
me. But I need to go right away. I need to speak
with the viscount," Della said, pushing Sarah's
soft hair away from her face. "You can stay here;
the girls will be downstairs soon anyway."

Sarah nodded. "Thank you." She made a vague
gesture in the air. "For everything. I had given
up reading the papers, it was too hard to be disappointed every day."

Della felt her throat close at her friend's sad
tone. Dear Lord, she hoped this captain-viscount
person would have something to tell her.

She took Sarah's hand and squeezed it, meeting
Sarah's gaze. Her friend smiled weakly at her.

"Do you want to get up?" Della asked.

Sarah considered the question. "I think I'd like
to stay down here for a bit."

Della nodded. "You do that." She looked up at
Mrs. Borens. "Can you stay with Mrs. Wattings
as she rests?" She looked back at Sarah. "Do you
want tea?"

"That is all you British people can think about,"
Sarah replied. "It is not as though tea is the cure
to everything."

"But it is," Della said with a smile. "And besides, you were born here too."

Sarah raised her hand toward Della.

"You want to get up so soon?" Della asked.

Sarah wrinkled her nose. "The carpet must have belonged to a family with a dog."

Another reminder that Della was no longer living with her parents—a duke's rug would be beaten regularly, and even if the duke had owned one hundred dogs, they would not have been allowed to do something so vulgar as to make it clear they were in residence.

This covering, however, they'd found on one of their foraging trips when they'd first arrived. Della couldn't bear waste, whether it was worn rugs or people or animals whose families had decided they were unwanted.

Della took Sarah's outstretched hand, helping her friend to rise. She wrapped her arm around Sarah's waist, then sat her back down in her chair.

"Tea?" Della asked again, patting Sarah on the shoulder.

She grinned at Sarah's eye roll.

"I was born here, as you remind me several times a day," Sarah said, sounding more like her usual self, "but I wasn't raised on tea. But we can't get good coffee."

Sarah's parents had come from the West Indies before Sarah was born, but according to Sarah, her parents had maintained their West Indian traditions at home, even though all their children were British-born.

They'd grown up working on and around coffee plantations, and therefore tea was apparently not allowed in their household. They'd arrived in London to improve their situation, and now Sarah's father was the owner of an import company that did a respectable business bringing goods, including coffee, in from the Caribbean. But since Sarah's parents were speaking to Sarah as little as Della's parents were speaking to Della, there was no possibility of obtaining coffee.

Like Della, Sarah had found an unsuitable man to fall in love with. Unlike Della, she had married him, at which time her family had disowned her.

Della nodded. "Fair point. I'm delighted that you are feeling well enough to argue national beverages with me. Stay here with the girls, and I will go hunt down the griffin viscount and see what he might know about Mr. Wattings."

"Thank you," Sarah replied. She stretched her hand out to touch Della's arm. "Thank you," she repeated in a more emotional tone.

Della's throat tightened, and she nodded and rose, smoothing her skirts. She paused at the door, looking back at Sarah, who was watching her go. A pang of hope skewered her heart, and she felt her chest constrict. If she could discover Mr. Wattings's fate—no matter what it was—

Sarah would rest easier. Her friend had suffered so much from not knowing what had happened to her beloved husband. And Della, even though she was a scandalous disgrace, was still a duke's daughter who could get answers where a woman of Caribbean descent, like Sarah, could not.

She just had to be able to ask questions.

Chapter 2

I know he is here. I demand you bring him out and release him."

Griffith opened his eyes slowly, staring up at the ceiling of his cell as he figured out where he was.

Swirls of dirt above him, a small filthy window too high for anybody who wasn't Griffith's size to see through, and marks on the wall.

Right. Naval prison, with charges still to be specified. He wondered if Clark had woken up and wondered where he'd gone. Or just assumed he'd wandered off in search of other pleasures to be found on land.

"He is the Viscount Stanbury. You cannot hold him."

Griffith frowned, swinging his legs over to the floor as he sat up on the bed. The bed was surprisingly comfortable, but that could be because he'd been sleeping in a hammock recently. Other ship captains demanded the captain's berth—hence its name after all—but some of the men had come down with dysentery, and Griffith had insisted the sickest one rest in his cabin.

"Viscount what?" a disgruntled voice replied. "He didn't mention any of that when we brought him in last night. Are you sure it's the same one?"

"Captain Griffith Davies, correct?" the first voice said.

"Yes," the other man replied slowly. "But wouldn't a nob mention he was a nob when we arrested him?"

"Not this nob," the voice replied in a rueful tone. Griffith began to reflexively smile as he recognized who was speaking. Of course it was Robson—the son of the Duke of Northam's steward, he was always the most serious of the Three Musketeers, as Griffith, his cousin Frederick, and Robson called themselves.

And since Griffith was by far the most adventurous of the musketeers, Robson was frequently called upon to talk him out of a difficult situation.

That was close to fifteen years ago. And Robson was still talking Griffith out of a difficult situation.

Some things never changed.

Although Griffith had; he frowned as he considered why the hell Robson was here. He would not return to that life, even if Robson tried to use his skills of persuasion on him. The queen herself might want him to resume being a lord of no fixed purpose, but he'd be damned if he'd ever agree to that. Not until he was the absolute last person that could be called upon. And even then he would have to weigh his own future happiness with what his lineage demanded.

"Griff, where the hell are you?"

Griffith rose, feeling his muscles complaining about having been in the same position all night. Neither they nor he were accustomed to this much stillness. "Down here, Robson." He spoke in a weary, apprehensive tone. He really did not want to have to go against his old friend, especially if said friend was rescuing him from jail, but he would if it meant Robson would try to prevent him from returning to sea.

Griffith heard quick footsteps, then froze when he saw Robson's face. He hadn't spared a thought for Robson, nor anyone he'd left behind, since he'd gone. Likely because it hurt too much to think about who he was missing. But when he saw his friend's familiar face?

All the feelings came rushing back, and he felt as though he'd been punched.

"What the hell are you doing here, Griff?" Robson turned to address the officer who'd scurried after him. "Release this man at once, he is required by the Duke of Northam."

"What the hell are *you* doing here?" Griffith echoed, his tone belligerent. He had no desire to see the duke, his father's brother, certainly not after all this time. *That* would feel more like a punch to the heart, given how little love they had for one another. He glanced around the cell. "I might rather stay here," Griffith said, "given the alternative. Why are you here for *him*?" he asked, feeling the sharp slice of betrayal cutting through him. Robson knew how he felt about his uncle, about his whole family except for Frederick. Had his old friend changed so much?

Well, if he had, he'd soon discover so had Griffith. For one thing, he was a lot bigger. And a lot more muscular.

"We don't have time for that," Robson replied. He turned to address the officer. "Get him out now." The man hesitated, looking from Robson to Griffith and back again. "Now," he repeated, "or I shall be forced to report you to the authorities."

"They *are* the authorities," Griffith pointed out.

"The Duke of Northam wants him. Now," Robson said, gesturing to the door. Griffith's jaw was clamped so hard his teeth hurt.

The officer unlocked the cell and swung the door wide to allow Griffith to exit. He stepped into the hallway, ducking to avoid getting slammed on the head by the metal of the bars.

"Well," Robson said, looking Griffith up and down, "it has been a long time, Griff."

Robson's widow's peak was more pronounced than before, but otherwise he looked nearly the same. He wore respectable, if somber, clothing.

He was carrying a satchel that bulged out on the sides, so there must have been a lot of papers in there.

Robson was always studious, a good thing since his father was an ambitious man who wanted more for his son. It appeared that Robson had achieved it. Although retrieving errant black sheep lords from naval jail cells must be one of the lower levels of tasks he was asked to perform.

Griffith thrust his hand out. "I don't know whether to shake your hand or strike you," he said, taking Robson's hand in a firm grip. "What's this about? Why does my uncle want me now?" *When he couldn't care less twelve years ago.* "And why are you his errand boy?"

"It's not your uncle anymore," Robson explained as they began to walk down the hallway toward the exit. "Frederick's the duke now."

Griffith froze. "Frederick? How on earth did he get the title?"

"The way most people inherit things," Robson replied in a dry tone. "People die, and then relatives get things. It's the way the world works, Griff."

Oh. The surprise of seeing Robson after all these years receded as Griffith processed this new and more startling information. Frederick, his cousin, was the Duke of Northam now. Many people had to have died in the interim. He had been away for a long time, hadn't he? Nor had he cared to follow anything that was happening in his family, so it should not be a surprise that things had changed so much.

But it was a surprise.

"To rephrase the question, then, what does the duke want with me?" When he did see Frederick, he'd make certain to tell him to bugger off with whatever it was he wanted.

Robson turned to look at Griffith. "Don't you realize? You're the heir now, Griff."

Griffith felt as though he'd been pummeled in the chest and had all the air knocked out of him. The heir? To something he neither hoped for nor had ever imagined?

"And," Robson continued in a softer voice as though he knew what Griffith was thinking, "Fred is sick. So there's a bit of urgency to it."

Sick? The third musketeer? No, it couldn't be. None of this could be happening, Griff thought to himself. Not Robson retrieving him from jail, not being told he was the heir, not hearing that Fred was ill.

But even as he denied it, he knew it was the truth. And he knew just how he felt.

"Fuck."

Robson chuckled grimly. "That's one way of putting it."

"HE'S GONE?" DELLA frowned at the officer, who frowned right back. "But where?"

"I couldn't say, ma'am," the officer said, in a tone that indicated not only couldn't he say, but he absolutely could not care either.

Della had made certain Sarah was recovered, then stepped outside of their London town house to find her way to naval prison. It had taken a lot of questioning to figure out just where the viscount-captain had been taken; it wasn't as though Della had ever known anything about the Navy, much less where they took people they arrested.

The building she was directed to was squat and forbidding, and even normally fearless Della had to take a deep breath before entering. The inside of the building was just as unpleasant as the outside, built of stone and grimness. The few windows were small, letting in a tiny portion of the already meager London light.

"Hmph." Della whirled around, gesturing to her maid to follow her.

That she needed a maid to accompany her everywhere when she was already ruined, for goodness' sake, irritated her, but Sarah had pointed out that it would reflect badly on the Society for Poor and Unfortunate Children, where both she and Della taught, if Della was seen gallivanting about London on her own. And she'd said "gallivanting," which had made Della laugh.

Sarah and Della shared a fondness for idiosyncratic phrasings.

"Where to now, my lady?" Becky sounded anxious. Not surprising, since she was barely sixteen years old, and was intimidated by the thought of being a duke's daughter's lady's maid, a fact she'd reiterated several times to Della.

Becky had been one of their first rescues when they'd arrived in London. She had been lured from the country with the promise of employment, only to discover when she arrived that *employment* was a genteel name for prostitution. She was sweetly pretty, with enormous blue eyes and a chin that seemed made for quavering.

"We're going to find this Viscount Whatshisname," Della replied determinedly. Because without him, Sarah might never know what happened to her beloved Henry.

At least in Della's own case, she knew perfectly well what had happened to her not-so-beloved Mr. Baxter: he'd stolen her jewels and snuck off in the middle of the night, leaving her and their daughter, Nora, to fend for themselves. She didn't need to know any more than that. Just as she didn't need to recall Lord Stanbury's title, even though of course she did; he was just another man, a *gentleman*, and the last thing she wanted or needed was a man. Ever.

Which was why she addressed him—in her mind, at least—so cavalierly. It was her own tiny rebellion, even though the gentleman in question was like her, as evidenced by his being a sea captain, not a bored aristocrat.

She was too protective of herself and her family to give anyone the benefit of the doubt again.

"How can we find him, my lady?" Becky's tone was even more apprehensive, if possible. Perhaps because in their short time together Della had already done and said things that were not at all ladylike?

But she wasn't a lady any longer, no matter what her title might say. She was a ruined woman, and so if it turned out that a merchant was cheating the Society by padding the bill, Della was going to call him out. And if some uncouth men decided to comment on Della's and Sarah's appearances while they were out walking with their charges? She was damned well going to say something about that too.

What was the point of being ruined if you couldn't speak your mind?

"We're going to the Duke of Northam's town house." Her sister Olivia had provided all of the information Della wanted, and more, in a frantically scribbled note in response to Della's letter asking for information on the viscount-captain. She could hear the words as Olivia would speak them, and smiled at how good it felt to be reunited with her sisters, even Ida, who tended to deliver lectures no matter what the circumstances.

It was endearing, Della had to admit. If also obnoxious.

"A duke?" Becky sounded wondrous now instead of terrified.

"Yes, a duke." Della couldn't help how grumpy she sounded. She wished this captain had not been a nobleman as well—a noble captain had to be a relative anomaly. It was just her luck that her captain was also a member of the aristocracy.

When she had a moment, she'd ask Sarah to calculate those odds. Sarah was much better at maths than Della.

But in the meantime, she would be braving the lion in his den. Or the viscount in the duke's town house, to be more accurate.

Roar.

THE LAST PLACE he'd ever wanted to set foot in again was this house. Home to so many bad memories. Where his father had berated him for not paying proper deference to his uncle. Where he'd spent a few holidays being neglected or chastised.

Where he'd seen the merchants banging at the door, clamoring for payment, as the house's inhabitants mocked them as they drank champagne.

Where he'd seen female servants suddenly discharged because of an unfortunate incident that had been caused by his father or his uncle.

Where he'd grown to hate who he was, and

what he was supposed to be, so much so that he had escaped with nothing but a vague urge to head to the sea.

The house itself wasn't much changed, at least not from the outside. It looked more welcoming, however; was that because Griffith knew his father and uncle were gone? And that Frederick was here?

He took a deep breath as he lifted the massive brass knocker and dropped it down. He heard the clang resonate within, then heard the snick of the door being unlocked. He braced himself for . . . *something*.

A return to his life, even if it was just for a few moments. Though he had the terrible suspicion that walking into the house, acknowledging the reality, would irrevocably alter his future.

"I'm here to see Fre—the Duke of Northam," he announced, his gaze sweeping the entranceway. There were more signs that things had changed for the better here—the footmen standing at attention didn't look as though they were being hunted. More as though they were being treated properly.

A maid holding a huge bouquet of flowers curtseyed on her way through the room. She didn't look beleaguered either.

And the butler who'd answered the door seemed as though he was in command, not as though he were waiting for some crisis to occur.

"I'm Cap—Viscount Stanbury. Mr. Robson told me the duke wishes to see me."

And I him, Griffith thought to himself. Even though the prospect of seeing Frederick after all these years felt both wonderful and horrible.

The butler's brow rose a fraction, but he merely cleared his throat. He nodded at Griffith, gesturing toward a door at the other end of the hall. They walked, their footsteps echoing on the parquet floor.

"Viscount Stanbury, Your Grace," he announced as he opened the door.

Griffith tensed when he saw Frederick. Robson hadn't exaggerated. Frederick was clearly ill. How long did he have?

Damn it, he hadn't asked Robson enough questions. He'd been too busy wondering if he should punch his friend for returning him to this life.

Priorities, Griffith, he reminded himself.

Frederick sat in a Bath chair, a blanket draped over his knees. He looked far thinner than Griff had ever seen him.

You've been away far too long, a voice admonished inside his head.

The room was on the ground floor, an office that had clearly been converted into a bedroom. Because Frederick couldn't walk up the stairs?

Griffith felt the implacable truth of it settling around him like a vise. Fred was ill, and Griffith was the heir. His future was unspooling in front of his eyes, and it felt like a death sentence.

There were throw rugs tossed on the floor, a large bed at one end of the room, an imposing desk at the other end. Bookshelves lined the walls, and a small table holding an array of bottles containing a variety of colored tinctures stood in one corner.

"Griffith!" Frederick's voice, at least, was still exuberant. "Come here, it has been far too long." Echoing the voice in Griffith's own head.

Griffith drew nearer, his gaze searching his cousin's face. Older, of course. Thinner. His face was nearly gaunt. But his eyes were still smiling, his mouth widened into a delighted grin. He stretched his hand out for Griffith to shake.

The last time Griff had seen his cousin was twelve years ago. Fred had been with him the night he'd left, had pressed a wallet full of bills into his hand, waving Griffith's protestations away. Back then, Frederick had been a reasonable specimen of the British aristocracy, with wavy blond hair, a medium build, and an easy smile.

Now only the easy smile remained. His hair was darker and thinning, and it was clear his body was wasting away from whatever disease was afflicting him.

"It's good to see you, Fred," Griffith said, releasing his cousin's hand. "Or Your Grace, I should say?"

Frederick waved his hand. "None of that polite stuff here, Griff. I'm still me and you are still you, I see." He looked him up and down. "A captain in the Royal Navy now?" He looked over at the butler. "Get Lord Stanbury a chair, for goodness' sake. And not my kind of chair," he continued, winking toward Griffith.

The butler nodded, then dragged a large arm-chair over, one that would nearly accommodate Griffith's size, to Frederick's side.

"Sit!" Fred commanded.

Griffith seized on the opportunity to lighten the mood. Or his mood, at least. "Always telling me what to do," he said with a grin, crossing one leg over the other. "And now you're the duke."

Frederick nodded. "And you're my heir."

"About that," Griffith replied, his moment of humor receding. "What the hell happened to your brothers?"

Frederick regarded Griffith as though he were stupid. Which, given what he'd just asked, wasn't that far-fetched. But Griffith had avoided reading the papers from home so he wouldn't have to stumble across mention of his past, so of course he'd missed this information.

"Daniel died of influenza just soon after you left, and Richard went to India to make his fortune, where he got shot and killed."

"I'm—I'm sorry," Griffith said.

Fred shook his head. "Don't be. Daniel was

too stubborn to come in out of the rain, while Richard was a foolhardy idiot. The dukedom would have suffered if either one of them had inherited."

"It wouldn't have been any worse than when Uncle Richard had the title," Griffith said bitterly. Frederick nodded in brief acknowledgment. He'd known what was happening too, but he hadn't gotten as much abuse as Griffith. Nor had he fought back so hard. "But what about you?"

Frederick's expression was rueful. "I am a decent enough duke, I suppose. But as Robson likely told you, and you can tell for yourself," he said, gesturing toward himself, "I won't be the duke for long. That is why I need you."

Griffith's breath caught at how blithely Frederick referenced his forthcoming demise.

"You don't need me," Griffith blurted out, a blind panic making him freeze in his chair. Knowing, even as he spoke, that there was no way he could refuse this. Not when Fred needed him. "I've got work, Fred. I can't inherit."

He'd lose his ship, his men, his captaincy. The things that made him feel as though he weren't an enormous waste of human on this earth, as his parents and his uncle had always inferred when they hadn't been actively telling him that. The only thing that had ever truly mattered to him.

And if he wasn't at sea, who would help those people who couldn't help themselves? He hadn't been able to help people less fortunate than he when he'd lived here before. But since leaving, he'd felt a moral imperative to do whatever he could to help people who needed it. Sometimes it felt like a compulsion, as though he was trying to correct what had happened in the past when he didn't have any power.

"You're the heir, Griff. It's that simple. You can't refuse, not without upending the whole system." Frederick spoke in an urgent tone. Articulating what Griffith already knew.

Griffith rose, unable to sit still any longer. Arguing even as he felt the vise tighten. "I've already upended the system." He turned to Frederick, his hands held palm up. "For God's sake, I left over twelve years ago. Nobody has called me 'my lord' or even knows who I am in the Navy. I got to where I am on my own merit, not because of some title. I cannot go back to this world, your world."

The silence hung in the room, Frederick looking thoughtful as he processed what Griffith had said. At least he was listening. Fred had always listened to him.

"No," he said at last. "I'm sorry, Griff, I really am, but you have to. It's not something you can simply turn down." Echoing Griffith's own thoughts. "Even if you went back to being a captain, you'd still be the Duke of Northam. Even if that's the last thing you want." He paused and took a deep breath. "I'm dying, Griffith. It might not be soon, but it is coming. And I will not leave everything to fall apart, not when I worked so hard to build it up."

Griffith stared at his cousin, hearing the truth in his words. *I'm dying.*

"You knew it would happen eventually," Frederick continued. "It's just a bit sooner than you might have wanted."

Griffith suppressed a snort. Because "a bit sooner" was a lot closer in time than "never."

"But let me show you," Frederick said. He gestured to his chair. "Push me out the doors. We can tour the estate."

Griffith walked over and gripped the handles on the back of the chair. He gave a hesitant push, then increased the force of his push at Frederick's sigh of exasperation.

"I'm not going to die right now, I promise. Not before showing you what I've done." He sounded proud, and Griffith felt a glimmer of something— was it hope?—that this wouldn't be as bad as he feared.

Griffith wheeled Frederick out onto the terrace, taking in the view. It was lovely here. It always had been, even through the times of neglect.

"Over there," Frederick said, pointing to the left, "is where I put in a small garden for the household staff." He swept his hand to the right. "And I've given the house where my father had his parties to the local parish. I believe they are going to set up a school there. I certainly never wanted to set foot in that house again, and I couldn't stand to see it just be vacant." He turned to look up at Griffith, an earnest expression on his face. "We've done so much more with the country estates too. I know neither one of us spent much time there growing up, but they were in terrible disarray. We've changed that. Robson acts as my eyes and ears, and we've made improvements. More can be done, Griffith." He had a look of fierce intensity on his face, and for that moment, it seemed as though Griffith could feel Frederick's passion.

"Not that I have a choice," Griffith said at last, "but I'll do it." *Because you need me to. Because people are now relying on the Duke of Northam to be more than just aristocratic deadweight. Because it's the right thing to do.*

Although the thought of remaining here made him almost physically ill. He wished he could enlist a first mate in this venture as he could at sea. This he'd have to do on his own.

Which would leave him vulnerable in this new world.

"My only requirement is that you seek more doctors' advice." Because he wanted Frederick to live, of course, but he also did not want to inherit too quickly.

Frederick responded with that easy smile. "Yes, if that is your stipulation. Not that they'll suddenly give me a clean bill of health." He nodded in satisfaction. "I knew you would say yes. You're too good a man."

Griffith snorted. "Tell that to the naval authorities."

Frederick gestured for Griffith to wheel him back in. "What did you do anyway?"

Griffith guided the chair back into the room. "The usual. Refusing to let an injustice stand, thumbing my nose at the authorities." He released his hold on the chair and sat back down on the sofa. He crossed his arms over his chest and cocked an eyebrow at his cousin. "Given that, are you certain you want me as your heir? I'm bound to do something to set someone's teeth on edge."

"I know that, but it's not as though I have a choice," Frederick pointed out. "One cannot just decide who will be one's heir, or at least one of the previous dukes would have chosen his favorite bottle of brandy or perhaps a particularly juicy roast of beef."

"I can be intoxicating," Griffith replied, waggling his eyebrows at his cousin. "And I am certainly rare."

Fred laughed as he shook his head, and then his expression turned serious. "I know this is the last thing you want, Griff, but it is the only thing that can be. You'll have to make the best of it and hope I don't die before you've learned everything that has to be done."

"How long?" he asked.

Fred glanced to the side, his lips pressed into a thin line. "I have six good months, if the doctors are correct, to teach you all you have to know."

Six months. Unless the doctors were wrong. No more months at sea. Griffith felt as though he were being strangled by responsibility, but he couldn't refuse, and not just because it was the law.

It was the right thing to do, to take up the reins of responsibility. To spend Frederick's remaining months reassuring his cousin that the dukedom wouldn't be falling into complete disrepair. Perhaps he could find time, at some point, to engage in more improper procedures that would suddenly be proper because he was too important to impugn. He'd definitely be able to rescue as many people on land as he had at sea, cold comfort though that was.

"I'll do it, Fred. I'll make certain you're proud of me."

It was an oath and a promise, even as it was a death knell for everything Griffith wanted and worked for just the day before.

"I know you will." Frederick wheeled over to his desk, gesturing for Griffith to follow him. "We have to get started, six months isn't a very long time."

AFTER AN HOUR, Griffith was regretting every altruistic bone in his body, his horror growing the longer Frederick laid out all of Griffith's new responsibilities.

Not only did he need to learn everything possible about the estates and the people whose lives he would be directly affecting, he also would have to venture into Society.

"I can't just hole up here?" Griffith said, glancing around Frederick's sickroom. "They want to meet me as little as I want to meet them."

"That is where you are wrong, cousin," Frederick said with a grin as he looked up from the accounts he was showing to Griff. "You'll dazzle them with your adventures, and they will have no choice but to welcome the black sheep into the fold. The flock, I should say," he continued. "Those Society vultures will welcome you into their glittering den."

Griffith shook his head. "Clearly you would much prefer to be a member of the animal kingdom than a duke—sheep, vultures, a den?"

Frederick paused, his expression growing serious. "There was one time when I wished I was as brave as you, Griff. Running off and doing whatever I wanted, regardless of who it affected."

Griffith winced at the implicit criticism—_it affected me_, his cousin might as well have shouted. Had he even thought about that when he'd run off?

He had to admit he had not.

"I understand," Frederick continued. "I know you don't want to do this, but it's your duty. It's not something you can run away from."

Not like you did before, Frederick didn't have to say.

He couldn't run away. Not this time. If only the thought of facing Society didn't make him want to run faster than he ever had before.

"DAMN IT," GRIFFITH muttered, glancing back toward the door.

The butler emerged, nodding to Griffith as he shut the door behind him.

"Thank you for coming," the man said in a stiff tone of voice. "His Grace has been concerned he would not find you." *In time*, he didn't need to say.

Griffith wanted to ask so many questions—how long had Fred been ill, what was his diagnosis, how many doctors had he seen already—but he could tell that the butler would not divulge his master's secrets. And honestly, Griffith wouldn't have respected him if he did.

Damn it.

He wished Clark were here. He needed to talk it out with someone. He was accustomed to having a full crew to navigate whatever course he'd set.

That he would have to do this on his own made it even more unpleasant. If only he had a compatriot to help him steer this particular course.

"I need to see him immediately." Both men turned at the sound of a woman's voice, a voice that spoke in a peremptory commanding tone, speaking at the front door.

"Excuse me, my lord," the butler said, walking swiftly toward where a footman was trying to hold back the woman.

"He is here, isn't he?" Griffith saw the top of a hat, and then a pair of wide, dark eyes peering at him over the footman's arm. "There you are. Lord Viscount Captain. I need to speak with you."

Griffith walked toward her, recognizing the lady from the day before. Stubborn little thing. "You'd better let her in," he said. "She might have a hat pin on her."

The butler turned to Griffith, a questioning look on his face.

"Never mind that," Griffith said quickly. "Just show her into one of the rooms and bring us tea." He wished he could ask for something stronger, but he didn't want to perturb the butler more than the man likely already was.

"Of course, my lord." The butler gestured for the woman to enter, then led the way down a side hallway and opened a small room that appeared to have been a lady's receiving area. Was Frederick married? There was so much he didn't know about his family anymore. But apparently was about to learn.

"Thank you," the woman said, raising her nose as she entered the room. A timorous maid followed, only to start at the woman's next words. "I'll speak with the viscount alone, Becky. You may sit and wait for me in the hall."

The maid glanced from her mistress to Griffith and back again, a clear look of terror on her face. Because of Griffith's size or her mistress's cavalier regard for her own reputation, Griffith couldn't tell.

"She'll be fine," Griffith said to the maid as he stepped into the room, closing the door behind them.

He turned to the lady, who was, as he'd seen the day before, remarkably pretty. What drew his attention immediately was her mouth—her lips were lush and full, with an enticing curve—not to mention that mole—that almost made him step forward and kiss her.

He would have, if this were yesterday and he was still merely Captain Davies. Even with the threat of a hat pin.

But now he wouldn't presume. He already hated being a gentleman.

"You know who I am, my lady," Griffith said. "Perhaps you can introduce yourself? And explain why you require my assistance so urgently?"

She spoke in a stiff tone of voice. "I am Lady Della Howlett."

The name meant nothing to him, of course.

Although it was a confirmation that she was, indeed, a *lady*, which meant her being at the pub yesterday was entirely untoward.

It was a damned good thing he had been there to rescue her, or she would have been in serious trouble. Not that she would acknowledge that, it seemed.

Griffith gestured for her to sit, then went and sat in the sofa opposite. The room was so small that their knees nearly touched.

"Well, Lady Della Howlett," Griffith said, stretching his arm over the back of the sofa, "what do you want?"

"You," she replied.

Chapter 3

$\mathcal{H}$e was even larger than she'd recalled. If she were anybody but herself she would have been intimidated by his size—he had to be well over six feet tall, with broad shoulders, perhaps the broadest she'd ever seen, and long, long legs that threatened to touch hers as he sprawled on the sofa.

But Della was not easily intimidated.

"Me?" he replied in an incredulous voice, leaning forward to stick his face close to hers. He glanced up to the ceiling as though exasperated. "You are not the only one. Perhaps it's a sickness that's going around."

He was exceedingly attractive in addition to all that size. Even though he was currently spouting nonsense.

Although she should not be noticing his appearance right now. But she couldn't help it; he had long dark curly hair, far too long for Society's liking, and it was clear he hadn't shaved in some time, judging by the thick stubble on his face. His eyes were dark also, and focused on her so intently she felt his gaze throughout her entire body. His mouth was lifted in a sly grin, as though he knew how he was affecting her.

He probably affected every woman who saw him the same way. Imagine all that force and power engaged in—*stop it, Della*! she chided herself.

"Yes, you." Della dragged her eyes away from his face to look in the corner of the room. There was a bookshelf with what appeared to be discarded knitting, and she wondered if this enormous viscount-captain had a wife. And if he did, Della envied that woman more than she would like to admit.

But this wasn't his house, was it?

None of that mattered. *Focus, Della.* "The thing is," she began, directing her words to the knitting, "you were the captain on the HMS *Royal Lady* three years ago."

He laughed. "I know that," he said in a condescending tone.

Hmph. "And the ship capsized."

"I know that as well," he interrupted, his tone less obnoxious.

"And some of your crew was lost."

She waited for him to say something cutting, but apparently even he could be silenced. "One

of the crew members was a Mr. Henry Wattings.
I am hoping you can tell me what you know
about what happened to him."

"What happened?" he repeated. "What do you
mean? He wasn't one of the lost crew members,
I know that."

She turned to look at him again. His expression
was just as intent, but it was far more somber
than before. "Wattings returned to London three
years ago. I set him up with letters of reference,
and I thought he was headed south."

Della exhaled. At least this behemoth hadn't
said Sarah's husband had been lost at sea, as
they'd feared.

"What is this about?" he continued. "Why is a
lady such as yourself interested in the fate of a
black seaman?"

Disappointment flooded through her. She hadn't
realized how much she had been hoping for a
miracle—*Mr. Henry Wattings? Oh, he is currently
in the prime of health aboard my ship now, even as we
speak. Allow me to take you to him.*

"Thank you for your time," she replied, not
answering his question.

She rose, and he leapt up also, meaning they
were a bare six inches apart from one another.
She addressed him midchest. "I was hoping you
could help me find him, but since you apparently
were last aware of his whereabouts three years
ago, you can offer me no assistance."

She dipped her head in thanks. The feathers on her hat likely poked him in the eye. Serves him right, she thought. Although why she had such a visceral reaction to him she couldn't say—or wouldn't say.

Because she knew damn well it was because he was so large, handsome, and forceful. Entirely everything that had gotten her in so much trouble before. Everything she had promised herself never to fall for again.

So much for not saying.

"Hold on a moment," he said, putting his hand on her arm. "If Wattings is missing, I want to help you find him. But I have obligations. Obligations," he repeated, as though to himself.

His expression shifted, and she could see when he arrived at some sort of conclusion in his head.

"I have a proposition for you."

Her eyes snapped up to meet his. He was grinning down at her, as though he knew how she might interpret his words. She felt her cheeks heat, and quickly returned to staring at the knitting. Much safer. With the added bonus that the knitting needles would make an excellent makeshift weapon, if she needed to defend herself.

"I need a woman," he continued.

So . . . was her initial interpretation correct?

She began to move toward the knitting, but his grip tightened. "Wait, I'm explaining this all terribly," he said in an amused tone. How could he find any of this humorous?

"You certainly are," she replied as she shook his hand off. "If you will excuse me?"

"I will help you find out what happened to Wattings if you do something for me."

"You're still not explaining all that well," Della said through a clenched jaw. Was it possible he was that dense not to realize what he was implying? No, of course he knew. Hence his laughing tone of voice. Was it possible he was that much of a lout?

Entirely possible.

"Do you mind sitting down?" he asked as he sat again. Not waiting for her to sit first. So perhaps her assessment of him as a lout wasn't far from the mark.

"Of course. Do explain," she said in a prim voice. Della lowered herself into her chair, placing her hands on her lap.

"It turns out I will be reentering London Society. As the heir to the Duke of Northam."

"Fascinating," Della murmured. She wished she could restrain her response to him, but she couldn't. It was either maintain her antagonistic facade or leap on him.

She knew which option she should take, even if it wasn't the one she wanted to take.

But he was speaking. She had to concentrate on what he was saying, not how he made her feel.

"I have faced battleships, fearsome storms, and the most voracious boll weevils while at sea. None of them terrify me as much as the thought of all those unmarried Society ladies discovering there is an eligible duke's heir in their midst."

She had to laugh at his horrified tone.

"It's not a laughing matter," he said, even though his expression acknowledged that it indeed was. "I want you to be my guide and to let these women believe I am already spoken for. Already engaged to be married, in fact. You will not, of course, be obliged to marry me. I would make it a part of our bargain that you do not."

"You're that irresistible?" she said, accompanying her words with an eye roll. Even though she knew the answer to the question.

"It's not that, although yes, I do believe I am," he answered, sounding entirely too pleased with himself. "It's that someone who is in line to inherit a dukedom, no matter what he looks like, would be irresistible. I do not want to end up accidentally married. I don't want to be married at all."

He sounded so decided she had to wonder what had set him against the tradition. He couldn't have had the same experience as she; he was a man after all.

But that was not her concern.

"So am I to understand that you want me to

pretend to be your betrothed so that young ladies won't fling themselves at your head?"

"Something like that, yes. And in exchange I'll
help you find Wattings."

"That sounds like a wonderful bargain," Della
said as she stood again, "but there is a flaw in your
plan." She hesitated, but she had to be honest.
Even to this loutish viscount. "I am not accepted
in polite Society."

He howled in laughter. Not the response she
was expecting.

"That makes it even more perfect!" He had a
wide grin on his face, and if he weren't currently
irking her so much, she'd find herself smiling back,
his smile was that infectious. "So when we break
things off, it will be entirely understandable."

Hmph. She didn't like the thought of being used
for her unacceptability, but if it meant he would
help her . . .

Damn it.

"Pardon me," he said, folding his arms over
his chest. He spoke in a serious tone, markedly
different from how he'd just sounded. "I mean to
say I would very much appreciate it if you could
do me a good turn, and I would endeavor to do
you one as well." He spread his hands out as he
continued. "You can be returned to Society, and
perhaps you can find yourself a husband, after
you have convinced all those fine people of how
you're truly not that bad. I am very persuasive,

as you can tell," he added with a wink. "Consider it my continued rescue of your fair person."

She didn't want any of that, although being accepted back into Society would help her sisters, at least. She definitely did not want a husband, but that wasn't any of his business. What she *did* want was his help, and she was fairly certain he wouldn't assist her with finding Mr. Wattings if she didn't assist him with this.

He gazed at her, one brow raised as he awaited her response. One corner of his mouth lifted as though aware she had no choice, not if she wanted his help.

"I accept," she said. "With a few stipulations."

"Name them." His tone was confident, as though there was nothing she could say that would make him change his mind.

"You might have me as a pretend betrothed, but I will not be told what to do, what to wear, or how to behave."

The brow rose higher.

"Not that I am going to behave improperly, of course," she added hastily. She would definitely have to restrain herself around him, for example. "I am a duke's daughter, I am cognizant of what is acceptable. But you have to promise you will allow me to make my own decisions at any time." She felt the tightness at the thought of being controlled again rise in her chest, and she had to take a deep breath to push it away.

"It's not usual to make this kind of request. I suppose you don't want to tell me why?"

Della gave a vehement shake of her head. "No, I do not. It has nothing to do with our bargain. And I do promise I will behave faultlessly and hold up the facade that we are truly betrothed."

He shrugged. "I have no intention of forcing you to do anything, so I agree."

She exhaled. She was going to do this, wasn't she?

"And we'll need to come up with some story of how we met." He nodded. "And, of course, how we're going to break it off." Even the thought of not having a planned escape from a pretend betrothal made her anxious.

She held her hand out to him. He was still sprawled on the sofa, his limbs seeming to take up the entire room. She would have to have a discussion with him about the appropriate behavior when a lady rose.

Teaching young children their multiplication tables, even given her own difficulty with maths, was likely far easier than teaching this man some manners.

"Excellent." Finally he stood, taking her hand. His hand was enormous, engulfing her own entirely. "It's a bargain."

As HE'D FIRST thought, the lady clearly had secrets.

Lady Della turned to him, her cheeks still delightfully pink. That mouth of hers, however, was pressed into a thin line, indicating just what she thought of him.

Blackguard, rogue, scoundrel. Nothing he hadn't heard before. Nothing that wasn't correct either.

"I reside at 568 Grace Court. Not the most fashionable part of town."

"Not that I'd know that," he interrupted with a grin. "I've just returned to London, remember?"

She rolled her eyes, clearly annoyed. Which only made him grin harder.

"Tomorrow. For tea. I will introduce you to Mrs. Wattings."

Mrs. Wattings. So Wattings had a wife? Now her interest in finding Wattings made much more sense. He wondered how his new betrothed had met Mrs. Wattings, but he suspected she wouldn't tell him.

"Until tomorrow, my lady." He took her hand, raising it to his lips. Placing his mouth on the back of her hand, wishing she weren't wearing gloves so he could taste her skin.

She snatched her hand back and nodded, then turned and marched out the door, the maid scurrying behind.

Griffith watched as she descended the stairs. There wasn't a carriage outside, so she'd come in a hansom. Was she too poor to afford a carriage? Or her situation didn't require one?

He realized he was desperate to know more

about this woman, a lady who did not appear to be at all daunted, either by his appearance or his lack of conventional manners. Just the sort of woman he had always longed for, but despaired of ever finding.

SHE LEANED ACROSS toward Sarah, taking her hand. "I would do anything to give you that peace of mind." She cleared her throat. "And he did say he wouldn't ask me to do anything I didn't wish to. It was part of our deal."

Sarah squeezed her hand in reply, still looking worried. "I wish you didn't have to is all. I know how cruel people can be, and I don't want you to have to suffer for me."

"It's not suffering," Della replied, waving her hand airily. "I get to buy some new gowns, attend a few parties with my fake betrothed as I fend off eager young ladies, and watch my parents wrestle with whether or not to acknowledge me. It will be delightful."

Besides which, how long would he tolerate being in her company when so many people were directly rude to her? She had warned him, it wasn't as though he could claim ignorance. And then she could remain at home while he continued to help her. Because she knew that under everything, he was a gentleman, and he would keep his word. And if he wasn't a gentleman, she would remind him that she was already ruined, so she wouldn't hesitate to spread rumors about him and his behavior if he stepped out of line.

In any scenario, she would get what she wanted.

Her friend shook her head, but Della could see that Sarah wasn't going to argue the point anymore. Perhaps because she knew it was pointless?

"Fine. But you have to promise me that if you become uncomfortable at any time that you won't continue."

That wouldn't happen. Or perhaps it would, but Della would never admit to any kind of discomfort, not while Henry's fate was unknown.

Sarah bit her lip, her eyes moist. "Thank you for doing this. I want to know. Whatever it is, I want to find out."

Della nodded. She and Sarah were both aware it was more than likely that Henry was dead, but they also both knew that Sarah would be agonizing over it until it was a certainty.

"And now that that is settled, how about we go visit the dressmaker so I can purchase some new gowns? I need to look appropriately outrageous as the scandalous Lady Della, the presumed betrothed to the Viscount—what's his name again?"

"Griffith Davies, Viscount Stanbury," Sarah replied with a soft smile. "You're going to have to know his name if you're going to be betrothed to him."

"Fine," Della said with an exaggerated sigh.

"Stanbury, Stanbury, Stanbury." Della rose, holding her hand out for her friend to take. "Let's go."

Sarah stood, allowing Della to lead her to the front of the house where they gathered their cloaks.

"Becky!" Della called. They heard footsteps, and then the maid appeared. For once, her chin was not quavering. Perhaps she was finally settling in.

"Mrs. Wattings and I are going out for a bit. Can you mind the girls? They're upstairs playing."

"Of course, my lady," Becky replied, curtseying.

"And we're off on our adventure," Della said as the two women walked outside.

"Heaven help us," Sarah murmured, at which Della just laughed.

Chapter 4

$\mathcal{G}$riffith arrived at Lady Della's house at what he presumed was teatime. At least according to his faulty memory.

Speaking of which—he should really find out what happened to Clark, and let his crew know he wouldn't be captaining them anymore. Not to mention figure out what procedure he'd need to follow to quit the Royal Navy.

Damn it, that hurt. He shoved the emotion away to deal with later.

Better to keep his mind occupied with thoughts of his new voyage than to obsess over trips he would never take now.

He knocked, and the door opened moments later. It was she, and not a servant. Again he wondered what was so different about her—why didn't she have a butler to answer the door? Unless she was so desperate to see him again she insisted on waiting for him herself?

The thought pleased him more than he knew it should. Especially since he knew it wasn't true.

"Good afternoon, my lord," Lady Della said, holding the door wider so he could enter. He stepped into the foyer, noting several cloaks hanging on the opposite wall, some of them clearly child-sized. A ball lay on the floor underneath.

"You live here with children?" he asked.

She glanced to where he was looking. "Yes, of course. My own child, and Sarah's. Mrs. Wattings's."

She had a child?

"So you are a widow?" he asked. He knew nothing about her; he'd resorted to looking in Debrett's for her name, but the only thing he discovered was her age and who her parents were. There was no mention of a husband.

"I am not married," she replied, an expression on her face that practically dared him to comment.

"Ah." He wouldn't ask when she hadn't volunteered more information, no matter how curious he was.

And he was intensely curious. Although that fact would go a long way toward explaining why she was unaccepted in Society.

"Well. If you would like to step into the parlor?" She gestured to a door at the far end of the small foyer. She began to walk ahead of him. Eyes up, Griffith reminded himself. Even though his eyes were not obeying orders, instead looking at the curve of her waist and the sway of her hips.

He really should do something about his needs

or he'd be subjecting his pretend betrothed to far too many salacious glances.

Although that thought, now that he'd met her, was not nearly as appealing as before. Any woman would pale in comparison to her.

She turned quickly, giving him just enough time to yank his eyes up to her face. Thank goodness for quick reflexes.

"Do you care for tea?" she asked.

"I doubt you have anything stronger, so tea is fine," he replied. She nodded as though that was the answer she'd expected and rang a bell.

"My lady?" It was yet another impossibly young girl, one who looked at him and turned white as a sheet. *If I could do something about my size I would,* Griff thought to himself. *It's not enjoyable to terrify any lady who comes near me.*

Except for her. She wasn't terrified at all. A remarkable woman, to be sure. Even without her hat pin.

"We would like tea, please. And if you could ask Mrs. Wattings to step into the parlor? Thank you."

The girl nodded and curtseyed, then shut the door behind her.

Griff looked at the closed door, his eyebrow rising. "Is it your custom that every gentleman who visits you has the benefit of being in a closed room alone with you?" He shook his head. "No wonder you are not accepted in polite society."

She glared at him even as her cheeks turned bright red.

"I did warn you about my reputation. It is you who thought that made our farce even more appealing."

Griff gestured for her to sit, then lowered himself down onto the sofa. She sat beside him at the far end, still glaring.

"So I did. I should ask, however. Am I likely to encounter any unexpected rivals in my claim to your person?"

Her eyes glittered. She was truly glorious, especially when her angry passion was so clearly raised.

"No, my lord. I live here with my friend Mrs. Wattings and our children. Every day Sarah and I go to the Society for Poor and Unfortunate Children to offer instruction. Sometimes, when we are feeling especially adventurous, we get ices and walk home. That is the sum of my existence. There are no rivals."

"Sounds fairly dull to me," Griffith said. "Are you certain you don't want to engage in any more scandalous behavior?" He winked at her, enjoying how she glared even harder at him.

"The most scandalous behavior I can imagine, my lord, is entering a ballroom on your arm."

Before he could reply, the door opened letting in two meowing kittens, and a striking woman around the same age as Lady Della entered the room.

The resemblance ended there, however; Mrs. Wattings, as Griffith assumed she was, was brown-skinned, with dark brown eyes and delicate eyebrows. Her hair was pulled back into a modest style, and her clothing was just as modest, and obviously that of a lady's. Her expression was gentle, and she glanced from his face to her friend's, her eyes widening as she assessed the situation. And how large he was, he presumed.

Griffith stood, holding his hand out to her. The kittens dove under the sofa. "You are Mrs. Wattings? I am Griffith Davies, Lord Stanbury. Lady Della tells me you are Wattings's wife?"

She nodded as she shook his hand.

"Please sit," Griffith said in a mild tone. He waited until she took a chair opposite, then sat back down.

"So you do have some manners," he heard Lady Della mutter.

He ignored her. He leaned forward, resting his hands on his knees. "Wattings was a good seaman. I am sorry to hear he has been missing. He was on my ship."

"The *Royal Lady*," Mrs. Wattings said.

"Yes, the *Lady*. A fine ship, at least until we ran into a fearsome storm. We were lucky there was another ship nearby."

"What happened then?" Lady Della asked impatiently.

"We boarded the other ship, which took us to the nearest port. From there we managed to find passage for the crew back to London. I stayed in that town until all of my crew had sailed. That is the last I knew of Wattings. I'm sorry."

"Oh. But you said—you told Della that you knew he had made it home?"

Of course. He'd left out the most important part. He was a thoughtless idiot. An opinion it seemed Lady Della shared, judging by her expression. "Yes, once I reached London and obtained another ship, I found records of my crew having landed, including Wattings. I would have liked to have him aboard again. I thought he was planning on heading south, but I could find no word of him. That is the last I know of him."

Mrs. Wattings started to tremble, and Lady Della was out of her seat immediately and bending over her friend. "Breathe, Sarah." She turned to Griffith. "Could you get a glass of water, please?"

"He's just as abrupt as you are," Griff heard Mrs. Wattings say in a shaky voice. He strode out of the room, nearly running into a woman carrying a tray of tea things. "Is there water on there?" he demanded.

She shook her head no, and he walked past her toward where he assumed the kitchen was.

"Water!" he called, his pace quickening. He

descended the stairs and ended up in a small, clean kitchen. A few startled young girls stared at him as though he were the devil himself. "Water for Mrs. Wattings, please," he said, trying to keep his tone reasonable so he wouldn't scare them further.

One of them jumped up and filled water from a tap, then held the glass out to him.

SARAH NODDED, GESTURING for him to sit, which he did. One of the kittens poked its nose out from under the sofa and then began to clamber up the viscount's leg. He didn't shake it off, though; instead, he drew the kitten up and cradled it against his chest.

Della had never envied one of her rescued cats more. Even though she wished she didn't have such urges. But his presence served to remind her of certain needs that had not been met in some time.

"Della will pose as your betrothed as you re-enter Society," Sarah answered. She frowned, tilting her head. "But that is what is puzzling me, my lord. Why do you have to do this in the first place?" She spread her hands out in an inclusive gesture. "From what I can see, you have no need of Society. Unless you want to settle down and raise a family? In which case having Della on your arm would be a strong impediment." That last part was spoken in a dry tone of voice.

"Just what I am hoping for," the viscount replied. "My cousin is the Duke of Northam. And he—" He paused as he took a deep breath. He looked pained as he spoke again, and he stroked the kitten's head for a moment or two before speaking. "My cousin is ill, and it seems I am his heir. He has insisted that I learn the ways of the dukedom before I inherit, which means reentering Society, among other things."

"But why?" Della asked, struck by Sarah's question. "I'm certain there are recluse dukes off somewhere, not having to bother with Society at all. Why do you have to?"

Lord Stanbury resettled on the sofa, a considering look on his face. "Frederick said that was part of it. That if I am not at least on reasonable terms with my fellow aristocrats that they will block anything I try to do. Not only that, but that they might bring up my unorthodox past. They can't take away my title, but they can meddle in my finances. Put restrictions on how I live my life. And I don't want to spend time or money fighting them. The estate is in reasonable condition, but there are needed improvements, and Frederick has been too ill to oversee it all. He needs the support of others to improve things." He swallowed. "Frederick has always wanted things to improve. It's just too bad that Frederick couldn't improve himself. So I have to do whatever Frederick wants. I—I owe him."

There was more there, of course. But it wasn't her place to pry, just for her to be on his arm as he did whatever it was he felt he had to do.

"I am so sorry about your cousin," Della said. She went to sit on the sofa beside him, resisting the urge to pat his arm or some other compassionate gesture. He would probably bristle at that kind of reaction. So would she, in that situation. They definitely were more similar than she wanted to admit. "I understand your family loyalty." She glanced at Sarah. "I have it myself," she said with a smile, which Sarah returned.

"Yes, well," he muttered, clearly uncomfortable with expressions of sympathy. "Also, perhaps not quite as important is that it will irk everyone I meet that I am the heir to the dukedom." He grinned in apparent pleasure. "So many of them warned my parents I was a troublemaker, and to guide me with a firm hand."

"I wonder why anybody would say that," Della commented.

"Besides which, it sounds as though you are in need of a reentry to Society yourself, judging by what you say. It will be a pleasure to watch their faces as we walk in. Worth any amount of fancy dancing and such."

"Ah, no wonder you are so pleased to have me along. I am an even bigger burr in their side. I'm the most disgraceful of the duke's daughters."

"Precisely," he said in an enthusiastic tone.

Sarah just looked from one of them to the other, her expression startled. Nearly aghast. Until she eventually sighed and threw up her hands. Her usual response to much of what Della did.

"Well," Della said in a bright tone of voice, "where do we start?"

Chapter 5

Where do we start?

Well, first I would undo your hair. I imagine it would flow down to your arse. Then I would lower my head to your neck, kissing it softly. Waiting for you to wrap your arms around me.

"Start?" Griffith said after a moment. A moment where his imagination had definitely run away with him. "I will consult with Frederick and review what invitations have come in."

She looked him up and down, a gleam in her eye. He liked it when she assessed him like that. He knew she could not possibly find him wanting.

"Do you have the proper attire?" she asked, her tone indicating she doubted it.

Well, she was correct in her assumption.

"No, not at all," he said, shaking his head. Which reminded him he probably should send to the ship for his belongings. At which point he'd have to tell his crew of his change in circumstances.

The thought hit him like a punch to the heart—not to be able to head off to sea whenever he

wanted, to be bound to the land. To take up responsibilities he'd actively run from so long ago.

"If you'll excuse me, my lord, Della, I want to
go see what the children are up to. I will leave
you to your sartorial discussion," Mrs. Wattings
said as she rose.

"Sartorial?" Della echoed in an amused tone as
her friend walked to the door.

Griffith got up and bowed, then retook his seat.
The kitten he'd picked up clung to his chest, and
he knew he'd have tiny marks on his skin as a
memento.

He wondered if she would scratch him as well.

"Will you need my help?" she continued. "With
purchasing the proper clothing?"

He didn't, he supposed. Surely Frederick had
some sort of valet tucked inside that grand house
of his. Or he could enlist Clark to act as his valet,
for that matter. If he could find him.

But the best-case scenario for that would mean
having to wait, and now that Griffith had made
up his mind—had set his course, so to speak—he
didn't want to waste time. Besides which, it
would be delightful to have her help rather than
anybody else's.

"I do, my lady." He spoke as though reluctant
to ask.

She narrowed her gaze at him. As though she
knew what he was thinking.

"I will have to ask my brothers-in-law where

they go. I do not have a list of fine gentleman's haberdasheries at hand."

"So perhaps you're not that shocking after all?" He couldn't resist asking, if only to see her reaction.

"Honestly," she said. "Are you going to vex me every time we speak?"

"Surely not *every* time," he replied. He grinned at her. "I imagine when I wish you a good morning I won't annoy you too much."

"Perhaps not too much." Her lips twisted as though she were trying to suppress a smile.

"Excellent. I will try to limit myself to all the good hailings I can imagine. Good morning, good afternoon, good evening. Will that suit?"

"Perfectly." She did allow herself to smile then, and he felt momentarily flattened by the brilliance of it.

And not only was she stunningly beautiful, she was also the barrier he would wield toward any ambitious debutante who thought a duke's heir might be worth the bother of him. Not to mention someone he could be himself with as he navigated these new waters.

She'd make an excellent captain herself, he could tell. She was obviously too stubborn and fierce to obey orders, as though he hadn't had her own words to confirm that. But she could give them with a lift of her imperious nose. And everyone would scurry to follow.

He would scurry to follow. He wondered if he could persuade her to issue some particularly intriguing orders after they'd gotten better acquainted.

His cock reacted predictably, and he shifted on the sofa.

"So how did we meet?" she asked. *She is not talking to you,* he reminded his cock. *Focus, Griffith.*

"Uh—perhaps we met when you came aboard for a tour of my ship and were struck by my remarkable handsomeness?"

She rolled her eyes.

"Or you dropped your handkerchief, I returned it to you, and you were struck by my remarkable handsomeness?"

She folded her arms over her chest.

"Let's just say we met at a park. We don't need to discuss your appearance."

"Fine," he replied. "What else?"

"How we'll break it off," she continued. "I think you should be the one to do it, since Society will forgive a duke's heir a lot quicker than they would a lady in my position."

"And what position would that be?" he couldn't resist asking, waggling his eyebrows.

She ignored him. "Not that I care about being forgiven, but it will help my sisters if I am somewhat respectable." She paused as she thought. "You can say that your duties have made it impossible to focus on marriage at this point, and that you wish me every happiness, etcetera, etcetera."

"I would never put duties over love." He held his hands up in response to her look of aggravation. "Fine, we'll do as you say."

"And when will we work on finding where Mr. Wattings might be?"

Of course. He'd nearly forgotten, he'd been so intent on teasing her. Not to mention his intense attraction to her.

There was a reason, a very real reason, that she had agreed to this bargain. She was so desperate to find her friend's husband that she was willing to subject herself to Society's ridicule and disdain.

That took strength of character, and he couldn't help but admire her.

"We'll start tomorrow. On everything."

"IN HERE." DELLA gestured toward the door leading into Dunworthy and Sons, Gentlemen's Furnishings. Lord Stanbury flung the door open, stepping in like a king entering his court.

To be fair, he seemed to behave like that most of the time, treating his surroundings as though everything was just there for his pleasure. A feeling that should not make her react, but of course it did.

He was just so—*so*. So big, so handsome, so irritating. Della had spent much of the night before lying awake thinking about their interactions. She was so keenly aware of his every word, every gesture. Although perhaps that would lessen the effect of returning to Society—she'd be too distracted by him to worry about people shunning her or whispering cruel words about her. So there was an upside?

He held the door for her and Becky, smiling gently at the girl as he shut the door behind them. Apparently he could be polite. To everyone but her.

"May I help you, my lord?" A clerk walked up, an apprehensive expression on his face. Because he didn't have clothing big enough for Captain Enormous, perhaps?

The clerk was of medium stature, with thinning hair and an impressive moustache. He wore a well-made suit that appeared to fit him perfectly. A good indication that this was, in fact, the correct place to shop. Despite what his own misgivings might indicate.

"Yes, thank you," Della said before Lord Stanbury could speak. "The gentleman needs a full wardrobe. Your shop came recommended by my brother-in-law Lord Raybourn."

The man's face cleared. "Oh, splendid!" He held his hand out to indicate a chair at the far end. "If your maid would like to take a seat, we can review what will be required."

"Go ahead and sit, Becky," Della said. Her maid

nodded, but not before giving Lord Stanbury an admiring look. Her fear of the gentleman seemed to have been replaced by a budding interest, one that should not make Della annoyed.

Even though it did.

"If you will come this way, we can discuss what types and colors of fabric you prefer."

"I don't prefer any type or color," Lord Stanbury said in a grumpy voice. "I just don't want anything that is too itchy."

"Stop being such a curmudgeon," Della said. She addressed the man who was waiting on them. "This is Lord Stanbury, and I am Lady Della Howlett."

"My betrothed," Lord Stanbury added.

"And you are?" Della continued, as though he hadn't spoken. Although she felt her cheeks heat as the truth of their deception—oxymoronic thought though that was—hit her. The news of his arrival, his impending inheritance, and their betrothal was likely to be known throughout London by the evening, given how much people liked to gossip.

She couldn't back away from their bargain now. Even if the thought of it, of returning to Society, terrified her, she had to follow through, if only to give Sarah some peace of mind. No matter what he did to her own peace of mind.

"I am Mr. Dunworthy. My father opened this shop, and I have continued his work, serving people such as your brother-in-law." Mr. Dunworthy's tone was proud and respectful.

"A pleasure, Mr. Dunworthy." Della shot a reproving glance at Lord Stanbury. "Ignore my betrothed, he is just peeved that he has to get rigged out in such fashion. He's a generally peevish person," she continued in a confiding tone, resisting the urge to giggle at Lord Stanbury's expression.

"If you care to assess these fabrics," Mr. Dunworthy said as he led them toward the back of the shop. "I believe you will find these to be the highest quality, suitable for a gentleman of your position."

"I am not peevish," he grumbled as they followed Mr. Dunworthy.

She gave him a pointed look before going to stand beside him, so close his scent filled her nose. He smelled wonderful, like cloves and wood smoke. She wondered if it was a cologne he'd gotten while on his travels—she certainly had never smelt anything like it before. Of course, she hadn't come close enough to any gentleman in years to sniff them. So perhaps it was common, she just didn't know about it.

But his scent was distracting her. As was his nearness and his general presence.

"Why are you doing this, if even this is burdensome to you?" she said in a low voice. "You try to hide it, but you must feel a strong sense of responsibility to be putting yourself through this. You do know that this is child's play compared to having to make the rounds in Society." She paused, then took a deep breath and exhaled. "Especially since you will be with me." She turned to look at him, drawing her brows together. "I will make things much more difficult for you."

He leaned in, brushing her shoulder with his. "Or you will make it much more pleasurable."

Oh. The way he said the last word, drawing it out through his mouth as though savoring it. As though he wanted to savor *her*.

She shuddered in reaction, trying not to imagine it. Unfortunately, the side effect of being a truly ruined woman is that one knew precisely what one was imagining. Mr. Baxter had been reasonable in that way, at least. If in nothing else.

And it had been so very long.

"Remind me to ask you again when you find yourself confronted by some disapproving lord." She spoke in a prim tone of voice, as much for her own benefit as for his. She could not allow herself to get distracted by the thought of all that. Even though he was entirely distracting, especially in that way.

"A disapproving lord who probably has some ninny of a daughter he'd much rather I end up with." He spoke in a disgusted tone. "No thank you. I far prefer the ruined woman in this scenario." He shrugged. "Besides which, it will give me an excuse to punch somebody in the nose if they impugn your honor."

Her stomach flipped at his words. Della hadn't had anybody but her sisters and brothers-in-law stand up for her, and none of *them* had ever offered violence toward someone who'd insulted her. Although Ida might, if provoked enough. It felt comforting, even though she would loathe it if he did it in truth.

Which reminded her to remind him. "You're not allowed to do that, remember? I can take care of myself."

He rolled his eyes. "Surely you'll allow me to do just a little bit of punching? If it was in response to a comment?"

She shook her head, even though the thought was appealing. But she knew men—if they thought they had permission for one thing, invariably they believed the permission extended far beyond the original limit.

"No, you cannot. But thank you."

They'd just met, and they had yet to get along, but he was offering, as though it was nothing, to support her. She would be safe with him, she knew that.

Although she wasn't certain she would be safe from herself.

Chapter 6

*T*hat wasn't so bad, was it?" she asked as they stepped out of the shop into the street. Griffith glanced instinctively to either side, taking her arm and drawing her close to him. Her maid trailed behind, and Griffith looked back to ensure she was safe as well.

"Stop manhandling me," she said as she twisted her arm away. "I am perfectly capable of walking down the street on my own."

He took her arm again, glancing down at her with an amused expression on his face. "I believe that, my lady. Perhaps I want the comfort of you by my side since I am unfamiliar with London?"

"Don't be ridiculous," she replied, but she didn't pull away.

"Thank you for your help today," he said as they walked. Toward where, he had no idea. He only hoped it wasn't to buy more clothing. "Do you have the proper attire for our upcoming adventure?" he asked.

"Sarah and I went shopping yesterday."

Damn. He wished he could have seen her trying gowns on, offering his opinion as to which was the most appealing on her. By which he meant the one that would show off her curves and creamy skin the best.

"There is a stack of invitations for us at Frederick's house." He spoke in a rueful tone. "News of my return traveled quickly. I believe there is a party tonight, should you be prepared for it. Unless you need more time?"

"I do not," she retorted, as he could have predicted. Lady Della was nothing if not predictably snappish, especially if it appeared one was questioning her being up to a task.

"Excellent. I will pick you up this evening, say around eight o'clock?" He glanced around them. "Where are we going now anyway?"

He saw her cheeks turn pink as she replied. "Since we are posing as an engaged couple, I thought it would be best if we have a ring. We're going to a jeweler's. Hopefully my mother won't have decided to go shopping today as well," she muttered, her tone as apprehensive as he'd heard from her thus far.

"A ring! I'd forgotten about that." He grinned at her. "Are you certain you haven't done this sort of subterfuge before?"

"You mean pretending I am betrothed to a duke's heir? I am fairly certain I would have recalled," she said in a dry tone.

He leaned his head back in laughter. She glanced up at him, a wry smile on her mouth, and then she laughed also, shaking her head.

This was already so much fun, and they hadn't even gotten into the teeth of Society yet.

"THAT ONE," LORD Stanbury said, pointing to a ring in the jewelry case.

Della frowned at seeing his selection. "That is far too large," she said.

"I am far too large, my lady, and yet you are stuck with me." The clerk in the shop raised her eyebrows, but didn't say anything. The clerk had introduced herself as Mrs. Harcourt, and judging by her placid demeanor, she was accustomed to seeing gentlemen purchasing jewels for ladies.

"You are not ostentatious and blindingly sparkling," she pointed out as the clerk withdrew the ring, laying it on the counter.

It was an enormous ruby, square-cut, surrounded by a ring of multicolored stones in a thick gold setting. It was, in Della's opinion, remarkably vulgar in its opulence, but she had to admit it drew the eye.

"I strongly disagree, my lady. I plan on being both ostentatious and blindingly sparkling this evening, when we attend that party."

"You will not," Della said firmly. "The point is for you to be accepted into Society, not to antagonize it. Even though you're insisting you bring me along, which will already be an impediment."

"Ah, but that is the whole fun of it." He winked at her. "Why should I compromise who I am? Who you are? Just so we can move through Society?"

"Don't be surprised when they turn their backs on you," she muttered.

He took her arm and turned her to face him. His gaze was intense, focused on her face. She inhaled at how fierce he looked. And how fierce he sounded when he spoke. "They will not. I understand these people. They pretend to be scandalized when someone in their world steps out of line, but they adore it when that someone does it with confidence. That is all you need, my lady. Confidence. We will succeed in our own storming of this castle, and we won't have to pretend to be anyone but ourselves."

Listening to him, seeing the look in his eyes, Della could almost believe it would be as easy as he said. Even though she knew that her situation—being a ruined woman—was far different from his. Not only that, but she'd be returning on the arm of a gentleman who would otherwise be fair game for single young ladies, so she would be despised even more.

It would not be enjoyable, not at all. But it was what he was demanding as the price to his helping her find Mr. Wattings, and she would face much worse than Society's disapproval if there was a chance she could help Sarah achieve some level of peace.

"Try it on," he urged. She picked the ring up and slid it on her finger. She stared down at it, at how the stone glinted in the light. It looked less terrible on her hand than it had in the case, and she could almost admit he was right in choosing this one. It said that there was no embarrassment to this engagement, that both the giver and wearer were proud to be open about their relationship.

"It looks lovely," the clerk said, her tone surprised.

Della looked up at the woman, her lips curling up into a smile as she met her gaze. "It does, doesn't it?"

"See?" he said in satisfaction. He addressed the clerk. "If you will send the bill to the Duke of Northam's house, we will settle the account immediately." He leaned toward Della to look into the case again, gesturing to something within. "And those earrings on the right, also."

"No, there is no need. The ring is plenty." Even though she couldn't suppress a gasp of appreciation as the clerk laid the earrings he'd indicated on the counter. They were ruby also, but simple teardrops on a plain gold wire.

"I say that there is." His tone allowed for no more argument. And besides, they were exceptionally beautiful. She could only resist so much.

"Shall I wrap these up?" the clerk asked.

"I'll wear them," Della said, scooping up the earrings. "And the ring too."

He watched as she slid the earrings through her ears, then tossed her head to make them dance when they were in. His gaze was appreciative, making her warm all over.

The clerk stepped over to the far side of the counter, writing up the order. Becky stood by the front door, her attention focused on the street outside.

"They suit you," he said in a low voice. "Richly beautiful, simple, elegant, in a color you cannot ignore. Like you," he finished. His words sent a ripple of pleasure through her body.

She bit her lip as she stared up at him, seeing the look of hunger in his gaze. Knowing that hungry look was likely duplicated in her own eyes.

This was so much trouble. He was trouble personified, and she would have to be wary in dealing with him that she didn't succumb as she had before. No pleasures of the flesh were worth the heartache that would inevitably come afterward. And she had no doubt that if she let him he would cause her plenty of heartache.

Better to keep her distance, no matter how much she wanted to close that distance for what she knew would be a passionate, intense kiss.

GRIFFITH FELT HIS breath catch in his chest as she looked up at him. Her expression was equal parts vulnerability and desire, and he swallowed against the urge to step forward and take her in his arms.

He had only known her for a bit over a day, and he could already admit he was besotted. He wouldn't act on it; it wouldn't be fair, given the inequity of their relationship already. If he approached her for anything beyond their current bargain, she might feel pressured to agree. Although he imagined she could take care of herself, but he wouldn't want her to have to, at least in regard to him. Lesser men would pester women, not understanding that a woman, especially a lady, had little recourse in that kind of situation. A hat pin was likely the most defense a lady could muster, and he'd seen what kind of result that had achieved.

But he would take her up on anything she might offer.

"And now?" she said, her tone returning to its imperious mien. "If you're done purchasing extravagant jewelry beyond what is required for this subterfuge, shouldn't we start looking for Mr. Wattings?"

He grinned at her. So she had felt it too. That was why she was being more than unusually prickly at the moment.

"Of course, my lady. As it happens," he said, quickening his steps, feeling as she scurried beside him, "I need to locate my first mate. The last I saw of him was at that pub."

"The one where you got arrested?" she asked pointedly. "The sleeping man?"

"Yes, that one."

"And will this be in pursuit of our goal of locating Mr. Wattings?"

Griffith nodded as he thought it out. "Clark will be less conspicuous than me. He can ask questions about where Wattings might have gone to."

"I want to go. I want to ask questions."

Griffith suppressed an urge to shake her. He knew he was stubborn, but Lady Della made him seem almost accommodating. Which he absolutely was not. "You, as you might have noticed when you came to the docks, are entirely conspicuous. Do you think anyone would answer your questions?" He raised his brow as he looked her up and down. "Never mind your person would be in danger. Sailors and the like are not accustomed to seeing anyone or anything nearly as beautiful as you."

Her eyes widened. In shock? Did she not know she was beautiful? Or more likely because it was him saying it?

And then her mouth flattened, and he saw as she marshaled her Della forces to deliver him some sort of crushing verbal blow.

"But I can see it is important to you," he continued. "And I did promise. So we will have to find you a disguise. Something to hide all of—" And then he gestured vaguely toward her so she wouldn't know if it was her face or her figure he thought needed disguising.

She looked as though now she didn't know how to respond, and he felt a moment of glee inside at having rousted her so thoroughly.

"A disguise," she said stiffly. "I suppose I can borrow something from somebody at the Society for Poor and Unfortunate Children. Mrs. Wattings and I teach there."

"As long as whatever you borrow hides the glory of Lady Della," he said with a grin.

And then she looked embarrassed all over again, and he wanted to take her in his arms and show her with methodical skill and patience just how beautiful he found her.

"But since we can't get your disguise until later, I'll go to the docks now to find my first mate. The last I saw of him," he began, thinking of Clark lying on that table, "well, I think he must be wondering where I am." Not to mention the rest of his crew, though they were likely pleased to have a reprieve from his orders, although he knew they'd be displeased to hear he wouldn't be their captain any longer when he did get to speak with them.

"As long as you don't begin the investigation without me."

"I wouldn't dream of it. I promise."

"And tonight we can announce ourselves to Society."

A shadow passed over her face as she spoke, and he wondered if she was going to share some of her hesitancy with him. He knew he didn't want to venture into Society, but he also didn't have the addition of Society not wanting him to venture into it, unlike her. How must that feel? And that she was willing to do it for her friend spoke volumes about her loyalty and the depth of her love.

But no, the moment passed; she raised her chin and took a deep breath. "This will be our first public appearance together."

"Yes, it will, my beloved."

She blinked, then her features cleared. "Oh yes. You're practicing. And I will have to practice saying Lord Stanbury."

"Or some other cozy nickname you might come up with?" he teased. "My captain? Lord Handsome?"

"Or the Duke of Arrogance?" she retorted. Her expression was amused.

"That would suit me very well," he said, putting his hands behind his back to thrust out his chest. He didn't miss how she glanced at him then, nor did he miss the look of interest in her eyes. "Although that would make you the Duchess of Arrogance."

"Not until I marry you," she reminded him. "And that will not happen."

It was unfortunate that this was only pretense—otherwise, he would be thinking about what she would be like in bed when they actually were married. How she'd tease and play with him there as skillfully as she was doing now on the street. Only she'd be naked and supine, and he would much prefer that scenario.

And he hadn't been lying when he said he did not want to be married. If he had to be shackled by his ducal responsibilities, he'd be damned if he'd add even more into his life. He'd seen his parents—seen how they might have once loved one another, only to become bitter and disappointed by one another's failings. And how his father had betrayed his mother so many times.

He wouldn't subject himself to that.

"My lord?" she said. She sounded impatient. How long had he been lost in thought?

"Apologies. Until tonight, then?"

She nodded, then beckoned to her maid and walked away, leaving him staring after her, this time able to look at her form, which was swaying enticingly.

Entering Society was going to be an enormous amount of fun, now that he'd found someone as fascinating as her to accompany him.

THE BUTLER PAUSED before announcing her name. Della smiled gently at him. She hoped he wouldn't be reprimanded for allowing her inside; it wasn't his fault that Viscount Huge had taken it into his head to bring her here this evening.

"Lady—Lady Della Howlett," the man said at last.

Della held her breath as she saw everyone in the room turn as one. If it weren't for his hand at her back—if it weren't for Sarah—she would have spun on her heel and run out of the room, no matter how bravely she faced scurrilous merchants, recalcitrant schoolgirls, and feisty kittens.

"Go on," he urged in a low voice. "You are betrothed to the most fascinating man in London. Nobody will scorn you, I promise."

"Griffith Davies, Viscount Stanbury," the butler said, this time as though he were actually pleased to be saying the name.

The crowd reacted again, their shocked expressions from before now tinged with curiosity.

Della saw a whirl of color approach her, like a pinwheel come alive, and realized it was Olivia and Eleanor, their eyes wide and their mouths hanging open in surprise.

She hadn't told her sisters she'd be doing this, so of course they were startled. That they had bolted out from the crowd so quickly to stand by her side made her relax just a tiny bit.

"We didn't know you were coming this evening," Olivia said, her eyes darting back and forth from Lord Stanbury to Della, avid interest in her gaze.

"My lord, allow me to present my sisters. This

is Lady Eleanor Raybourn, and Lady Olivia—" She paused, frowning. "What is your name anyway?"

Olivia stuck her hand out to Lord Stanbury. "Lady Olivia Wolcott," she said.

"I am pleased to make your acquaintance, my lady. And yours, Lady Eleanor."

"We're just thrilled you were able to persuade Della to come out," Olivia said in a delighted tone. "I have told her that it would be fine, but she would not listen."

"I have already discovered your sister is stubborn," he replied in a sly tone of voice. "But I was . . . *persuasive*." And that additional comment made it seem as though—well, as though something was happening that absolutely was not.

Which Della could tell because of her own reaction, but also because of her sisters' faces.

"Look," she said, speaking in a low tone of voice, "do not be shocked when you hear that Lord Stanbury and I are engaged."

"You are!" Olivia exclaimed. She started to wrap her arms around Della, who shook her head, sharing a commiserating glance with Eleanor.

"We are not, but we are saying we are so as to—so as . . . ." She turned to Lord Stanbury. "What are we doing anyway?"

He grinned. "You are helping me keep the ladies at bay." He swept into a bow. "You see, ladies,

I am irresistible. Especially now that it will be known that I am a duke's heir."

"That is very clever," Eleanor commented. "Although you should have kept it a secret from Olivia."

"I can keep a secret as well as anybody!" Olivia retorted, far louder than Della would have liked.

"Yes, I can see how good you are at not drawing attention to yourself," Della replied dryly.

"Hmph," Olivia said, but her eyes sparkled and it looked as though she was pleased to be in on the subterfuge.

"Lord Stanbury," a soft voice called from a few feet away. A handsome older woman drew toward them, a smile on her face. "I am Lady Linden. It is so lovely you were able to attend our gathering. I am hoping the duke is feeling better?"

A shadow crossed Lord Stanbury's face, so quickly Della might have missed it if she hadn't been looking at him at the time. Come to think of it, she spent a lot of the time she was with him just—looking at him.

Damn him for being so attractive, and stirring up all those feelings.

"Yes, he sends his greetings. And sends me, of course," Lord Stanbury said.

"And you are Lady Della?" Lady Linden said, turning to Della.

She braced herself for the inevitable look of disapproval. But the lady's face was just warm and welcoming, and she felt something inside her relax.

She still had the remainder of the guests to face, of course, but at least one person wasn't going to be unpleasant.

She would take it as a win.

"Yes, thank you, my lady," Della said.

"If you will excuse me," Lady Linden said. "I will leave you with your sisters and Lord Stanbury. Thank you so much for coming." She sounded sincere, and Della thought perhaps this wouldn't be as bad as she'd anticipated.

She felt a pinch on her arm. She turned around, not surprised to see it was Olivia.

"What is going on?" Olivia said in a whisper. "You have to tell us, I am dying of curiosity!"

Behind her, Eleanor nodded her agreement.

"If you will excuse us, my lord?"

"You can't desert me," Lord Stanbury said in a pained voice. It sounded as though he was serious. Was it possible that Lord Exuberant was actually terrified of meeting Society people? Was that what made him run off to sea? Or was his current attitude because he had so thoroughly thumbed his nose at these people—and now he was back among them.

"Come with us, then," Della said. "We can surround you in a phalanx of Howletts so nobody will speak to you."

She heard Eleanor smother a snort, and saw

Olivia's face brighten. "Oh do come. Let's go get some wine. Lord Linden is famous for his wine cellar."

"No beer, I suppose," she heard him murmur as they walked toward the refreshments.

"Did you find your Clark?" Della asked.

Lord Stanbury shook his head. "No, I wonder if he is still sleeping it off somewhere. I'll look tomorrow."

"I'll go with you. So we can ask for your first mate as well as see what we can find out about Mr. Wattings. Sarah found a disguise that will work."

"So stubborn," he said, and the admiring warmth in his tone made something happen low in her belly.

She couldn't blame the wine, since she hadn't had any yet. It was just him, and his outsized presence, and his surprisingly sweet trepidation about entering Society.

Oh dear, she thought as she walked beside him. *I am in so much trouble.*

"THAT WASN'T SO terrible," Griffith admitted as they waited for their cloaks. She had remained by his side the entire evening, sending pointed glances toward any young lady who appeared to be overstepping. He'd had to smother several grins at seeing how the young ladies wilted under Lady Della's proud gaze.

Her sisters had protected her all evening as well, stepping in whenever it seemed as though some Society member was about to mention Lady Della's scandalous past.

He'd never had that kind of protective family himself; the closest had been Frederick, who'd helped him run off to sea, but who had been too cowed by his father to stand up for Griffith when the duke had berated him.

"I suppose not," she said, smiling at the servant who arrived with her cloak. The servant blinked, as though startled. *Yes, she is beautiful*, Griffith thought. *And she is mine*.

Damn it, where had that come from?

He nearly glared down at his cock, since he knew perfectly well which of his parts had instigated that idea.

"Are you ready to leave?" she asked in an impatient tone.

"Yes, of course," Griffith said, shrugging into his own cloak, the voluminous fabric swirling around his body, hopefully hiding his reaction to her. He did not want her to know just how much he'd been thinking about her. About all that fierce passion of hers playing out in bed sport. Wanting her to tell him what to do and how hard to do it.

"Tomorrow we'll find Clark and begin our investigation," he said, as much to confirm their plans as to get his mind off her body.

"Yes, we spoke about that." Her tone made it

clear she thought he was being dim-witted, and he smothered a grin at how she'd react if he told her just why he was repeating himself—*I want to worship your body, Lady Della. I want to make you see stars. I want to hear you tell me just what you want me to do to you.*

So I tried to derail my thoughts by reminding us both of our plans for the next day.

They descended the stairs to Frederick's carriage in silence, the coachman holding the door open for them. She allowed him to assist her inside, and he followed, shutting them in together. Alone.

In a dark carriage with at least half an hour's worth of travel time before he deposited her back at her house.

His mind raced frantically for topics other than what was uppermost in his mind—and his trousers.

He was annoyed at himself for being so easily distracted. Yes, she was lovely and proud and stubborn and wickedly sharp. But he had a purpose in reentering Society, and it was not to engage in sexual congress with her.

Never mind that she would likely slap him if she had a hint he was so inclined.

"Thank you," she said in a soft voice, startling him—thankfully—from his thoughts.

"For what?" he replied in surprise.

He heard her shift on the seat next to him. "For staying by my side all evening. I noticed."

He chuckled, crossing his arms over his chest. "That was at least as much for my benefit as yours, my lady. I was telling the truth when I said the thought of those people terrified me. Knowing you were there at my side, quelling any potential awkwardness with a glare from your lovely eyes made it bearable."

Silence as she digested his words. "Why are you so terrified?"

He hadn't expected her question. Although he probably should have, given how forthright she seemed to be. She did not seem to be the type of person who would hold back from asking something that crossed her mind.

Which of course led him right back into thinking of her in his bed.

"I wasn't in Society at all when I was last a respectable member of the Davies family," he began. "I was too young. And I ran off to sea before I could leave home to get more of an education."

"So your terror is because it's unknown?" she said in a speculative voice. "Though that doesn't seem likely. You ran off to sea, for example, not knowing anything about it."

"Leaving the familiar has always fascinated me." Odd how he had never articulated that to himself. He shrugged. "I think that what I loathe is all the protocol. The having to be polite to people you despise, having to attend parties and pay attention when you'd rather be doing something—anything else."

"But if you never did it, how do you know it's as terrible as you say?"

Griffith bristled at the idea that he was prejudiced against something he hadn't experienced himself. Even though what she was saying was true.

"I don't know," he admitted at last. "Perhaps it isn't as bad as I'd imagined. Perhaps all the young ladies who obtained introductions this evening truly wanted to converse about the weather and the party." His tone was skeptical.

She nudged him in the arm with her elbow. "Stop. Those young ladies are far more trapped than you will ever be. They are trotted out like show ponies for inspection, with the prize being stuck with one person for the rest of their life." Her tone made it clear what she thought about *that*. "I know your fear is that you'd accidentally wind up married to one of them, but imagine how *they* feel? Knowing that their future existence depends on being chosen by some lord because of how well they danced, or what they look like?" She snorted. "That is my idea of torture. Pretending to be your betrothed is far more pleasant, at least."

"I am glad I am the lesser of two evils," Griffith

replied. "Is that what you went through before—before?" He paused, not sure how to reference her past scandal. Since he didn't even know what it was, but since she had a child and no husband he could likely guess. Not to mention how strongly she'd advised him against asking her to pose as his betrothed. Or the requirements she'd insisted upon. Which, of course, had only made it seem that much more intriguing.

"I had a season," she said. "I went to parties and spoke with gentlemen and wore pretty gowns. It wasn't all awful. I got to dance, and I do love to dance." She emitted a rueful laugh. "Which is what got me in trouble." She paused. "But I do not want to speak of that now."

He knew it would be a matter of simply asking someone, anyone, what her scandal was, but for some reason he wanted to hear it from her. And he wouldn't press until she felt comfortable enough to tell him.

"What do you wish to speak of, then?" he asked. "Or we can sit in silence. I will leave the decision up to you." He wasn't trying to tease her now.

For a moment, he thought she had made her choice because she was silent.

"Thank you," she said at last, sounding surprised. "Not many men—that is, no man of my acquaintance—would leave any kind of decision up to a woman. Which is why I insisted upon it. But I hadn't guessed you'd be so amenable."

"As you've noted, I am a remarkable man," Griffith couldn't help but reply.

"A remarkably conceited one," she said in a dry tone. "But I can't fault you for that." More silence as he wondered what she could possibly mean by that. "Which is why I choose to do this."

And then she moved closer to him, putting her fingers on his jaw and turning his head toward her, bringing his face down to hers until, at last, she pressed her mouth against his.

Lady Della was kissing him.

OH. SHE'D BEEN thinking about doing just this, honestly, since the first time she saw him in that dingy pub by the docks. Even though she hadn't wanted to admit it, not even to herself.

About how all that strength and size would feel in a moment of passion.

But her imagination could not live up to the reality.

Her fingers slid up from his face to his hair, and she tugged on some of the long strands, eliciting a soft chuckle in his throat. She could tell he was smiling against her mouth, and she drew his bottom lip between her teeth, biting gently before sliding her tongue inside.

His tongue met hers, but he didn't immediately take over in the kiss; instead, he allowed her to explore, holding himself still as she devoured his mouth.

But she could tell he was affected, and holding himself back, because his hand was on her arm, his fingers gripping her so tightly she knew he would leave a mark. A mark she would bear gladly, a reminder that this attraction was mutual, and she had instigated it. He wouldn't have, she knew that. Just as she knew that he felt it as strongly as she did.

Oh, but she'd missed this. Focusing entirely on a kiss, a caress, as though there was nothing else in the world. Nothing but the rumble of the carriage, of how his mouth was warm, and his tongue was now on the offensive, ravaging her mouth as though he was laying waste to all of her defenses.

Which she had to admit he was.

It was a good thing they were in a moving carriage or she would have torn his clothing off already. Her breasts felt sore and achy, but in a yearning way, while lower down that place throbbed, clamoring for attention. *His* attention.

It had been far too long since she'd been touched like this. Her own ministrations were fine, but there was nothing to compare to having a passionate partner.

She heard a moan, low in her throat, as his fingers moved up her arm to her neck, teasing in between the fabric of her cloak and her bare skin.

She shifted, thrusting her body up closer in

an implicit wish for him to touch her more, on her breast. Squeeze her nipple, if he were so inclined.

Oh, please be so inclined, she pleaded.

He stroked her skin, his thumb resting on the pulse at her neck. She ran her hands down his neck, rubbed the broad expanse of shoulders. Goodness, he was huge.

Was he huge everywhere? If forced to guess, she would say yes.

Dear Lord.

And then his fingers were dipping into the top of her gown, sliding down to the curve of her bosom, and she wanted everything. She wanted him to strip her bare, to plunge into her, to ride her to climax. *Her* climax, of course. He would have to wait for his.

The thought would have amused her if she weren't so focused on what he was doing—his fingers had found her nipple, and he was playing with it, sliding his fingertip across the taut peak. She shuddered, and arched her back, her mind frantically trying to do the necessary equation for coupling inside a coach.

He was too big to manage it satisfactorily, she would imagine.

Although he would likely take her up on the challenge, which would be pleasurable in and of itself—to watch as he twisted that huge body to successfully enter her. To push her into the carriage seat as he thrust into her.

He was kissing her more urgently, his fingers rubbing her nipple, then sliding around the globe of her breast as she ached and yearned and wanted everything from him right now, despite the logistical problem.

And then she couldn't take it any longer, not without feeling as though she were going to explode, and not in the way she longed for.

She drew back from him, staring up into his face. He was gazing intently at her, his eyes sparking with passion, his mouth wet from her kiss.

"That was even better than I'd thought it might be," she admitted. She was annoyed that she was speaking in a breathy voice.

"So you've been imagining this?" His voice was ragged, the masculine equivalent of breathy.

Good to know they were equally affected.

"Yes, of course," she replied. He closed his eyes for a moment, as though savoring her words.

"And how was it?" he asked, his voice resuming its usual arrogant tone. Although she couldn't fault him, not now. It was tremendous.

"You know how it was." She took a deep breath. Reminding her, as she inhaled, that his fingers were still on her breast.

She didn't want him to take his hand away. Even though they should be nearly home soon.

"It was." He paused, and then he extricated his hand from her gown in as graceful a manner as was possible, given the circumstances. "What do you propose we do about it?"

She lifted her chin, meeting his gaze forthrightly. "I propose that we have an affair."

Chapter 7

*I*t's the only thing to do," she continued. For the first time in possibly ever, Griffith felt unable to speak.

"We are clearly attracted to one another," she pointed out. "Also, neither one of us wants to get married, so there is no danger of a continuing relationship. We can give in to our attraction in the most logical way with neither one of us getting hurt."

It sounded so reasonable, how she put it. So naturally he wanted to object, since the last thing he ever aspired to be was reasonable.

But if it got him into her bed—and her into his—he'd swallow his objections, no matter how reasonable they were.

"How would this work?" he said. He was pleased he could manage to utter a complete sentence, given how startled and intrigued and, of course, aroused he was.

"Are you saying you don't know how it works?"

She spoke in a teasing tone, and he felt even more flustered.

"Not that," he said through his clenched jaw. This woman was the only person who had managed to get under his skin, for both good and bad.

He had the strange suspicion that it would take more than an affair to get over his obsession with her.

"Ah, I had thought your skills particularly . . . persuasive," she said in a low, knowing voice.

He resisted the urge to preen.

"But as to your question." She spoke in a matter-of-fact tone, not as though she was suggesting anything shocking at all. "I suppose we will look for Mr. Wattings, get you accepted into Society—as we'd agreed to—and we can also add a physical relationship to our agreement. It is that simple, there isn't much to it working. It either is pleasing to us both, or it isn't. If it's the latter, then no hard feelings." She stuck her hand out between them and he took it, allowing her to shake on the bargain. Another bargain on top of the first one.

This one was far more compelling.

The coach slowed, and she glanced out the window, her face lighting up at whatever she saw out there. Well, he knew it wasn't another gentleman; her desperate kiss had made it more than apparent that it had been as long for her as it had been for him, if not longer.

"I will see you at ten o'clock tomorrow," she commanded as the coachman swung the door open for her to alight. "To hunt for your first mate as well as Sarah's husband."

"Good evening, Lady Della," Griffith replied, but she was out of earshot long before, bounding up the steps to her house in clear excitement.

He saw the ladies peering out from the door; Mrs. Wattings and two small girls. One of them was obviously Mrs. Wattings's child, while the other one must belong to Lady Della. Or Della, he should think of her; it wouldn't do to address her so formally when he was about to embark on a clandestine relationship with her.

Unless she wished to be formally addressed: *May I ravish you, Lady Della?*

You may, my lord Handsome, she might reply in that peremptory tone of hers.

Her proposal was making his being an heir to a dukedom rather than aboard his own ship much more pleasant. Although eventually the affair would pass, and he would be left on shore with responsibilities and steady land under his feet.

Still, it would do for the moment.

"WHY DO YOU look like that?" Sarah asked. They had gotten the girls to bed at last—Nora and Emily had peppered Della with questions about the party because parties were not a usual part of their lives.

That hurt. Not so much because she was missing out on the parties, she didn't care one way or the other, but that her reputation and situation made it impossible to be social. Although the tiny town they'd lived in until about six months ago, Haltwhistle, didn't have any kind of Society to speak of anyway, so even if Della's reputation had been pristine, there wouldn't have been anywhere to go.

They were sitting in the small parlor where they took their afternoon tea. It was cozy, and much more pleasing to Della than her father's enormous town house.

Or that could be because of all the love and warmth she had here as opposed to what she had felt there.

"Look like what?" Della replied, knowing her friend would not be deterred.

"As though something happened." Sarah narrowed her eyes as Della tried to repress a reaction. Even though Sarah knew her better than anyone, sometimes better than Della knew herself. "Something did happen! You have to tell me everything."

Della exhaled and looked away from her friend's face. "Uh—I might have accidentally kissed Captain Enormous."

Silence, and then Sarah whacked Della on the arm. "What do you mean, accidentally kissed him? Did you mean to whisper something in his ear and your mouth accidentally collided into his?" Sarah's voice let Della know that her friend did not actually think that occurred. "Did you like it, at least?"

"Oh yes," Della said. "It was tremendous."

Sarah blinked at Della's enthusiastic tone. "Well. So there is that, at least. Did he like it?"

Della thought about how he had caressed her, how he had kissed her so thoroughly that she still felt the ripples of pleasure flowing through her body. "Yes."

"And . . . ?" Sarah prodded.

Della winced. "Well, I might have suggested we have an affair."

Sarah's sharp inhale was about the reaction she expected. "Good for you!" her friend cheered, which was absolutely not what she had expected.

"Good for me?" Della repeated. She leaned forward to place her palm on Sarah's forehead. "Are you feeling quite well?"

Sarah swatted her hand away. "I'm not feeling as well as you are, apparently, but yes. I think it's a wonderful idea. As long as . . ." she said, her words trailing off as she made a vague gesture in the air.

"No, of course not," Della replied hastily. She did not want to have another child, even if its father was Lord Captain Handsome.

"Then it's wonderful," Sarah concluded, settling back in her seat with a smile of satisfaction.

"But why? I mean, shouldn't you be warning me about doing something so reckless and scandalous?"

Sarah rolled her eyes. "As though I could stop you from doing any such thing. You are the most recklessly scandalous person I know, and also the person I love most in this world." She shrugged. "This adventure will keep you from doing something even more reckless, I imagine."

Della felt her eyes widen. "What could possibly be more reckless than embarking on an affair with a sea captain–viscount?" She shook her head. "I wish he were just a sea captain. It would make things much simpler." And might also make it possible for them to have a future together, although she wouldn't share that judgment with Sarah. If her friend so much as suspected that Della wanted more—not that she did, she assured herself—she would go to extreme lengths to see to Della's happiness.

But Della knew Society much better than Sarah did, and though they might accept her initially because of the novelty of Lord Stanbury, eventually they would realize that they could not stomach seeing the duke's most disgraced daughter in a respectable position. It would be a relief to everyone when she and Lord Stanbury revealed that they were no longer engaged.

So their time together would have a very specific end date—namely, when he was comfortable enough in his position not to need a buffer against the young ladies. Or when they grew tired of one another.

But she strongly suspected the former would happen a lot earlier than the latter. She felt a twinge of sadness, but shut that away. She hadn't even started to have her scandalous affair with him, so she shouldn't already be mourning its ending.

Perhaps he would end up being a terrible lover?

Although she knew, even as she thought it, that there was no possible way that was the case.

"GRIFF! LOOK WHO is here," Frederick said as Griffith entered the room that seemed to serve as Frederick's office and bedroom all at once.

Griffith had been surprised when the butler had told him Frederick was still up and was asking for him. That Clark was here explained all of that.

Clark rose from the sofa, a warm smile on his face. "I tracked you down, and now I find that you're some sort of lord?" Clark stuck his hand out to Griffith, who took it and shook it vigorously. "Why didn't you ever say?"

Griffith released Clark's hand. "Would you have said in my position?"

Clark considered it. "No, I suppose not."

"Your first mate has been regaling me with stories of your adventures at sea. I didn't realize you were such a rascal, Griffith."

Griffith grinned at his cousin. "Sure you did, Fred. Your Grace," he amended, at which Frederick shook his head. "You were the one who rescued me when we were young."

"Sit down, sit down," Frederick commanded. Griffith and Clark both sat on the sofa, Griffith crossing one leg over the other.

"Where did you come from anyway?" Griffith asked Clark. "I went to the docks to see if I could find you, only nobody knew where you'd gone after that pub."

"No thanks to you."

"You mean my heir left you on your own without a word?" Frederick demanded, his eyes glinting with humor.

Griffith had missed his cousin. Even though being with him required being on dry land.

"He did, Your Grace," Clark replied, shooting a wry glance toward Griffith. "But I was a bit under the weather at the time, so it wasn't as though he had much of a choice."

"Not to mention I was being pulled away by the naval police," Griffith added. "If it had been possible to stay there until you awoke, Clark, I would've."

"Ah, so that's when you were arrested."

"Arrested?" Clark echoed.

Griffith shrugged, shooting a conspiratorial glance toward his cousin. "Arrested because of what happened in Africa, I believe. Once they found out who I was, the charges were dropped."

"The benefit of Griffith's position," Frederick said pointedly.

"Oh," Clark said. "But if the case did go to court, then you'd have the opportunity to share what terrible things they did over there. Despite all of us being allies." His face darkened, and Griffith felt the injustice of it all over again.

"It'd be easier to enact change if you're in a position of power," Frederick added.

The only solace to his current situation was that as a duke he might be able to address some of the problems with far more effectiveness than as a renegade captain.

"Well, since you won't be heading out to sea again, my lord, would you mind writing me a letter of recommendation?"

Griffith shook his head. "No."

Clark leaned forward, his expression confused. "No?"

"No, because I want you to come work for me as my valet or secretary or whatever it is you think you'd like to do."

Clark's face cleared, and it was obvious the notion pleased him. "Yes, absolutely! I have no obligation to the Royal Navy as of the moment we came ashore." He grinned. "As long as I don't have to climb rigging any longer."

"There is a scarcity of rigging involved in being a duke," Frederick said dryly.

Griffith took a deep breath. His friend, his closest friend for the past five years, would be on hand for him to talk to. To work out just what this new life might mean. It had only been a few days, but he'd felt strangled with all this new responsibility. Not knowing what to do, or how to do it.

Clark's presence would help that, even though Clark had no idea how to be a nobleman either. As far as Griffith recalled, Clark came from a family of turnip farmers or something.

"Well, as your new employee, I shouldn't be sitting in this fancy room as though we were all the same," Clark said as he sprang up from his seat.

Griffith winced. "No, the whole point is that we are the same."

"Except that you have a title and will own more land than my family has ever seen," Clark replied.

"He is not wrong," Frederick commented.

"Be quiet, both of you," Griffith replied, glancing from one to the other. "And sit down, Clark."

Clark sat, a grin on his face.

"Fred, if you expect me to be the kind of duke that sits around musing on his own importance, you might want to reconsider asking me to stay. Because I won't do that."

Frederick smiled. "I know you won't. What I do know is that I'll be leaving the title in good hands when I am gone."

When I am gone. Fred spoke so matter-of-factly, as if his dying wasn't something to be feared. Perhaps it wasn't, since it was obvious that the event had been coming, and had been foreseen, for a long time now.

"And if he does get to musing," Clark added, "I'll knock him over the head."

Frederick's smile widened. "Excellent." He paused. "But not too hard, or we'll be out another duke. You don't have a child somewhere about to inherit, do you?" he said, addressing Griffith.

Griffith swallowed. "Uh—no." A good reminder that since he was planning on taking Lady Della up on her offer, he had to ensure that his answer remained accurate. He'd have to ask Clark to figure out where one might go to purchase some discreet items.

Likely his first mate wouldn't anticipate "find out where to buy condoms" as one of his first on-shore duties.

"So not too hard, then," Frederick admonished Clark.

"Aye, aye, Your Grace," Clark replied.

"Bring the decanter over, Mr. Clark," Frederick said. "Let's have a toast to our new situations."

"Your cousin, has he always been ill?"

Griffith and Clark had spent another hour with Frederick, swapping stories of life aboard ship as Frederick listened, his face alit with curiosity and excitement.

Now they were upstairs in Griffith's bedroom, a room at least five times larger than his captain's berth.

"He was fine when I left," Griffith replied. His hands reached up to his cravat, only to have Clark swat them away.

"That's my job now."

"So you want to be my valet?" Griffith asked, lifting his chin so Clark could more easily undo the fabric around his neck.

Clark shrugged. "I'll be both valet and secretary, at least until we figure out what either job is. If that's all right with you, my lord," he added in an obsequious tone.

Griffith glowered, at which Clark laughed. He bowed, then stepped in front of the wardrobe and began to open various drawers.

"What are you looking for?" Griffith asked.

Clark turned to regard him. "Well, I see some clothing here—yours, judging by the size—but you don't have any of your own items here, as far as I can tell. Should I send to the ship for them?"

Griffith nodded. "Yes, thank you. I—things have happened so quickly I forgot."

What with being hauled off to prison, just as suddenly released, and then made heir to a dukedom.

"And I'll need to send an official letter to the

Royal Navy letting them know I am resigning my commission. I forgot about that too."

"That is why you need a valet-secretary. Or secretary-valet, I'm not sure of the right sequence of words," Clark said with a grin.

It was good to have his friend around. He hadn't realized just how off he'd felt being on his own. Was that why he was so interested in Lady Della? Because he was lonely?

No, you idiot. It's because she's intelligent, quick-witted, and beautiful. You'd be interested in her if all of London was standing in one ballroom, and she was on the other side.

Not to mention, it appeared she was as interested in him, which couldn't help but increase his own interest.

"What are you thinking about?" Clark's question snapped him out of his reverie.

"Uh—" Griffith began, only to have Clark raise an eyebrow and look him straight in the eye. Difficult, since Clark was so much shorter than Griffith was.

Griffith admired his friend's dexterity.

"Out with it. What are you doing? What are you planning on doing?"

He never could keep a secret from his first mate, could he?

"Well, there is a lady."

Clark's expression cleared. "Oh, is that all? I should have expected that."

Griffith wanted to bristle at Clark's easy acceptance, and his implication that Lady Della was just another of his passing fancies.

Even though she was, by her own definition. And they hadn't done anything but kiss yet. And he'd stroked her breast, which it seemed she thoroughly enjoyed.

He felt as he did when he had first noticed the opposite sex; how could one sharp, beautiful woman set him so askew? As though he were half his age and desperate for notice?

He would have to remind himself of his own skill in matters of passion when he actually got to touch her. Or she'd be disappointed in his quick . . . resolution.

"Do you need anything else, my lord?" Clark said, a sly gleam in his eyes. "Should I help you dress for bed?"

Griffith grabbed a pillow off the bed and flung it at Clark, who dodged it easily, laughing.

"I take that as a no. If you will excuse me? I'll just go to my room."

"Good evening, Clark."

"Good evening, my lord," Clark said as he left the room.

Leaving Griffith alone to recall the kiss, and the proposal she'd made, and imagining just how delicious she would taste.

If it weren't close to midnight, he'd be tempted to walk over to her house right now to take her up on the offer. Perhaps she'd already be in bed, all sleepy and rumpled, and he could curl up alongside her, rousing her gently with his mouth and hands.

But—damn it!—he knew he could not do that, and now he had a massive cockstand and only his own hand to take care of it.

But soon. Soon he would be able to thrust inside her, to bring her to release, to ravish her thoroughly so that both of them would be left in a boneless heap.

He couldn't wait.

Chapter 8

*L*ord Stanbury is arriving at ten o'clock this morning so we can go down to the docks and make inquiries."

"Oh, he is, is he?" Sarah replied in a deceptively innocent tone. As though they both weren't aware of what he and Della were planning on doing—besides pretending to be engaged to thwart single ladies in search of an eligible gentleman as well as trying to find Sarah's husband. Those tasks should have been enough, but then Della had to find it impossible to resist her own reaction to him.

She shook her head at her own foolishness. Even though that foolishness was, she also had to admit, going to be entirely and absolutely pleasurable.

She just knew he was going to be an excellent bed partner.

"Della?" Sarah's tone made it clear it wasn't the first time her friend had said her name.

"Sorry, what?" She put a bright smile on her face as she looked at Sarah.

Sarah rolled her eyes. "I was asking if you would mind if I took Nora and Emily and some of the girls with me to the zoo. We started talking about animals at the society yesterday, and I thought it'd be a good opportunity to take them out. They'll learn something in spite of themselves."

"Oh yes, absolutely." A thought struck her mind. "And you should take Becky, she can help." And that would mean that Della and Lord Stanbury would be unchaperoned, but that was what Della wanted, wasn't it?

Honestly, it was remarkable more women hadn't just gone and gotten ruined since it made life so much easier—not having to have a maid tagging along with you wherever you went, not worrying if you were seen alone with a man.

In exchange, you were ostracized from your parents and regarded with suspicion by every member of Society you might meet. So perhaps not entirely easier, but certainly easier to manage.

"Mmm-hmm," Sarah said, her tone indicating she knew precisely why Della had suggested Becky be included. "We'll be gone all day," she said pointedly, "so you'll have the upper floor to yourself."

Oh. Well, then.

Della reached across the table to clasp Sarah's hand. "You truly are an excellent friend, aren't you?"

Sarah squeezed her fingers, a knowing smile on her face. "I am. But you are just as excellent since you're trying to find Henry for me. I never could have done it by myself."

"It's the least I can do. Especially since you're clearing out the house," Della added with a wicked grin.

Sarah laughed and shook her head.

"GOOD MORNING."

It was her opening the door again. Griffith stepped inside, shutting the door behind himself.

"Don't you have someone who can do that for you?" he asked.

"Do what?" she replied.

He gestured to the closed door. "Open the door to visitors? What if there is some ne'er-do-well who decides to pay a call?"

She snorted, making him feel entirely nonplussed. Per the usual, he had to admit.

"A ne'er-do-well? I have to remember that one for Sarah."

"You haven't answered the question," he said. "I am concerned for your safety."

She patted him on the arm. "Thank you for your worry, my lord. I am just fine. I can open and shut doors all by myself."

"That is not the issue, and you know it."

She exhaled in an exaggerated way, sending strands of hair flying up into her face. "I cannot imagine anyone more ne'er-do-well than you, my lord. Unless you're suggesting I refuse you entry?"

"At least let me get you some sort of protection," he grumbled.

She looked taken aback. "What kind of protection? A pistol?"

"Of course not," he said quickly. "You'd likely shoot your own foot as an intruder. I meant that I could hire some of my crew to stand guard here. It will take them all a while to find new assignments, and I might as well try to make use of them so they can earn something while they wait."

"Ah, so you are pretending to be worried about my safety so you can disguise your altruism toward your crew. Well done, my lord," she said.

"That's—never mind. Yes. That is what I am doing, you annoying woman."

She gave him a bright smile. "Well, now that that is settled, shall we head to the docks?"

Griffith glanced around the hallway. "Don't you need that girl to come with you?"

Della grinned wickedly back at him. "No, she is with Sarah and the girls. I do not need a chaperone when I am with my beloved betrothed, Lord Hugely Handsome."

Griffith leaned his head back in laughter. "Well, then, Lady Stubborn, let us go make our inquiries."

"Took you long enough," she grumbled, but with a humorous note in her voice.

"WATTINGS," GRIFFITH REPEATED. "Henry Wattings. About five feet ten inches, broad in the chest. A black man who might have been looking for work as an able seaman."

The man paused in winding the rope around his elbow, and Della had a moment of hope, only to be dashed when he shook his head. "Nope, don't recall anybody like that. We've got plenty of sailors about, but nobody matching that description."

"It would have been about three years ago," Della added.

The man grunted, then spat on the ground. "Yer gentleman said that already."

Della opened her mouth to snap back at him, only to remain quiet as Lord Stanbury put a hand on her arm as though cautioning her. He wasn't wrong, even though she wanted to shake him off.

"The Holdfast Arms is where most of the black sailors drink when ashore," the man said. "You'd be best asking there for your missing man. It's that way," he continued, gesturing down the docks to the right.

"Excellent, thank you," Lord Stanbury said.

They headed off in that direction, Della holding on to Lord Stanbury's arm as his long legs chewed up the ground.

She could have asked him to slow down, but she found she liked the pace. Far too often she'd found herself frustrated at the slowness of other people around her. Lord Stanbury—Griffith— was just as energetic as she, and she liked how breathless and energized she felt.

Which, of course, reminded her that they would be engaged in other physical pursuits that would hopefully make her feel both energized and breathless.

And the house was empty now, so it made sense to try to hasten this errand. Was that why he was walking so quickly? Because he was eager to get her into bed?

Not that he knew of her plan, so perhaps not.

"Why are we searching this way instead of applying directly to the Navy?" she asked. She looked up at him, noting how his dark hair was flying about, nearly as wild as he was. He only needed a gold hoop through his ear to look like the most dangerous of pirates.

"I'd rather not remind them of my existence," he replied wryly. "Given that the last time the Navy and I met I ended up in jail."

"How did you get out anyway?"

He looked down at her as though considering what to say. "My cousin's solicitor came to get me. It turns out a duke's heir should not spend time in any type of jail, no matter what they did."

"What did you do?" She couldn't help but ask;

hopefully it was not "asked a lady to be his pretend betrothed and then dumped her into the ocean" or something equally terrible.

"I did what was right," he replied, his tone making it clear he did not want to discuss it further.

"What was that?" Because even though Della could read a tone as well as the next person, that did not mean she paid attention to the cue.

"I captured a slaver ship and then released everyone aboard when it was clear that the authorities were going to let the matter drag on." He shrugged. "Apparently I should have waited for justice to take its course. But it seemed to me," he said, sounding more vehement, "that justice was taking far too long, and some of those people would have died in the interim."

"You did the right thing, then. Even if the Navy disagrees. But I understand why going through official channels—"

"So to speak," he interrupted.

"—would be something you would prefer to avoid."

"At the moment, yes. So we'll ask at this pub and try to find Wattings without having to inquire of Her Majesty's Navy."

More questions occurred to her, but there was no opportunity to ask them, since they were in front of the pub. He turned to her and adjusted the hood of her cloak lower over her face.

"You're still too damned beautiful," he murmured as he tucked a strand of flyaway hair behind her ear. "But I also know you're too damned stubborn, so you wouldn't let me do this on my own."

She smiled up at him. "And you're far too handsome, but I assume you won't let that impede you from asking questions."

He grinned back as he pushed open the door to the pub.

They stepped inside, him close at her back as though for protection. *Not that I need it*, she thought. Although it did feel nice to feel the solid warmth of him.

He strode to the bar at the other end of the pub, her trailing along after him. The pub was half-full of men, some white and some black. All of them staring at them, making Della feel nearly uncomfortable.

If she ever felt uncomfortable, that was. Which she did not.

"We're looking for someone," Griffith announced. He placed a few coins on the bar and addressed the room. "A Mr. Henry Wattings, he would have come ashore about three years ago, right after the *Royal Lady* capsized."

Della held her breath as the men glanced at one another. A man, one nearly as large as Griffith, rose slowly to his feet. "And who is asking?" he said in a soft voice, but one that held a menacing tone.

"I'm Captain Griffith Davies. Wattings was under my command, and now I want to find him."

The man paused, his gaze assessing the two of them. At last, he nodded. "I've heard of you." Della exhaled. "Wattings hasn't been here for at least a year. He went to—where did he go, John?" he said, turning his head to address a man at another table.

Was it going to be this simple? And once she had found Sarah's husband, did that mean her agreement with Lord Stanbury would be finished?

"I can't say," John said, shrugging.

Damn it.

Lord Stanbury tossed a coin to the first man, and then to John, leaving the rest on the bar. "If you hear anything about Wattings, send word to the Duke of Northam's address."

The first man looked askance at Lord Stanbury. "You're a duke?"

His mouth thinned. "Not yet I'm not." He nodded at the two men, then slid the remaining coins to the barkeep as he took Della's arm none too gently.

SHE WAS GOING to do it. She was on her way to taking Lord Enormous into her bed, where she'd discover if his enormousness extended everywhere.

She was fairly certain it would.

Lord Stanbury—or Griffith, since she supposed
that their imminent sexual congress would put
them on a first-name basis—walked so quickly
she had to scurry to keep up. They had left the
docks and were in the shopping district now,
close to home. He kept her close to his side, his
hand clamped on top of hers where it rested on
his arm.

"My lord!"

He kept moving as quickly as before.

"My lord!" the voice said again. She nudged
him with her elbow, and she heard him sigh in
exasperation.

"Yes?" he said, nearly as curtly as earlier. She
nudged him harder, and he responded by holding tighter to her hand.

"My lord, if I may presume to introduce myself." The gentleman who'd approached them
was older, a young lady at his side. An explanation for his insistence on hailing Griffith. *I'm
here to prevent your daughter from ensnaring him,*
Della thought. *And let me keep up my part of the
bargain by making that very clear.*

Not to mention she was very eager herself to
get him home. Since then they could embark on
the most pleasurable aspect of their bargain.

"Lord Thwaite, my lord. I know your cousin
the Duke of Northam. Terribly sorry to hear of
his illness."

She felt Griffith's posture get rigid. And knew it was because he didn't want anyone to speak of his cousin, whom Della could tell was someone Griffith cared about.

"Thank you."

"I know you are recently arrived in London, and I believe you don't have many acquaintances as of yet," Lord Thwaite continued, apparently oblivious to Griffith's clear aggravation. "So I would introduce my daughter, Lady Amelia."

The daughter nodded at Griffith, looking pained. Perhaps she was aware of her father's encroachment?

"A pleasure, my lady." Griffith's tone was softer, as though he wouldn't punish the daughter for the father's sins.

That shouldn't have surprised her, given how kind he was to any lady he'd met besides her. Should she take that as a reverse sort of compliment?

After all, he wasn't planning on having sexual relations with any of the ladies he was pleasant to. At least she hoped he wasn't, or he'd be too tired to venture into Society.

Not that she had claim to him in any way about that, but she did hope he would devote himself exclusively to her, at least while they were in agreement as to their relationship. She deserved and desired his full attention.

"My lord."

"This is my betrothed, Lady Della," Griffith said.

Lord Thwaite's face fell. Just as his daughter's brightened. She glanced at Della with a wry look on her face, as though acknowledging her father's disappointment, but also relieved by it.

Della liked her already.

"Lady Della, a pleasure. I believe I have met your sister Ida, Lady Carson?"

Ah. No wonder Lady Amelia was relieved not to have to cast her lures to Griffith—if she knew and had spent time with Ida, and was also willing to admit it, chances were good she was as intelligent as Ida and as unwilling to get married simply because that was what one did.

"If I may, could I persuade you to share a dance with me this evening? I believe we are scheduled to attend the Chartleys' party?" he said, looking down at Della.

"Yes," Della confirmed, even though now was the first time she'd heard of the party. But she shouldn't have been surprised; there were parties every evening. His surprising her with the information wasn't the same as being told she would have to go.

And she wouldn't have been invited at all if she weren't on the arm of an eligible gentleman.

It was remarkable how that would open doors for someone who'd expected all the doors to be shut in her face on her return.

"Thank you, my lord, I would be delighted," Lady Amelia replied.

"Good, good. Now, if you will excuse me, my betrothed and I have to be on our way. We have strategizing to do."

He whisked her away before Lord Thwaite and his daughter could see her break out into laughter.

Chapter 9

$\mathcal{D}$ella fumbled for the key to the house, only to have him snatch it away from her and put it in the lock, pushing her inside with his big body as the door swung open.

"You're home!"

Both of them froze, his front pressed against her back, their faces likely wearing equally startled and probably guilty expressions.

"Mrs. Wattings said you likely wouldn't be home for hours, and I shouldn't wait, but see, you are here, and much earlier than expected." Olivia beamed at both of them. "My lord, a pleasure to see you. I didn't realize the two of you were together."

Sarah peered over Olivia's shoulder, her expression bemused. Not unusual, given Olivia's enthusiastic mien. Likely Sarah had done her best to dissuade Olivia from staying, but Della knew her sister would not be deterred if she had a purpose.

And her purpose today—even though she did not know it—was to keep her sister from embarking on an illicit affair.

Drat.

"Do come into the parlor, Olivia." She might as well accept that nothing passionate would be occurring today. "Sarah, do you mind ringing for tea?"

Sarah nodded, her expression still rueful. *There was nothing you could do*, Della wanted to say.

"Lord Stanbury, would you care for tea?" He hadn't moved from where he had been when Olivia had hailed them. His face was still frozen, as though in shock. And disappointment, Della knew. Since she was feeling vastly disappointed herself.

"I should return home," he replied, his voice clipped. "We can meet to strategize later, I will leave you to your sister."

He didn't wait for a response, just spun on his heel and went out the door.

"Good-bye, my lord!" Olivia called.

Della took a deep breath before turning back around. She didn't want Olivia to have any kind of suspicion as to what had almost happened; a pretend betrothal was one thing, but a very real affair would make Olivia determined to interfere.

It was unfortunate none of her sisters had been able to keep her from running off with

Mr. Baxter. But if she hadn't, she wouldn't have Nora.

"Where are the girls?" she said. She hadn't been able to spend as much time with her daughter since returning to London as she would have liked. What with hunting for Mr. Wattings and attending parties with Lord Hugely Attractive. She'd barely gotten to work for the Society for Poor and Unfortunate Children lately. She missed it, actually.

"They're upstairs with Becky," Sarah said. The three ladies began to walk toward the parlor. "We decided to visit the zoo another time, since Emily was sneezing this morning. They told me today that you and I are too old to play with, so we're being shunted aside for a younger version."

Della snorted in response. "Also because if they don't spend time with us they're not having lessons."

"True," Sarah confirmed.

"Della, you have to tell me how you came to meet Lord Stanbury," Olivia said as they settled into their seats. "Why are you pretending to be engaged to him? I am delighted to see you out again, but I worry about you, you know."

"I know. You don't have to, but it is lovely that you do." Della smiled at her younger sister, by far the most exuberant of the duke's daughters. "Apparently Lord Stanbury is not accustomed to Society, and he thought that he might get entrapped by some conniving female if he entered this world as an unattached gentleman." She shrugged. "It suits me to pretend, and he has promised to help me locate Sarah's husband."

Olivia turned to look at Sarah. "Oh! I didn't realize—that is, I—"

"You thought I was like Della, relieved to be free of the burden of a gentleman in my life?" Sarah gave Della a fond look. "I admire your sister's independence and refusal to be constrained by what people expect, but I did love—do love—my husband."

"Refusal to be constrained by what people expect is a delightful euphemism for 'won't be told what to do,'" Della remarked dryly.

Sarah burst into laughter, nodding her agreement.

"Is there anything I can do to help?" Olivia asked.

Della shook her head. "Lord Stanbury and I asked at the docks this morning." She didn't want to raise Sarah's hopes by telling her Mr. Wattings had been in town a year prior. Better to wait until she had something definitive to share. "But we will not quit until we know something," she said, a fierce tone in her voice.

Sarah gave a soft smile. "Thank you," she replied.

"What happens after you find Mrs. Wattings's husband?" Olivia asked.

One of the maids came in bearing a tea tray, setting it down on the table between them. Olivia immediately snagged a biscuit, but Della knew her questions wouldn't cease merely because her mouth was full.

"I mean," she said, her words emerging between bites, "how are you and Lord Stanbury going to explain when you don't get married after all?"

Sarah arched her brow as though curious to hear the answer as well.

"Well," Della replied, fixing her tea, "we decided Lord Stanbury would announce that he is too busy with ducal things to consider marriage at this time." She shrugged. "And everyone will assume it is my fault, since I am so extremely fallen."

Olivia frowned as she swallowed. "But doesn't that just mean you acquire more scandal? Don't you want to find someone you actually want to marry?"

Sarah bit her lip as though feeling Della's emotions herself. It was lovely to have a close friend, but not when your friend suffered alongside you.

"I won't ever get married," she replied, trying to keep her voice light. "What kind of man would want to marry me anyway?"

Olivia snorted. "A wise one? You're intelligent, brave, a good mother, and beautiful besides."

Della felt herself start to blush. If only she'd had as much confidence in herself five years ago as her sister did in her now. She would not have run off with Mr. Baxter, who'd exploited her insecurities and persuaded her to do a very foolish thing.

"Thank you, Olivia, but I have to assure you, I have no interest in marriage." Della felt her chest get tight as she pondered it. "A husband can do with his wife whatever he wants. He might say during the courtship period that he can overlook a woman's past, but what would happen the first time we had a disagreement? Or the twentieth time?" She shook her head. "Far better not to risk it at all."

"That is such a shame," Sarah said, her tone gentle. "I have to believe that any man you would choose would never betray you so."

"But I cannot be certain. Because clearly I have very poor judgment in men," Della replied wryly. "Mr. Baxter was a blackguard of the highest order, and I chose him. Who's to say I wouldn't make such a terrible decision again?" She shook her head. "No, the safest thing is to remain unmarried. I have my friend, my sisters, my daughter. I don't need anything else."

Except that she did. She needed passion, and she knew where she would find it. If only Olivia weren't so stubborn she would even now be discovering what lay beneath Lord Stanbury's clothing.

But she would never conflate her desire with love. With commitment. She wouldn't put him under that obligation. As much because she didn't want to be obliged. She might like him as a bed partner—although she had yet to confirm that—but she did not want him, or any man, as a husband.

If not for her own self, then for Nora.

"Well," Olivia said, gesturing with her biscuit at Della, "we've all made mistakes in our choices, but that doesn't mean we all don't deserve a happily-ever-after."

Sarah nodded. The traitor.

"And there might be someone who could persuade you that marriage, that love, is worth the risk." And then her expression got all spoony. No doubt thinking of her own husband.

Della wouldn't argue with her sister, even though she knew full well that she would never find anyone worth the risk. Because the risk was too great. But if she said that to Olivia, her sister would spend the next hour—and an enormous amount of biscuits—trying to convince her otherwise.

The duke's daughters didn't always have a lot in common, but they did share one trait: stubbornness.

Which meant that Della would stubbornly persevere in her attempt to gain Lord Stanbury as her lover.

IF BEING SEXUALLY sabotaged was a crime, Griffith would never emerge from a jail cell again. He stalked back to Frederick's town house, frustration oozing from every fiber of his being.

What was it about her that felt so different? He'd been with plenty of women before, all different sorts, the only commonality being that they found him worthy of their consideration.

As they damn well should.

Griffith wasn't conceited—or, perhaps he was, but his conceit was well deserved. He knew he was handsome, charming, and attentive in bed. He'd gotten so accustomed to having whatever desire he wanted almost immediately granted that he didn't know how to react with this latest impediment.

Of course it was only an impediment, not a stoppage. It had been she, after all, who had made the initial proposal. And he knew she was just as eager as he to begin.

But what if she changed her mind? What if her sister and her friend discovered what she was planning and talked her out of it?

He'd have to ascertain she was still of the same mind when he saw her again. And if she was not, he'd have to accept her change of heart and with-draw gracefully, albeit frustratedly.

"My lord."

How had he arrived back at Frederick's so quickly?

"Good afternoon," he replied to the footman who'd greeted him. The door swung open, revealing the taciturn butler.

He would have to figure out the man's name eventually. Since he was going to be Griffith's own butler at some point. His throat tightened as he thought about what that change would mean.

Please don't let Frederick die, he pleaded. *Now that I've returned home.*

"Lord Stanbury, the duke is hoping to see you before dinner. If you would—?" he said, gesturing to Fred's room. Griffith removed his cloak, relieved to have something to think about besides her and what they were not doing right now.

"What is it, Fred?" Griffith said as he entered Frederick's room. His cousin was seated in front of a blazing fire, the warmth of it heating Griffith even from the doorway.

His cousin turned his head and smiled. "It's nothing. Can't I want to see my cousin and heir?"

Griffith suppressed a sigh of relief. He strode into the room, shrugging off his jacket and placing it on the back of one of the chairs. "You don't have to make me feel a physical hell, it's enough that I am being forced to go out into Society," he commented, nodding toward the fire.

Frederick chuckled in reply. "But tell me the truth," he said, fixing Griffith with a keen gaze, "it is far easier than you feared, isn't it?" He rolled his chair closer to the hearth. Griffith was surprised Fred wasn't on fire already.

"Being a duke's heir smooths the path far more easily than being the rapscallion relative from a noble family."

Rapscallion. Griffith would make sure to share the word with Della and Mrs. Wattings. "Perhaps," he said, wondering why he felt so reluctant to admit Fred's point, "but it really shouldn't be." He spread his hands out. "I have nothing to recommend me but my expectations. I ran off before anyone could come to know me, but I am certain I left a reputation behind."

Frederick shrugged. "It doesn't matter. None of it matters as long as your title is old and your money is good."

Griffith snorted in disgust. "That shouldn't be all of it." He recalled Della, and what she'd said about her own reputation. If it was as Fred said, then perhaps he could leverage his standing to help hers.

And then she'd marry someone else, a voice whispered inside his head. He couldn't let that happen.

But you don't wish to be married.

Did he?

He thought about it, thought about her as his wife rather than his lover. Though even that hadn't happened yet. And immediately felt the chafing tug of responsibility at his neck. He'd run away twelve years ago to avoid that very thing. Even though she was alluring, he would not be tied down. It was bad enough he had to inherit a dukedom—and then he wished he could punch himself, he sounded so entitled—but he did not want the added binding of a wife.

So, yes, he wished for her company for a short time, as long as they had their bargain, but he did not want, nor would he expect, any more. They were agreed on that, at least, even though it seemed they agreed on nothing else.

Another reason not to marry her specifically. All she would do was argue with him. Perhaps in several years, when he'd finally become resigned to being a duke he could look for a wife. When he was too old to care.

"Speaking of making it easier to go about in Society," he said, "I do have a young lady, a Lady Della, who is my betrothed."

Silence, but Griffith could see his cousin's face. He was wincing, as though Griff had dealt a painful, if expected, blow.

"Your betrothed. Lady Della Howlett?"

"You know her."

Frederick's jaw tightened. "Everyone knows her. Everyone knows she—"

"Stop." Griffith held his hand up. "I don't want to hear it."

"But she—"

"No."

Frederick heaved a clearly exasperated sigh. "I hadn't expected when I said you could get away with practically anything as a duke's heir that you would already be testing those limits. Although I suppose I should have, knowing you."

"It's not true." And why was he telling Fred anyway? Was it because of Frederick's disapproval, or in spite of it? "We're not actually engaged. She and I have made a bargain. She has agreed to keep me company as I return to Society, and I am doing something for her."

What that something was entailed either giving her the benefit of his cock or helping her locate her friend's husband. Depending on what aspect of the bargain one was looking at.

"But why?"

Griffith shrugged, unwilling to admit that the thought of entering Society on his own was as terrifying as it was.

"I suppose it is because she is like me."

He hadn't thought of it that way before. But it was true, wasn't it? She had spurned Society to chart her own course, as had he. He'd seen how she was around her sisters and her friend. He knew she wanted to be able to see them, to have her family.

As he did. He knew he would be the duke no matter what—lineage being what it was—but he also knew he couldn't just continue as though he weren't the duke, so he was obliged to learn what Frederick had to teach him. And to use his power to try to enact some change, no matter how small.

Frederick chuckled. "I suppose she is, now that I think about it. From what I understand, she is very much her own lady. Determined to make her own way in the world." A pause, and then he continued. "And she behaved in a way that affected her family profoundly."

Griffith winced at the implied criticism. He hadn't given a thought to the family he'd cared about that he'd left behind. He'd just known that the life his parents wanted for him wasn't the life he wanted.

"I'm sorry, Fred."

Frederick shook his head. "Don't be. You did what was right for you. I just wish I had been that brave before—" He gestured to himself, clearly indicating his illness. "Speaking of which, I promised you I would consult with another doctor. I have one scheduled very soon. Not that I am hoping for a miracle, or anything."

Griffith felt his chest tighten at the reminder of Fred's illness.

"You know I will do my best to prove a worthy successor." He meant it, even though it originally felt as though it were foisted onto him.

Poor Griffith, he thought ruefully. Forced to become a duke, with estates and wealth and power.

He was ridiculous.

"I know you will. That's why I am relieved to hear that Lady Della will not be your duchess." Frederick's eyes crinkled. "She would make a terrible duchess, always doing just what she wanted to, not behaving with proper decorum."

"Oh, like me, only she's female."

It was unfair, but that was the way of their world. And if he could help her regain some of her previous standing, at the very least so she could appear in Society without people whispering about her?

He would.

"My lord." Clark stepped into the room after a cursory tap on the door.

"What is it?" Griffith said, turning to look at his first mate. No, his valet now. Always his friend. Clark's expression was drawn.

"You're needed."

Griffith didn't wait to hear any more; he strode to the door, pushing it wide to accommodate his body as he walked through. Clark held his hat out, and Griffith smashed it on his head with barely a pause. "They weren't able to arrest you, so they've taken Hyland." His sailing master.

"What are the charges?"

"Same as yours, I suppose. Interference with

property and then he resisted, so they're charging him with assaulting an officer."

Hyland was as stubborn as Griffith, but didn't have Griff's size and his aristocratic background to protect himself.

Griffith shouted at the butler as he and Clark walked out the door. "Send to Robson, have him meet us at the naval police station. And a note to Lady Della that I cannot meet her this evening after all."

He really should get the man's name.

"Yes, my lord," the butler replied.

He and Clark kept a quick pace as they exited the house.

"I don't have any money," Griffith said, recalling he'd forgotten to put his jacket back on.

Clark looked over at him, not slowing as he replied. "All you have to do is wave your privilege around. That'll get him out better than a hundred pounds would."

Griff felt the weight of it on his shoulders, so heavy it felt as though it would break him. And he had very broad shoulders, well used to holding responsibilities.

But there were significant differences in being the captain of a ship and the incoming heir to an ancient title. The former—well, the former he could control with his actions. The latter he could only act under, knowing the only effect he could have would be a negative one.

Marrying the wrong woman, saying the wrong thing to the wrong person, ruining livelihoods with the wrong decision.

While he was determined to do the best he could, as he'd promised Frederick, he also knew how quickly he could foul it up.

Was it any wonder he longed for an escape into oblivion in her arms?

Chapter 10

I couldn't dissuade her, you know that." Sarah flung her hands up as she continued to speak. "Your sister is even more stubborn than you are!"

She was walking back and forth in their small parlor, irritated frustration emanating with every step.

Olivia had finally left after demolishing no fewer than half a dozen biscuits and asking ten times that amount of questions.

Della couldn't help but laugh at Sarah, even though of course she was frustrated as well. In so many ways.

"Olivia is—well, the most determined of the duke's daughters," she replied.

Sarah whirled to face her. "We should ask her to make inquiries about Henry. I am certain she would get answers."

"Yes, if only so that she would go away. Lord Stanbury and I will continue our search tomorrow." Even though they hadn't gotten the chance to discuss that. Which made her think— "And if you will excuse me, there is an errand I have to run."

Because if the mountain—in this case, Lord Stanbury, who was indeed a mountainous man—couldn't come to Mohammed—her—then she would have to go to him.

"Do be careful," Sarah warned, the tone in her voice indicating she knew precisely where Della was going. Or at least what she planned to do once she got there.

Della nodded, giving Sarah a sly grin as she walked out. "Tell Nora I will be home to tuck her in."

She caught a last look from her friend, who appeared to be both wistful and concerned. The former likely because Henry was still missing, and the latter—well, she'd seen that same expression on Sarah's face often enough to know that it was directly related to her.

She took her cloak off the hook in the hallway, relieved nobody was there to insist she take someone with her. Perhaps it was foolhardy, but if she had Becky with her, she'd have to figure out what to tell the girl to do with herself when she went to discuss . . . strategy with Lord Stanbury. It wasn't customary for ladies to care what their servants did when they were busy, but Della certainly wasn't the usual sort of lady.

Nor was Becky the usual sort of servant.

Like everyone who was in the Howlett/Wattings household, Becky was a stray. Della and Sarah had found one another, and then they had kept going, collecting people and animals and even furniture that it seemed nobody else wanted.

That was why there were seven young ladies living with them at the moment as well as a multitude of kittens. Not to mention a few wobbly chairs.

Neither Della nor Sarah could resist rescuing someone or something that had been abandoned. Della didn't have to examine her own life too carefully to understand her own impetus. And she knew Sarah had been tossed out by her family when they believed her to have married below her station.

Had Lord Stanbury been tossed out too? Was that why he had run off to sea?

"My lady." Mrs. Borens placed her hand on Della's arm as she was getting her cloak on.

"Yes, Mrs. Borens? What is it?" Della couldn't help the note of impatience that crept into her voice. Because Lord Handsome was at the other end of her journey, and now that she'd asked, and he'd accepted, she couldn't wait to engage in some illicit pursuits with him. Or licit ones, but the gist of it was that she was aching to be touched by him and touch him in return.

"There is a young female person in the sitting room." Not a lady, or Mrs. Borens would have said. "She seems in . . . distress." And then Mrs. Borens kept Della's gaze as though to communicate through an intense stare rather than words.

Thankfully, Della spoke unspoken communication as well as English.

There's a young woman in a delicate condition in the sitting room who needs your help.

Della sighed and withdrew the one arm she'd been able to slide into her cloak out again. "I'll go speak with her. Do we have any room?"

Mrs. Borens's expression cleared, as though in relief. Was she imagining that now that Della was hobnobbing—she'd have to share that word with Sarah—with a duke's heir that she wouldn't give help to the women who found her?

Bosh.

"We don't have a separate room, but she might be about Becky's age. I could put her in there."

Della grimaced at someone having to share a room with Becky. The girl was fine, but she was a bit silly. But that was no cause for not offering help, although she did feel badly for the potential new arrival. Although sharing a room with a silly girl was likely far better than whatever she'd escaped.

"Bring us tea, Mrs. Borens. And tell Mrs. Wattings I have not left after all."

"Excellent, my lady."

Della shook her head as she headed toward the sitting room. Thwarted in her desires first by her sister, then by some random girl who'd heard about Della's soft heart.

Lord Handsome would have to wait, although she wasn't certain she could.

The girl stood by the window, turning when Della entered. Her condition was obvious, although she was probably not more than four months along. Della gave a reassuring smile as the girl's eyes widened at seeing her.

"You are—drat, my housekeeper did not tell me your name. I am Lady Della," she said, extending her hand to the girl to shake.

The girl's hand was soft, so she was likely a governess or something where she wasn't doing manual labor. She looked awfully young, and Della bit back the anger at the person who caused the situation—probably some young nobleman down from college, seeing a vulnerable girl who could not refuse his advances.

"I am Miss Mary Ol—that is, Miss Mary," the girl said, nodding her head in confirmation.

Della gestured to the sofa. "Would you care to sit down, Miss Mary?"

The girl glanced at the sofa, then stepped over and lowered herself down, her hand on her belly.

"How can I help you?" Della asked as she sat in the chair opposite. "Do you need a place to stay until the child is born? We have some funds, although not a lot. But enough to get you somewhere else, if that is where you want to go."

The girl stared at Della for a moment, her eyes wide. She was very pretty; Della could see why some blackguard would want to seduce her.

And then the girl burst into loud, sobbing cries, which meant that Della couldn't waste time thinking about what might have happened to her. She yanked a handkerchief from her pocket and went to sit beside the girl, wrapping her arm around her shoulders and holding the linen square up for the girl to take.

The sobbing continued for a few minutes, Della murmuring nonsensical words that she hoped sounded reassuring.

Normally Sarah handled the sympathy portion of the females who came to them for help, while Della was the one who made all the arrangements and helped to decide what might happen in each particular case.

"Thank you, my lady," Miss Mary said at last. She raised a tear-streaked face to Della. "I don't know why I am crying so much, I just—" And then she began sobbing again as Della tried to curb her impatience.

"The thing is," Mary began again, speaking down into her lap. Her hands clutched the now sodden handkerchief, worrying the fabric with her fingers. "I am here because I don't know where else to go."

Well, Della knew that. Why else would a pregnant stranger arrive at their door if she had somewhere else she could possibly go?

But Della did not point that out to Miss Mary, since she did not think it would be helpful.

"Can you tell me more about your situation, so I know how I can help you?" Della tried to recall what Sarah would usually say in such a moment. She hoped she sounded gentle enough; sometimes, Sarah said, she asked questions as though expecting to be argued with.

As if you could argue with a question, Della thought to herself.

"I am a governess to two children," Mary began. *I was right!* Della cheered inside her head. But that was not helpful.

Even though she *was* right.

"And I became involved with—with a relative of my employer's family," Mary said, sounding chagrined.

"It isn't your fault," Della replied, clasping Mary's hand. "These gentlemen, they think because—"

"No, it's not like that," Mary interrupted. She sounded stronger now. "I knew just what I was doing, I just didn't expect—" And she gestured toward her stomach.

It was on the tip of Della's tongue to ask what she did expect, if not this.

Again, not helpful.

"And when it was discovered, my employer insisted that Mr. Robert marry me, only he didn't really wish to, and I discovered I didn't either." She took a deep breath. "I have gotten to know Mr. Robert, and it is my belief he is not as kind as I first thought. When he heard of my situation, he—he threatened me, although my employer soon put a stop to that. She offered a dowry, which she did not have to do, not at all, and he was willing to take me." She exhaled. "But he does not wish to marry me, and I cannot trust that he wouldn't harm me or the child. But once we were married, he can do with me as he wishes." She swallowed. "Can you imagine a worse fate?"

Della understood what Mary was saying, but she also knew that it wasn't always sensible to refuse a future that promised more solidity than just running away.

But she'd be the worst kind of hypocrite if she said that, given her own behavior. And she felt Mary's words—not wanting to be beholden to any man, not wishing to give up your own sense of self to someone who wasn't you—as though it were words she'd spoken herself.

In fact, she had likely said them many times to Sarah when they were discussing their pasts.

Thank goodness Mr. Baxter had run off before she had to break with him. She would have, she knew that. There was nothing any man could promise her that was worth her freedom. Or Nora's, more importantly.

"You don't think I've made a terrible mistake, do you?" Mary asked in a pleading voice.

"No, I—" But Della was interrupted when the door swung open to reveal Sarah, a look of concern on her face.

"I heard we had company," Sarah said in her usual soothing tone.

Della felt an almost palpable relief, then horrified at herself for her reaction.

But the fact was, as Sarah had gently pointed out on a few occasions, that Della was not nearly as good at the comforting aspect of their lives as Sarah was. Exemplified by Sarah's fainting spell of a few days before.

"Mrs. Borens is bringing tea, and, Della, you have an errand to run?" Sarah said.

Della rose, nodding. Even though now the thought of indulging in carnal relations with Captain Enormous made her hesitate.

What if she got pregnant? She didn't think she could be ruined twice—once appeared to be sufficient—but she didn't want to have to confront that possibility.

But she knew herself well enough to know that once she'd made her mind up she wouldn't be dissuaded, so she'd just have to take pains to protect herself.

But meanwhile, there wouldn't be any harm in going to see Lord Stanbury, would there? Just to make plans for the next day?

"HE'S NOT HERE?"

Della shifted on the stoop as the butler gazed at her impassively.

"No, my lady. Although the duke is, if you would like to see him?" The man didn't wait for a reply, but widened the door to allow her to slip inside.

The household had been in enough of a tumult so she didn't even have to prevaricate about not taking anyone with her—she just left, after telling Sarah she'd be home in time for dinner.

So now she was here, only he wasn't. Drat the man. Why couldn't he have stayed at home if there was even the remotest possibility she would be arriving to discuss strategy?

"In here, my lady," the butler said, gesturing toward a door at the other end of the hall.

The duke's house was much closer in size and majesty to her parents' house; the foyer alone was as big as four of their bedrooms combined.

Small wonder it was difficult for anyone to believe she would rather live on her own with her friends and her rescues than return to that splendor. But that splendor came with a price, and that price was slow suffocation.

Her heels made a sharp clicking noise on the

parquet. It would be difficult to arrive without someone noticing, she thought to herself. Better invest in soft-soled shoes to better facilitate an illicit affair.

On the list now, then: protection against unwanted pregnancy and some secretive footwear. If it got any more expensive, she'd have to consider scrapping the entire idea since she might not be able to afford it.

But then she wouldn't get to see him naked, she thought wistfully. *I can go without tea for a time.* Sarah would be fine with that.

Although she wouldn't want to have to explain why.

"My lady."

The duke—since Della presumed it was him—was seated in a large rolling chair in front of the fire. A blanket was draped on his knees, and a table filled with bottles of liquid was to his right.

Della had visited enough sickrooms to know that the duke was ill. How ill, of course, she couldn't say. But it explained why Lord Stanbury was so determined to succeed at reentering Society if the current duke was on the verge of dying.

She felt a pang of sympathy for both of them—one for obvious reasons, the other because he so clearly did not wish to be foisted into his current situation, but he was too honorable or obliged or whatever it was he felt to refuse.

"Forgive me for not getting up," the duke continued. He had a quiet voice and a friendly smile. He was nothing like her father, that was for certain.

"Of course." Della went to sit on the couch that was perpendicular to his chair. It was luxurious, and she nearly closed her eyes in bliss at the sensation—the furniture at her house was worn because it was all hand-me-down, so the last sofa she'd sat on had lost most of its plushness.

But this was heaven.

There was something to being a duke, wasn't there? Even if she had long ago decided there wasn't enough to being a duke's daughter. Or a duchess, for that matter, given her current subterfuge.

"Lord Stanbury explained everything to me," the duke began. Della froze, wondering just what he'd explained. There was so much that could be explained. "That you and he had agreed to pretend to an engagement to ensure his return to Society wasn't tinged with the strong likelihood of his being in the sights of so many young ladies."

He spoke with a note of amusement in his voice, but it was laced with a clear affection. "And I do understand—back when I was in Society it felt as though I were constantly under scrutiny."

Della repressed a snort.

"But why am I telling you that? You would

know about that, wouldn't you, given your own history?"

Apparently she hadn't repressed enough. And, of course, he knew about her scandal. Who didn't?

Well, except for all the young women who arrived at her doorstep looking for help. And likely most of the kittens that had wandered in to be rescued as well. She couldn't speak to the furniture's knowledge.

"You know my history. Do you know everything?"

The duke shrugged his thin shoulders. "I believe so. That you eloped with an ineligible man, that you returned to London a few years later with a child and no husband. That your sisters have been desperately trying to maintain their own status in Society but have only caused their own scandals."

Della felt herself bristle. To speak so cavalierly about her sisters, as though all that mattered to them were their reputations. Although she supposed that to any outsider it would appear that way; she wouldn't have known what was behind their actions if they hadn't kept writing one another.

She should remember to thank them, all of them, for keeping in contact with her. She hadn't thought much about how difficult it must be for them, to have a sister such as her.

She hadn't thought much at all those years ago

when she'd eloped either. Just that she had not wanted the future that lay before her, presented on a gold tray with ducal strawberries.

But it was a few years later, and hopefully she was wiser, and knew what she wanted. Which at the moment was a very large former sea captain. And she also knew for certain what she did not want—the same thing as before, only more definitively. Not only did she not wish to be married to some lord who took her because of her family, not because of her, but she did not wish to be married to anybody.

"I apologize, did I offend you?" the duke asked, interrupting her thoughts.

She began to shake her head instinctively, then considered it and nodded. "Yes, you have."

His eyes widened. As of course they would; ladies never cast blame toward any gentleman, much less a ruined woman such as herself toward a duke.

"My history is as you say," Della continued. "But my sisters—there was more to what they were doing than merely salvaging their reputations." She thought about them, from earnest Eleanor, to fierce Olivia, to stubborn Ida, to resolved Pearl. She also hadn't realized, those years ago, how much she loved her sisters. Sarah was the sister of her heart, but her actual sisters were just as beloved.

"I apologize to your sisters for inferring they

were concerned for themselves." He drew his brows together in thought. "It can be difficult to discern the line between selfish and independent." He gave a rueful sigh, and Della knew he had to be referring to Lord Arrogance.

"What happened?" Della asked in a quiet voice.

The duke shrugged again. "Griffith has always found himself on the other side of the usual opinion. His parents—my father's brother and his wife—didn't make it easy on him either. They wanted him to conform, and he wasn't built that way." He snorted. "Literally. I mean, it's impossible for him to fit in anywhere, given his size."

"And then he ran off to sea? He must have been so young." Younger than she was, even, when she made her disastrous mistake. Although the mistake had brought Nora to her, and eventually Sarah. So perhaps not a mistake after all.

"He was sixteen." The duke took a deep breath. "I helped him go. I gave him money, I kept his parents from discovering where he had gone until it was too late for them to fetch him. Even though I was terrified my own father would punish me."

"Did he?" Della asked.

The duke shook his head. "No, he didn't seem to care one way or the other. He had my two older brothers to worry about. I wasn't even the spare." He looked up past her head as though struck by a memory. "Griffith was the only one who cared about me." A pause. "I wish he didn't have to go through this."

"Go through what? Return to Society?"

"Yes. Even when we were young, Griffith hated anything that had even the remotest whiff of privilege. It's ironic that he ended up as a ship captain—in charge of all those people—"

"Capable people who presumably wanted to be aboard," Della pointed out.

The duke nodded as though conceding her point. "True. He despised having to endure what he thought were pointless conversations."

He'd said, but she hadn't believed him, that he would hate it so much. But now, seeing how the duke spoke about him, she felt more sympathetic toward him. Yes, she had it harder. She was a ruined woman whom nobody wanted to see return to their midst. But given what the duke had said, it seemed as though perhaps Lord Arrogance's attitude was bluster disguising something else. Shyness? Awkwardness? Self-consciousness?

And she wished she hadn't had this revelation, because she hadn't even had relations with him yet and she was already feeling softer toward him.

You are not allowed to feel more than pure lust, she reminded herself sternly. *He is not for you. You know what life as a duchess is like, and you want no part of that. Nora cannot be part of that either. The Society that might be willing to tolerate me because of my presumed relationship with a newly arrived heir would tear my daughter to shreds.*

"I don't know when Griffith is returning, by the way," the duke said. "I do appreciate your visit, although I suspect my butler gave you little choice in the matter." He winked at her, and she smiled in return. "He worries about me being on my own so much. But I tell my staff that I am fine; I have them to keep me company, and now I have Griffith and Clark. Clark is Griffith's valet," he explained at seeing Della's confused look. Ah, Clark the first mate! He'd found him after all.

And it should not hurt that he hadn't mentioned it to her, but she couldn't deny that it did.

It's what you want, she reminded herself. *He should not confide in you.* The only thing he should do for her was locate Mr. Wattings and give her several paroxysms of pleasure.

"I should be on my way," Della said, beginning to stand. "But I would like to visit you again, if I may." And not just as a way of getting into Lord Handsome's bedroom. She found she liked this duke quite a lot. "And perhaps I will bring my sisters? Not all of them at once, though," she added quickly, more for her sake than his. She wasn't certain she could handle all of her sisters at one time. Perhaps that was why her mother was so difficult to be around?

But no, Della recalled when it was just her and

Eleanor, before the twins and Ida arrived, and the duchess had been just as unpleasant.

"That would be a pleasure," the duke replied. "And I will inform Lord Stanbury that you came by. Did the two of you have plans this evening?"

Della shook her head. "No, he sent a note saying he couldn't keep our plans. I am promised home to dinner and will be putting Nora to bed. My daughter," she explained.

"Perhaps you would like to bring Nora for a visit at some point?"

Della felt as though she'd had the breath knocked out of her. That someone in his position would extend an invitation to her daughter without seeming to care about what it might look like.

"Thank you, Nora would love that." And she would—her daughter was a sociable person and there was nothing she liked more than talking an adult's ear off, as Della well knew. "I will come again soon," Della said, holding her hand out to the duke. He took it and raised it to his lips.

"Thank you."

"THAT WAS A close one," Hyland said in a gleeful tone.

Griffith paused in his stride just long enough to shoot a glowering look at his sailing master. Or former sailing master, unfortunately.

"You assaulted an officer."

Clark smothered a laugh into his hand.

"He said I'd interfered with property. But how could I, I said, when I didn't have any property to interfere with?" Hyland's tone was outraged.

"So you punched him in the nose?" Griffith replied.

"You would have done the same," Hyland retorted.

"As a matter of fact, I would not. I got arrested and spent a night in jail."

"You're getting soft, Captain." Hyland punctuated his words by nudging Griffith in the shoulder. Or actually the middle of the arm, since Hyland wasn't nearly as tall as Griffith.

"I am not!" he replied. Was he?

"He's living the nob's life, being a duke's heir now," Clark explained. "He can't go around punching people just because he wants to."

Griffith felt a twinge of discomfort. As though he'd like to go find some deserving person to punch in the nose just to prove Clark wrong. A cheating shopkeeper or a cruel master or an oblivious ship captain.

"What does a nob do?" Hyland asked. "Besides not punching people."

"I get to sleep in a real bed, wear clothing that isn't drenched in seawater, and sometimes get to attend parties where most of the people have all their own teeth."

"It's pretty dull, from what I can see," Clark said in an aside.

Griffith resisted the urge to punch him.

"But why are you doing it, then?" Hyland asked. He gestured in the direction of the sea, even though they were a few miles from the docks. "When you are the captain of your own ship with the best crew in England?"

"It's not that simple," Griffith said. His tone was sincere, making both Hyland and Clark drop their grins and look intently at him.

"So what is it, Captain?" Hyland asked.

"I owe it to my cousin Frederick, if not my family." Griffith's mouth tightened. "We sail for queen and country, do we not?"

The men nodded.

"And if things are tumultuous at home, there is no queen. No country."

Clark frowned in thought. "But why does it all rest on your shoulders?"

"Not all mine. Ours." Griffith shook his head. "I have never wished to be a part of it, but the truth of the matter is that I am a member of the aristocracy, and part of a quite ancient title to boot. If not me, and people like me, then the system crumbles."

"And what if it does?" Hyland always wanted to challenge authority, which was one of the reasons Griffith liked him so much—if he saw a ridiculous custom being maintained simply because it was the way things always were, he would challenge it.

"I am not knowledgeable enough about the system to answer that. Except that if it does, then good people, honest people, will lose their way of life. Their livelihood."

He recalled what he'd been thinking about earlier, with Frederick. "What if I am able to effect a change because of who I am?"

He imagined that was how Della felt, leveraging her status as a duke's daughter—even if she was currently disgraced—to make a difference. To help somebody.

"You'll have to tell the crew," Clark pointed out.

Not to mention he had yet to tell the Royal Navy.

"We're with you," Hyland added, as though it were that simple.

And to someone like Hyland, it was. Black and white, right and wrong. Griffith liked having someone like Hyland on his side, even if it meant that people's noses got punched now and again.

"Thank you," Griffith replied, glancing between the men. His men. "Thank you both."

Chapter 11

*D*id you have an interesting afternoon?"

Sarah's voice was deliberately mild, although Della noticed her friend's laughing eyes. Or not laughing, but smirking.

"I did," Della replied as nonchalantly. "I ended up visiting with the Duke of Northam, he is a really kind gentleman."

"Oh!" Sarah sounded startled. Not surprising, given that she thought Della had gone off to meet with the man currently dominating Della's fantasies. Captain Passion, or something like that.

"Yes, I had hoped to see Lord Stanbury, but it turned out he was away from home."

"So disappointing," Sarah said. Della shot her a look.

"A duke?" Nora asked. "Like my grandfather?"

Della's heart twisted in her chest. Nora had yet to meet her grandfather, but Della had told her all about their family, wanting her little girl to know she had people in her life, some of whom cared about her.

She'd met all of Della's sisters, and already loved them; Ida was her favorite because she was willing to answer any and all of Nora's questions. But the duke and duchess had kept themselves steadfastly away, refusing to speak of Della to their other daughters.

The sisters had wanted to cut ties with their parents entirely, but Della had stopped them; what if they had a change of heart? What would it do to the sisters' own children, not to know their grandparents?

"Yes, like your grandfather," Della replied at last. "And he has invited you to visit him."

"And Emily?" Nora asked, looking at her friend who sat beside her.

Della and Sarah shared a look, and Della shrugged. If the duke wouldn't receive a call from Nora's friend Emily, then he wasn't worth cultivating as an acquaintance. She just hoped she could discover what his response would be before she exposed the children to the potential unpleasantness.

It would be easier, she admitted to herself, if she were just able to conform to what Society expected. If she had married as she'd ought to have, socialized with the right people, and left the unfortunates to fend for themselves.

But, of course, then she wouldn't be Della.

"I will send a note to the duke asking when it would be convenient to visit him." That way she

could ascertain if he was amenable to receiving a
visit from Emily as well as Nora.

"Does he have any dogs?" Nora asked.

"I have no idea," Della replied.

"If he doesn't, we should bring him one of our
kittens," Emily said.

"Let's wait to see when he might want to see
you before we start bringing him gifts of live animals," Sarah chided.

Della smothered a laugh. Sarah was constantly
having to rein all of them in, Della included.
Della felt for her, but she couldn't resist diving
into trouble if it seemed as though it would be
fun and worthwhile. Occasionally both.

*Which is why you are so intrigued by Lord Hand-
some*, a voice reminded her.

"Are you feeling all right?" Sarah asked as she
moved a gravy boat that was perilously close to
Nora's elbow.

"Yes, why?" Beyond being sexually frustrated,
but she wouldn't be sharing those details with
her friend.

"You exhaled. Deeply, as though you were
troubled."

Della bit her lip to keep from bursting into
laughter. "I am fine, thank you." She rose, placing
her napkin on the table. "If we are done, perhaps
we can play a game before bedtime?"

Emily and Nora both scrambled out of their

seats, while Sarah kept a worried glance on her. *I'm fine*, Della wanted to say. *It's you I worry about. That's why I want to find your husband so desperately. I want you to be happy in a way I doubt I ever will.*

The next time she saw Lord Stanbury, she'd have to make him commit to firm plans to look for Mr. Wattings. They had only gone to the docks once, and he hadn't made it clear when they would go again. He'd mentioned Clark making inquiries; had he sent him instead? Without telling her?

Then again, he'd been distracted, as she had, by their mutual plans for strategizing.

So. New tasks: purchase shoes suitable for slipping in and out of houses for clandestine relationships; get protection so Nora wouldn't wind up with a sibling; and require Lord Stanbury to lay out his plans for finding Mr. Wattings.

"Della?" Sarah was holding the door of the dining room open. Della had apparently been thinking on her feet for far too long.

"Oh yes. Sorry," Della said, walking out the door and down the hall. She heard the sound of their daughters' giggling, and shared a warm look with Sarah. "Oh, and Miss Mary? Is she here?"

Sarah nodded. "She is. I've put her in with

Becky. I have asked her to help out with the girls' lessons. She is delighted to be able to assist."

"Oh excellent." This was family. This was the most important thing in her life.

"I MET YOUR lady today," Frederick announced, holding a glass of sherry in his hand, a sly look on his face.

"Oh?" Griffith frowned at the table with all the liquids. He wanted whiskey, but the various bottles could have held medicine or could have held liquor, for all that he could tell.

"The one on the right," Frederick said.

Griffith grunted as he picked the bottle up and gave himself a healthy pour.

"What did you think of her?" Not that it mattered, not really. It wasn't as though they were actually engaged. And yet he realized it did matter to him. He would have to consider that later. Or not; it wasn't as though he was particularly analytical. Just that he apparently cared what his cousin thought of his fake betrothed.

"She's delightful. Even though she is not duchess material."

"You said that already," Griffith said in a curt voice. He tilted the glass up to his mouth and drained it, then immediately poured another one.

"I invited her and her daughter to visit. I liked her quite a bit."

And then Griffith wished Frederick didn't have

such a good opinion of her, even though not a minute earlier he'd been hoping he did.

What was happening to him? Could he just attribute it all to sexual frustration? He certainly hoped so, because if there were other forces at work he wasn't certain he wished to acknowledge them.

"What happened with your man? The one you rushed off to rescue?"

Griffith turned to take a seat on the sofa, stretching his legs out in front of him. "I got him out. Apparently being a duke's heir is good for something. People tend to blanch when you start waving your title around."

Frederick chuckled, taking a small sip of his sherry. It must have gone down wrong, because he started to cough, tilting the glass so it was in danger of spilling. Griffith leapt up and took the glass, put it on one of the side tables, then stood next to Frederick's chair feeling helpless as his cousin continued to cough.

"Anything I can do?" Griffith asked. He glanced around for the bell, then spotted it and shook it vigorously.

The door burst open moments later and the butler ran in, his eyes wide.

"Your Grace?" he said, kneeling on the carpet next to Frederick. Frederick waved a hand, then straightened again.

"I am fine. Merely a bad swallow."

Griffith and the butler shared a glance, and then the butler rose, smoothing his trousers. "I will just fetch you some tea, Your Grace."

"Thank you."

Frederick leaned against the back of his chair, closing his eyes.

Griffith glanced over at the butler, who was regarding his master with an expression of concern.

The man's look made it seem as though this was not a usual occurrence, and Griffith felt his blood run cold at the thought of losing Frederick so soon after finding him again. Or, to be more accurate, Frederick finding him again.

"Don't look at me like that." Frederick spoke in a quiet voice.

Griffith didn't pretend not to know what he was talking about. "I don't want you to die."

Frederick snorted. "Nor do I, and yet here I am."

"Not just because I have no desire to take over. Although that is part of it," Griffith said with a grin, trying to lighten the mood. And then he spoke in an earnest tone of voice. "I didn't realize until I was back here how important you are to me. All this time, I assumed you and the rest of the family would be here, as though you were preserved entirely as you were when I left. Not that I care about any of the other members of the family, but I do care about you."

"Thank you," Frederick said gruffly.

"Which is why I want to learn everything I can from you."

"I look that bad, hmm?" Frederick asked.

Griffith froze in horror. "No, it's not that." He grimaced, then looked at Frederick who was laughing.

"You bastard," Griffith said. "I just want to do what is best."

Frederick pointed at Griffith. "And that is why you were such a good captain. And why you'll be a good duke."

Griffith wished it didn't sting that his being a captain was in the past tense.

"And I saw that other doctor," Frederick continued. "He seems to think it's not as bad as the previous doctors. I don't know if it's because he wishes to keep me as a patient, or what, but I am seeing him again."

Griffith felt his breath catch at the thought—if there was a chance Frederick would be alive in six months, and six months after that—well, he'd get to have his cousin and his friend around for a lot longer than he'd expected. And, perhaps, Griffith could resume his captaincy after all.

Though he wouldn't tell Frederick that, or his cousin might just get more ill, just to keep him on dry land.

"Good afternoon. Is Lady Della at home?" For once the lady herself had not answered the door.

The girl nodded. "She is, I'll get her. If you would come inside?" She spoke in a cultured voice, although her clothing was plain. Her belly was round enough to make him wonder if she was in an interesting condition.

Not your business, he could hear Della snapping in his head.

"Thank you." Griffith stepped into the hallway, shutting the door behind him.

He hadn't planned on seeing her this afternoon; he'd sent word that he would escort her to another party that evening, but then he'd spent the morning with Frederick going over accounts, and it had gotten to the point where Frederick had tossed him out of the house because he was so restless.

Naturally, he'd walked over here, barely realizing he had until he'd been striding up the steps.

"Good afternoon." Lady Della walked up to him with a puzzled frown on her face. "Is there a change in plans? You could have written a note."

Griffith glanced around the hallway, making sure nobody else was there, and then he placed his hand on her waist and drew her up against his body. "I couldn't wait. I've been thinking about you all day."

He held his breath, waiting for her to react, wanting to be certain she was of the same mind as before.

But it seemed she was, since the corner of her

mouth drew up into a sensual smile, and then she licked her lips as she met his gaze. "I thought of you all night," she replied, reaching up to thread her fingers through his hair and draw his head down to hers.

Their mouths met in a ferocious clash, and he nearly groaned aloud at how good she tasted. Her tongue slid into his mouth where it tangled with his, and her hands gripped his hair, tugging him closer still.

He had initiated the kiss, but now she was the aggressor, taking one hand out of his hair to slide it down his back, then under his jacket to rest at the small of his back, edging up against him so they were pressed against one another.

She took her other hand out of his hair and put it on his hand, the one resting at her waist, then moved his hand up so his fingers were just under her breast. He took the hint, cupping her breast, rubbing his palm against her nipple, feeling it press through the fabric as it stiffened.

His cock was stiff as well, pressing up against her lower belly. He knew she felt it because she made a low noise in her throat and shifted so his cock was fully pressed against her. And then she moved again, causing a delicious friction.

If he weren't an experienced man of twenty-eight years he would have spent by now. As it was, the only thought in his head was that he absolutely should not lay her down on the floor in the hallway, shove her skirts up to her waist, and thrust inside.

Even though he was seriously considering it.

She kissed him deeper, harder, making low moans in her throat, pulling him closer to her, so close his fingers were crushed against her breast, not that either one of them was complaining about that.

And his cock throbbed in his trousers, so hard that each of her movements felt like a delicious torture.

He heard a noise above them, and they sprang apart, both of them panting, staring at one another.

The noise receded, and her mouth—moist from their kiss—curled up into a knowing smile. "Well. It seems we have something in common, even if we can scarcely agree on anything."

He wanted to argue about not agreeing, but realized how that would just prove her point. Besides which, the most important thing was that they did agree on one thing. Namely, how soon they could tear one another's clothes off.

"So what are we going to do about our common interest?" His voice was roughened by passion.

She licked her lips, and he groaned aloud, making her smile more wickedly. She drew her hand up her body, her fingers touching her stomach then trailing up to touch her breast. She splayed her fingers out around her breast and squeezed, emitting a soft sigh. "I touched myself last night, thinking of you," she said.

"Fuck, woman," he growled. He wanted to take her in his arms again but he knew that was dangerous, since clearly neither one of them was thinking straight.

"That is what I want," she answered, her gaze sliding down his body to settle on where his cock thrust out from his trousers. "I want you to fuck me." And he swallowed, his throat dry. He knew he would recall just how she'd said that for the rest of his life, likely an integral part of his fantasy when it was just him and his hand. "I just don't know where to go so we're not interrupted." She lifted her gaze back to meet his. "I want to have plenty of time for exploring," she said, biting her lip.

"A room." His voice was ragged. "We'll get a room. Tonight. After the party."

She smiled. "As long as I am home in time for breakfast, my lord."

He gave a brief nod, then couldn't keep himself from reaching down to give his aching cock a squeeze.

"That's for me," she said. "Don't do anything there until tonight." She raised her chin challengingly. "If you are able to."

He'd do it, even though he'd be walking around with a cockstand for the rest of the day. Damn. He couldn't wait to give her all the pleasure he could.

"Tonight," he repeated, then turned on his heel to walk out the door, knowing if he stayed he wouldn't be able to resist anything about her.

DELLA WATCHED IN appreciation as he walked away. She was startled at how forward she'd been, but he seemed to like it. And so did she. She hadn't been with Mr. Baxter long enough to figure out what she did and did not like in bed, except that he did have some skill in that arena, even if he was not who she'd hoped he was.

But it felt, with Lord Handsome, as though *she* were in charge. It felt exhilarating. She wanted to explore what pleased her, what pleased him, and how they could please one another.

And since she had no expectations of him beyond that, she would not be disappointed, as she had been in Mr. Baxter.

She hadn't been selfish in any way since before Nora was born. She'd focused on the child growing in her belly, their survival, and then keeping them alive. Then she'd had Sarah in her life, which was selfish in that she loved Sarah, and claimed her as her family, but there was also a measure of rescue there. Although Sarah had rescued her equally.

But this—she only had pleasure to gain from the sexual bargain they'd made. It was a simple, selfish act. It was only about her pleasure, although of course she hoped—and knew, to be honest—that he would derive pleasure from it as well.

It felt empowering to be so selfish, honestly. To claim what she wanted and make strides toward getting it. To know that the only objective was something she longed for. Not something that would benefit her materially, or raise her standing in the world, or help her and her family's future. Just something for her.

Like buying a pretty hat even though you had dozens at home. But he would fit her far better than a hat would, and the satisfaction she'd gain as a result would be far greater than being told she looked lovely that day while wearing the hat.

Damn it, she could not wait until after the party. The party itself would be a tortuous delight, both of them anticipating what would be happening in a few short hours, and yet not able to hasten the moment.

She'd have to make certain to wear one of her most beautiful gowns that was also the easiest to remove. Although there was something to be said for his stripping her bare, undoing each button as she felt herself start to unravel. Feeling those big hands sliding on her skin as he undid her.

She'd told him not to touch himself until this evening. She supposed she'd have to promise herself the same thing. Even though the thought of her fingers touching herself as she thought of him and those big hands and that bigger body was an enticing one.

It was going to be exquisite torture until she could get him alone.

Chapter 12

"*A*re you certain you are all right?" Sarah asked in a skeptical voice as she held the gown out for Della.

Della nodded far too emphatically. "Yes, of course." She would not share with her friend that she'd been in a torment of sexual anticipation for the past few hours. They were close, but Sarah didn't need to hear of Della's urges.

"Lord Stanbury is coming to pick me up in half an hour," she continued, glancing at the clock. She frowned. "I'll be ready by then, won't I?"

She wouldn't want to keep him waiting. Or herself, for that matter.

"If you stop fidgeting you will," Sarah replied in an exasperated tone. The one she usually used for one or the other of their daughters.

"Fine." Della stood exaggeratedly still, biting her lip not to laugh at Sarah's aggrieved expression. It was far too easy to needle her friend. Nearly as easy as it was to needle Griffith, but she didn't want to annoy him at the moment, even though that was her general philosophy.

She wouldn't want him to cry off from their later activities because she was being aggravating.

"Fine," Sarah repeated. She helped Della tug the sleeves of the gown down her arms, then leaned over to smooth the skirts.

Della looked down at herself, pleased that she'd splurged on this gown. Thank goodness she had some funds set aside for pretty things—what was the point of existing if there wasn't some joy in one's life? Which, of course, brought her back to the topic uppermost in her mind.

She really needed to stop thinking about it.

The gown. She'd focus on the gown. Not how it would feel when he removed it from her body, not how she was anticipating what his expression would be when he saw her in it. None of that.

She should try this again. The gown. It was a dark purple color, nearly burgundy, and plain except for the black lace ornamenting the hem and the bodice. It was cut low, revealing plenty of her bosom, with tiny puffed sleeves that rested just on her shoulders.

She wore a black velvet choker around her neck with a dark purple stone set in the middle of it. It tied with gold wire, and she wore a pair of gold-and-purple earrings that dangled nearly down to her neck.

Mr. Baxter hadn't seen fit to take those items,

since he knew they were paste. But they were pretty nonetheless.

"You look lovely." Sarah's tone was sincere, and Della smiled at her friend.

"I wish you could come."

Sarah rolled her eyes. "And have to watch you and Captain Handsome flirt the entire evening?" She shook her head. "No, thank you, I will stay here."

"And tomorrow we will go again to look for Mr. Wattings, I promise," Della said, touching her friend on the arm and squeezing. "I feel that he is out there somewhere, we just have to leverage the power of the duke's heir to get the information."

Sarah snorted. "The power of the duke's heir sounds like some kind of dark magic."

Della waggled her eyebrows. "Captain Handsome is some sort of dark magic, and I intend to let him cast a spell on me."

Sarah laughed as she poked Della in the shoulder. "Stop it, I don't want to know." A moment as she tilted her head in consideration. "But you will tell me everything, won't you?"

"I will."

Della looked at the clock, then picked up her skirts and began to walk out the door. "I don't want to be late. You are certain I look all right?"

"You know you are gorgeous. Captain Handsome is lucky to have captured your interest."

Della felt a warmth right around her heart at hearing her friend's words; Sarah didn't care about Della's ruined reputation or that any gentleman might think she was fair game given said reputation. She only loved and supported her, and she would doubtless object if Della tried to settle on someone who wasn't—in Sarah's eyes, at least—worthy of her.

Della knew that situation would never happen, since she wouldn't settle herself, but it was nice to know her friend was so solidly in her corner.

And she had to repay the love by finding out what happened to Sarah's husband.

DEAR GOD. GRIFF nearly said the words aloud, but they choked in his throat.

She had been waiting at the door for him— apparently she was relieved of door duties only the once—and he had stepped inside without registering her appearance.

But now that he had—*Dear God.*

She was a spectacularly beautiful woman, he knew that already, but in the gown she was wearing she was practically irresistible. The fabric was shiny, in a color that looked somewhat like a bruise on its third day.

Not that he would tell her that.

It was molded to her figure on the upper half, and cut low enough to please even him. She wore an enticing strip of black fabric around her neck, and her hair was swept up, showing the graceful lines of her neck and the earrings that bobbed as her head moved.

"Are you going to stand there gawking?" she said, but in a tone that indicated she knew what he was thinking, and she was glad he was thinking it.

"If you'll let me," he replied honestly.

"We have to go do more of your Society establishing," she replied, shaking her shoulders to adjust her gown. Making Griff even more tongue-tied at the sight. "Otherwise I wouldn't be wearing this gown." She twirled in a circle. "Do you like it?" she asked in a mischievous tone.

He stepped forward so he was within a hand's breadth of her. But he didn't touch her, because he knew he wouldn't be able to stop. "I like it," he said in a low tone, watching as she reacted to his voice. "I'll like it better when I am underneath its skirts." And then he watched as her eyes widened, and she took a few deep breaths as she realized what he was saying.

"Let's go to this thing before I forget I am a fake betrothed," she said in a strained voice.

She stepped to the door and he followed, his gaze riveted on the back of her neck, on where the tiny black buttons were like a treasure map to what he knew would be a treasure just for him.

This was going to be a long night.

"LADY DELLA HOWLETT." The butler announced her name tentatively, as though he knew what the likely reception would be. "And Lord Stanbury," he added, this time much more confidently.

Della lifted one eyebrow toward Griffith, who was glowering in a particularly possessive—and yes, intriguing—way.

"It's fine," she murmured as they walked into the ballroom. He tucked her arm into his, practically sweeping her into the middle of the floor.

Unfortunately, since it was a ball, he had just walked her into the middle of about two dozen couples.

"Nice work, my lord," she said in a dry tone. "I think we have to dance now."

He grinned at her, apparently oblivious to the sea of people swirling around them. "If it means I can touch you in public, then we'll dance." He took her in his arms and swung her immediately into the rhythm of the dance, making her nearly breathless. Whether that was because he had taken her unawares or because she could feel the heat of his body, she didn't know.

And actually, she mused ruefully, he hadn't taken her at all yet, either aware or unawares.

Stop thinking about it, Della, she admonished herself.

"What is on your mind?" he asked, sounding merely curious. Thank goodness it didn't seem as though he could read her thoughts.

"Uh—well, we have to return to looking for Mr. Wattings."

"That's not what you were thinking about." He stared pointedly at her mouth, so intensely it felt as though he were kissing her here, right in this ballroom.

And so much for not reading thoughts. It seemed he could, but he was also very good at hiding his reactions.

What would it take for him to show his reactions? She felt her mouth curl into a smile as she pondered it.

"Stop that," he said in a growl. "Unless you want me to—"

She didn't hear the rest of his words because just then a dancing couple slammed into them, making her stumble, and making him release his hold on her.

She blinked, startled, as she regained her stability, glancing at the other couple, her mouth opening to ask if they were all right.

"Lady Della, it seems you are impossible to keep upright," a voice said, louder than was necessary. A few heads turned to look at them, and then more, a cascading effect of salacious interest rippling through the crowd.

"If you weren't so determined to be horizontal," the voice continued, "you wouldn't have the reputation you do."

Della felt her breathing quicken as she glared

at the man speaking. Of course it was someone she'd known, before, when she'd had her first season. Before she eloped with Mr. Baxter. She didn't recall his name, but she did recognize his face, even though it seemed he had been doing some hard living while she was away from London.

"You don't even recognize me," the man said, sounding affronted.

"I recognize you're an ass," Della replied without thinking.

The crowd gasped. Of course it did, because a gentleman impugning a lady's honor was far less horrible than a woman calling him out on it.

It felt as though she were staring at him through a red haze, fury clouding her vision, making her fists clench and her stomach tighten.

"Shut. Up." It was Lord Stanbury, who had stepped over to her side, and was trying to pick her hand up. He directed his words to the gentleman, and she felt a flash of gratitude until it was swept up by her self-righteous anger.

"I will handle this," she said in a low tone. She shook his hand away, taking a few steps away from him.

He did not relent, however, coming to stand right up against her and dragging her arm up so he was able to tuck it into his.

"No," she said, shaking her head. "I will not—" *I will not rely on you to fight my battles, I will not al-*

*low another man to make me feel ashamed of what I've
done, I will not, I will not, I will not.*

"Is that the first time you've said no?" the gentleman continued, only this time he spoke in a much
lower tone. As though he knew that the crowd
wouldn't like this meanness, but he had to get in a
few more shots before he was done.

Lord Stanbury advanced toward the gentleman
at that, and Della was suddenly grateful that he'd
taken ownership of her arm because she was able
to drag him back, yanking on him so he couldn't
move forward and do whatever it was he was going to do.

Which was hit him. She knew he was planning
on hitting him.

But that would cause a far worse scandal than
this man saying terrible things to her. It would
mean that the duke's heir would be seen as a
low-class brawler, not a gentleman worthy of his
forthcoming title.

And the whispers would start, as Della well
knew—that he'd run off to sea, that he cavorted
with his lessers, that he had even spent an evening in jail.

So she held on to his fist with all her might,
making him turn his head to glare at her because
she was impeding his movement.

*Yes, because this is the kind of rash impulsivity you
absolutely do not wish to engage in*, she wished she

could say. *This is why you enlisted me as your pretend betrothed, so you could fake respectability and keep determined young ladies at bay.*

"Stop it," she said in a fierce whisper. "You do not wish to do this."

"Oh, but I do," he said through a clenched jaw. "He's maligned your honor."

That fiery spark of anger flared through her, making her throat tight and her heart hammer against her ribs. "*My* honor. Not yours. It is mine to defend or not. That is *my* choice. I do not want—I will not have—you leaping to my defense."

He took a step back, giving her an incredulous look. "You don't want me to hit this bastard?"

The man in question was just over Lord Stanbury's shoulder, looking smugly at her. *I should just let him hit you,* she thought. *But I won't, because I am a better person than you.*

"No. This is bound to happen, I did warn you. The best thing to do," she said, moving closer to him so only he could hear her, "is to ignore it. People like that one just want to get a reaction." She lifted her eyes to his face. "And he did. I can barely speak I am so angry, and you are on the verge of stomping about and smashing things with your fists." She took his hand in hers, wrapping her fingers as best she could around it. He had an awfully large hand.

"I couldn't just accidentally trip him or something?" he asked in a mournful tone, as though he knew what her answer would be.

She snorted. "No, you can't."

He gave an exaggerated sigh. "You are by far the most respectable pretend betrothed I have ever had." She had to laugh at how disappointed he sounded—had he expected her to be some sort of Jezebel or Lady Godiva wandering into a ballroom wearing only a horse?

"But I am glad I was here," he said, nearly baring his teeth again. "He might have said worse if you were a lady on your own."

And just like that all her amusement at his primal urges disappeared, and she was angry all over again, that he'd be so presumptive as to assume she couldn't take care of herself, that she required a man to rescue her from situations.

A man was the one who got her into her situation, thank you very much. Without him, she wouldn't have eloped, or been ruined, or returned to London as an unwed mother.

She'd be one of those debutantes dangling for a husband, perhaps assessing Lord Stanbury here as a potential husband. If she were one of those women, she'd be terrified, not intrigued, by his size and his past. She'd be willing to overlook his rough behavior and occasional lapses in manners because he was a lord, and part of the aristocracy into which she was supposed to marry.

She wouldn't see his good qualities, like his intense loyalty, his steadfast ferocity, his humor, his abundance of self-confidence.

So he should be grateful she was who she was, and in no need of his protection. Or anything of his, for that matter.

"Should we leave?" A pause, and then he spoke in a soft rasp, so low she had to strain to hear him. "I promise it will be better than this."

She jerked her head up to stare him in the face. He frowned, as though confused. He didn't understand how truly angry she was.

"I want to leave, yes," she said in a normal tone of voice. A few of the people still gawking around them nodded as though in agreement.

"Allow me to escort you home, my lady." He held his arm out to her, and she nodded as she took it. She hoped he had learned his lesson and wouldn't attempt to assert his dominance over her again—if she wanted his arm, she'd take it. If she wanted anything else of his, she'd take that too.

GRIFFITH NEARLY HOWLED in relief as they walked out of the party. They'd only been inside for a few minutes, but it had been long enough to remind him that he hated these kinds of functions, that most people were terrible, and that what he really wanted most was to get her naked and underneath him. Or on top, he wasn't particular.

"I have a—" he began, only to swallow his words as she cut him off.

"No."

The coachman opened the door, gesturing for them to go inside.

He waited until she had settled herself, and then he stretched his legs onto the opposite seat. "No what?" he asked.

He felt her shake her head. "No, I do not want to proceed with what we had talked about earlier. I don't appreciate your manhandling me, I definitely do not like being treated like a possession for two men to wrangle over, and I do not feel inclined toward you in that way at this particular moment."

He blinked at the vehemence of her tone. He hadn't realized she was so affected by what had happened.

Although that wasn't what she had said, was it?

"It's because of what I did?" He couldn't help the rising note of incredulity in his voice. "Not that one who basically said you were—you were—?"

"A loose woman? A trollop? A wagtail?" He felt her shake her head again. "No, his comments were to be expected. But I had thought you knew me. That is, I had hoped you knew me well enough not to intercede." She sounded hurt, and he felt an answering ache in his heart.

"A wagtail?" he said in a lighter tone. "I must have missed that one. Perhaps I was too young when I was last living here." He took a deep breath. "I apologize. I didn't mean—I only meant—"

"I know." She sounded dispirited. "I know you only meant well. And if I were someone else, I would appreciate your standing up for me there. But I am not someone else. And I thought you knew that."

He winced at the soft loss in her voice, and he bit his lip, not wanting to say anything that would diminish what she was feeling or try to salvage the situation.

Yes, he wished he were currently sliding his hands up her thighs, perhaps kissing her belly and moving lower, but he didn't want her to conflate his remorse with his desire for her.

So even though he'd had an erection for the past few hours, and he'd have to do something about that when he got home, he would not press the issue. He thought, or at least he hoped, he knew her well enough to know that she would reflect on tonight and realize what he hadn't done as much as what he had.

"I'm sorry," he said again. "We should be at your house in a few minutes. I'll come in the morning to continue the search for Mr. Wattings." No intimation that there would be anything but their earlier bargain—a pretend engagement in exchange for a hunt for a missing man. He owed her that much respect, since it seemed he didn't know her as well as he had thought.

"Thank you," she said at last as they arrived at her house.

Chapter 13

$\mathscr{I}$t wasn't necessarily the right thing to do, but it was the only thing he could do.

Griff slid his hand down his chest toward his aching cock. He was entirely naked, having shucked his clothing without waiting for Clark. He didn't want anybody to see him in this state—this wanting, desperate state where all he could think about was her.

Thank goodness only the butler had seen him when he returned, and he had sprinted up the stairs to his bedroom without even waiting for the man's greeting.

He'd slammed the door behind him, the flame of the candle lit on his nightstand flickering from the disturbed air.

And then tossed his clothes to the floor as quickly as he could before sliding into his bed.

"Ahh," he heard himself moan as his hand curled around his shaft. He held it for a moment, relishing the sweet tension prior to beginning to move.

And then he did, sliding his palm up and down the warmth of his cock, grasping the top and twisting before sliding down again to its root.

Damn it, he wished he hadn't erred so tremendously earlier this evening. If he hadn't, it might be her soft hand curled around him, tugging on his cock as she licked her lips, all that dark hair falling around her gorgeous breasts.

Not that he'd seen them yet, but he knew they'd be gorgeous. Just like the rest of her.

Her small hand might not even fit all the way around him. She'd have to tighten her grip to grasp him, squeezing his girth as she stroked up and down.

Would she be sitting upright in bed, perhaps straddling his thighs?

The image sent a bolt of lust through him, so he decided that yes, she would be straddling his thighs. Her wet warmth spread out in front of him as she touched him.

Perhaps her other hand would be touching her breast, those delicate fingers trailing over her nipple, which stood erect, practically begging for his mouth.

Maybe he'd ask if she wanted him to suck her nipples. Would she like him to talk during sex, or would she be too focused to concentrate on words?

He gripped himself harder, images in his mind of her touching him as she rubbed herself on his thighs as he stroked faster. Wishing it were her, but knowing that there was a distinct possibility it wouldn't happen, and he'd have to make do with his hand.

Thinking how he'd let her stroke him close to breaking point, then tossing her on her back and pushing all the way inside, making sure to use his fingers on her little button so she would climax.

Biting her shoulder as he thrust in and out, grabbing her legs so they wrapped around his waist, feeling her breasts rub against his chest.

"Unnnggh," he groaned, feeling his balls tighten as he drove inexorably toward his climax.

He spent a few seconds later, arching off the bed with the impact of the orgasm.

He felt the satisfying release flow through him, relaxed back down onto the bed, his stomach wet from his spend, his whole body shaking.

Damn it. This was good, but he knew that being with her for real would be far, far better.

He resolved to do whatever he could to make it right—not just so he could get her into bed, although that was a strong motivation—but because he wanted to feel her trust again.

And he wanted to see her naked and shaking with as much passion as he was.

"Good morning, my lady."

Lord Stanbury was as subdued as an enormous

handsome man could be. His tone was low, his gaze respectful, and even his hair seemed tame.

"Good morning, my lord." Della nodded as she took her cloak off the hook. "Thank you for coming so promptly this morning. I wasn't certain if you—" And she paused, wishing she hadn't started to say what she had.

Because of course his whole mien changed. He froze, and it felt as though his whole body was vibrating. Although, truth be told, she much preferred Exceedingly Angry Lord Viscount Whatever to Lord Meek. Much to her dismay.

"Did you think I would renege on my promise because of what did not happen last evening?" he said in a growl.

Damn it, and now she wanted to leap on him. Contrary, contrary Della.

"No, I didn't," Della replied, lifting her chin. "It was a thoughtless thing to say, I apologize."

He took a breath, as though to argue, then blinked as he realized what she'd said. "Oh."

"Oh," Della echoed. She took a deep breath. "Let me begin again, this time without being so careless of your feelings. Thank you for coming this morning."

"We have a bargain," he said gruffly. And then his eyes widened. "Not that one, I mean. The first one."

She had to laugh at his reaction—aghast that he might seem to be dismissive of her desires.

When actually if she let him, she had no doubt that he would encourage her desires.

Damn it.

"Are you all right?" he asked, returning to his more considerate tone.

"I am," she said firmly.

"Because I didn't mean to upset you last night."

She rolled her eyes as she shook her head. "Of course you didn't mean to upset me. Who sets out to upset someone?" Besides her father the duke and Mr. Baxter, that was. But she would not tell him that—he was just as likely to go hunt both of those men down and punch them, which of course would be the exact opposite of what she wanted.

Which was the problem in the first place.

He absorbed her words, then burst into laughter. "I never thought of it that way. Although I will admit that I believe there are occasions where you try to deliberately upset me."

His expression was tentatively hopeful, and it made her heart get all mushy. Because he was flirting with her, naturally, but not forcing anything upon her. Allowing her to take the lead, but letting her know how he felt.

"Let's go," she said, wishing she were less of a good friend so she could take Lord Aghast and Thoughtful here into her parlor and have her way with him. But she *was* a good friend, and Sarah had been waiting for so long for news of her Mr. Wattings that Della couldn't and wouldn't justify waiting any longer just because she had feminine wants and needs.

"Of course," he said, his hand going automatically to the small of her back, but then hesitating right when he would have touched her.

She turned and nodded at him in acknowledgment. It was a small gesture, but it was an automatic one for most, if not all, gentlemen. That he would hesitate because he was uncertain if she wanted it spoke more than a thousand apologies.

Although she might take those as well. It could be fun to see him grovel.

"I THINK I might've seen him." And then the man paused, making Griff want to shake him until his teeth rattled in his head.

Not that that would help. But it would be most satisfying.

"He was here mebbe six months ago?"

He and Della had gone straight to the docks where a ship had just arrived, its crew spilling out in search of companionship and alcohol. Probably not in that order.

They'd asked nearly forty sailors if any of them knew Mr. Wattings, and none of them did, until this one scratched his head and squinted and surmised that perhaps he did.

He and Della had whisked the sailor away to the closest pub, where Griff bought him an ale, buying one for himself as well, waiting impatiently as the man downed his drink, belched, and then scratched his head some more.

"Where was he?" Della asked.

The sailor paused in his head-scratching to give her an appreciative glance. Griff was pleased that he did not immediately want to punch the man— mostly because he already wanted to punch him for taking so long to answer the question.

"He was aboard the *Righteous Lady,*" the man replied. He was thin, his skin sallow, as though he hadn't been let on deck during his voyage. "Last I saw him he said he was leaving London. Said there was nothing for him here."

"But there was!" she replied in a fierce tone. "His wife and child were here."

The man shrugged, looking wistfully at the bottom of his glass. Griff gestured to the barmaid for another, at which the man brightened considerably.

"All's I know is how he looked when he left." The barmaid put the glass down on the table, removing the empty one. "Like his heart was broken."

Griff glanced over at Della, not surprised to see her eyes moisten and her chin wobble. She was fierce, certainly, but she was also fiercely loyal and passionate, so anything she felt would immediately reveal itself on her face.

It was a good thing she didn't play cards.

"Did he say where he was going?" She spoke in a low tone, as though it was the most important question she'd ever asked. Perhaps it was.

The man shook his head. "No, but if I had to guess . . ."

Another pause.

She shook her head at Griffith as though she knew he wanted to leap up and drag the man's words from his throat.

". . . I'd think he went somewhere to work with animals. He kept saying animals wouldn't betray you, not like people."

He heard Della's sharp intake of breath, and wished he could do something to ameliorate her reaction.

"He must think Sarah abandoned him," she said in a tremulous whisper. "And that is why she can't find him. He left because he thinks she broke his heart." She rose, shoving the chair behind her, the legs screeching along the rough wooden floor. "We need to find him, Griffith."

He rose as well, something blooming in his chest at hearing her use his name so naturally. She hadn't before, at least not that he could remember. And he knew he would have remembered it.

He wanted to hear her say his name again. Only in a more desperate way, when she was on the verge of her climax and she knew he could bring her there.

"Uh, yes. Find him. We will," Griffith said, realizing she was waiting for a reply. Impatiently,
he had to say.

Would she be as impatient when—? He really
needed to find this Mr. Wattings. Or resign himself to his hand for the rest of eternity.

"THE NAVAL OFFICE is the next natural step,"
Della said as they exited the pub. "I know you
might not want to go there, because of your past
interactions with them—"

"You mean getting arrested and accused of
treason or whatever it was?" he replied in a lazy
voice, as though it didn't come within inches of
irrevocably changing his life.

She had to admit, he had remarkable aplomb.

"We can go there. I'll wave my title around and
see if we can get some answers. Besides which,
eventually I'm going to have to tell them I'm not
coming back." The last part he said as though he
were dreading it all.

Della nodded, pleased he was so willing to
venture to a place she doubted he ever wished
to return to again—a place where the future he
wanted was housed, while also being the place
that had attempted to rob him of his freedom.

He is not doing it for you, she reminded herself.
It was all because of their bargain. And to find
his missing seaman, since it was clear it rankled

his masculine pride to have lost someone so thoroughly.

Although she knew he was doing it a little bit for her. And she knew why.

The question was whether she would be able to allow him that much control over her body without immediately wishing to rescind it.

"We can walk," Griffith said, gesturing ahead of them. "It's only a mile or two. I presume you're not too much of a lady to balk at some brisk exercise?"

Della began to frown in outrage, then realized that was exactly the reaction he was looking for. "Of course, my lord," she replied in a silky tone. "I wish only to proceed with the investigation and locate our missing sailor."

"Mmph," he grunted, beginning to stride ahead, making no accommodation for her shorter stride. Or if it was accommodating, it wasn't quite accommodating enough. But she relished his brisk walking. It meant that he knew she could handle it, that she would adjust herself to work alongside him. That she didn't need special treatment because she was a lady.

She knew that he would treat her as an equal if or when they ever managed to find their way amicably to the bedroom. She'd be more than able to keep up with him there, and she couldn't wait to challenge him with some of her own wants and desires, and discovering what his were.

So the faster they located Sarah's husband, the more swiftly they could proceed to a bedroom of their choosing to explore.

No wonder he was walking so quickly.

Chapter 14

$\mathcal{D}$o you have an appointment?" The prim man seated behind the desk looked as though the closest he'd come to being on board a ship was walking over a puddle.

Not that there was anything wrong with that, Griffith amended in his head. If there wasn't paperwork and management on land, captains and their crews would have to deal with it themselves, and that was the last thing Griff ever wanted to do.

Good thing he was on his way to becoming a duke, where paperwork and management seemed to be the entirety of the position, tossing in a few awkward moments in ballrooms for a little added fun.

You're being ridiculous again, he chided himself.

"We're looking for a sailor," Griffith announced. Della stood at his side, despite his trying to shield her from most of the men they'd passed on the journey.

Of course they'd stared, no matter how much

he tried to block her with his body. Even catching a glimpse of her was bound to make anybody's eyes start out of their sockets.

"Well," the prim man said, a trifle less primly, "this would seem to be the place to find one."

Della leaned forward, placing one hand on the desk to address the man. "It is actually one sailor in particular. A Mr. Henry Wattings, he was aboard the *Royal Lady* three years back. And perhaps the *Righteous Lady* six months ago?"

The man was shaking his head no before she had even finished her words.

"You haven't heard all of it," Griffith said, feeling a fierce desire to punch the man in the nose. His usual reaction, to be honest. "I am the Viscount Stanbury, heir to the Duke of Northam, and the family is quite desirous of locating this particular sailor. So if you could scurry on back through your records perhaps we won't have to involve the House of Lords in the investigation."

Griff had no idea if the House of Lords would care or be allowed to become involved in such a situation, but he suspected this desk worker didn't know either. Or if he did, he certainly wouldn't argue the point with a duke's heir.

"Let me check." Apparently the duke's heir mention did work after all. "Three years ago, you say?" The man rose, pushing his spectacles farther up his nose. "You can wait in this office while I take a look. The *Royal Lady*?"

"Yes," Griff confirmed.

The man nodded and walked through a small door behind his desk.

Griff gestured to two chairs in the corner. "It appears we will be stuck here for a moment, unless our assistant is a lot more adept at unraveling naval paperwork than anybody I've ever seen."

Della smiled in reply, going to sit down in the farther chair. It was reminiscent of a chair Griff might have seen in his own captain's quarters, if he cared about making a good impression on his men. Or more accurately, if he cared about making that kind of good impression on his men; his preferred method included a focused mission, clearly defined goals, and the tools needed to achieve them. Not fancy chairs.

But at least she would be comfortable for the next few hours.

SHE HAD TO admit to liking it when he got all aggressively masterful. Even though that made her a thorough hypocrite; after all, she definitely did not like it when he focused that masterful aggression on her.

Or perhaps she would, given the right circumstances.

He caught her eye and smiled, a slow, lazy smile that made it seem as though he knew what she was thinking. He probably did; she hadn't been very shy about what she wanted.

And what she didn't want, she recalled, thinking of the night before.

He had to know she had changed her mind, but he also had to know her well enough by now to realize she would have to be the one to tell him. And she would. As soon as they had gotten some sort of news about Sarah's Henry, and Della could see the crease of worry leave her friend's face.

And she had taken care of purchasing a method to prevent adding a sibling to Nora's life. As well as some soft-soled shoes.

So many things to take care of.

"Well." The man had returned, easing himself back into his seat, putting a binder on his desk. Whorls of dust rose into the air, proof that the Naval Office did not consult these records often.

The man withdrew a large handkerchief from his inside pocket just in time to sneeze. Della wished some of her pupils were as prescient.

"I believe we have a record of your Mr. Wattings," the man said, opening the binder and pulling out a yellowed slip of paper. She and Griffith both leapt out of their seats, going to either side of the man, whose eyes widened in alarm behind his spectacles.

"Uh," he began, touching his fingertip to the paper, "Mr. Wattings was last at this address near Timber Wharf." He looked up, first at Della and then at Griffith. "Surely this will help locate him."

"That's at the docks?" she asked. Griffith nodded in confirmation. "So if we go there to this address it's likely someone will know where he went?"

Griffith straightened, holding his hand out to the desk clerk. "Thank you for your help, Mr.—?"

"Hastings," the man replied. He took Griffith's hand and shook it vigorously. "Yes, you are welcome. I do hope you find your missing seaman."

Griffith clapped his hand on the man's shoulder, making him jump. "I will be sure to mention how helpful you've been to the House of Lords."

"Thank you, my lord." The man looked awestruck. Della would not point out that speaking to the entire House of Lords about one desk clerk was not a thing that was usually possible.

"And, my lady, I need to get you home, it is getting late."

Della narrowed her eyes before she glanced at the clock on Mr. Hastings's desk. It was late. How had she lost track of time?

Being in his undeniably intoxicating presence was probably the reason, a sly voice said inside her head.

She inclined her head to Mr. Hastings before exiting the room, Griffith close behind her.

He stepped in front of her to begin the descent down the stairs, Della appreciating the consideration even though it was not necessary. Her whole being felt as though it had been zapped by some kind of kinetic energy. They had a clue about where Sarah's husband could be, and it only took pretending to be his betrothed—not a difficult assignment—for it to happen. She couldn't keep herself from waving her hands in the air in her excitement. "We're so close! Henry could be home with Sarah tonight!"

He paused on the stairwell in front of her, turning to meet her gaze. His expression was serious, and her stomach fluttered.

"Have you thought of what you'll do if it turns out that Wattings is—?" He paused, waiting for her to fill in the word.

She bit her lip. Then raised her chin and replied. "I can't believe that a love so true could die. I won't believe it. Not until I see absolute proof. Until then?" She tossed her head. "Until then, he is alive."

And she strode past him on the stairway, keeping up a brisk pace until they reached the bottom.

I CAN'T BELIEVE that a love so true could die.

Had he only just realized that underneath the bright acerbity of Lady Della's personality was a romantic? A hopeless one at that?

And why did that make him feel just slightly better about the world?

Although knowing she was a romantic should make him run far, far away. What would happen if—no, forget that, *when*—she fell in love with him?

Because she would fall in love with him.

He knew he was irresistible. But unfortunately she was as well—he was unable to resist the allure of her, no matter the danger of coming too close to her flame. He would get burned. They would both expire in some lustful fiery conflagration, and he would die a happy man.

He beckoned to a hackney, then opened the door for her to get inside, wrinkling his nose as he followed after her. Judging by the smell inside, the cab had apparently been egalitarian in its ridership, having borne a horse or two to their eventual destination.

Or the cabby was just not that clean.

She met his gaze, her wry smile acknowledging the odor.

"It's a good thing I am not fussy," she remarked, pulling a handkerchief from her pocket and holding it up to her nose. "But I wish it were not quite so fragrant in here. I don't want to arrive at where Mr. Wattings might be smelling like a stable."

"I had thought we would go tomorrow," Griff said, taking his own handkerchief out from his pocket. "If we are attending a party this evening, which I presume we are, we won't have enough time to prepare and find Mr. Wattings. Especially now that we both likely smell."

She lowered her handkerchief and leaned over to him, sniffing his shoulder, then gave him a mischievous look. He slid the cloth from over his nose and raised his eyebrow, daring her to do what he knew they both most wanted to.

And, thank God, she did.

"At least it'll keep me from smelling it all," she murmured before grabbing his head and bringing his lips down forcefully on hers. He placed his hand on her waist, then lower so he was cupping her arse. Her delicious, fulsome arse. She responded by moving closer, keeping one hand in his hair and putting the other one on his thigh, squeezing it as they kissed.

His cock reacted immediately to her hand's proximity, of course, stiffening and straining against the cloth of his trousers. He shifted, and she chuckled against his lips, clearly enjoying the situation.

He responded by moving his hand so he could reach the skirts of her gown, gathered the fabric in his fist and began to draw it up. Slow enough so she could stop him if she wanted to.

She didn't stop him.

He extended his hand to slide his fingers over her leg, continuing to bring the bottom of the gown up. Up her shin, over her knee, until he was able to roll it up and rest it on her thighs.

His eyes were closed, but he couldn't resist opening them for a moment to look at what he'd done. And then he couldn't stop staring—her revealed thighs, the juncture between her legs beckoning him.

Damn, he wanted her. Even in this ridiculous-smelling hackney cab, barreling through London's streets en route to take her home, he wanted her.

It was the first time he'd ever begrudged his size; if he were a smaller man, he could take her against the carriage seat, her holding on to his arse as he thrust into her.

He'd have to make do with what he had, however. He slid his fingers on her thigh and then curled down between her legs. Not quite there yet, but just shy of there. Waiting to make certain she was on board with what he was doing.

She moaned into his mouth, edging her body closer so his fingers touched her soft wetness. She was definitely on board with what he was doing, then.

He felt the damp curls, and then his finger found her nub and he rubbed it gently. She broke their kiss, tilting her head back and closing her eyes as she bit her lip.

"Do you want me to touch you, Della?" he asked in a rough voice. Even though he knew what her answer would be. He needed to hear her say it.

"Yes," she gasped. "Touch me, please, Griff."

He felt a deep current of satisfaction flow through him at hearing her speak his name so pleadingly. He placed his other hand on her neck and caressed her soft skin, sliding his fingertips along her jawline.

She exhaled sharply as he increased the pressure of his fingers down below, and she squirmed as he found the rhythm she liked.

Within a few minutes, she was clutching his arm and biting her lip, her eyes closed as he felt her rush toward her climax.

She was so beautiful. He never wanted to stop watching her.

And then her eyes flew open, meeting his gaze as she cried out, and he could feel her shuddering in deep satisfaction.

"Oh," she sighed, keeping her eyes on him. She relaxed her hold on his arm but didn't let go.

Don't ever let go, he wanted to say.

Her face was flushed and she felt soft and wet where he'd pleasured her.

He drew his fingers away, then brought them to his mouth and licked her taste off them, her eyes widening as she watched what he was doing.

"You need to kiss me right now," she commanded, tugging on his arm to bring him closer. Their mouths met, and he slid his tongue inside, tangling it with hers. His cock was rigid, and it took all his will not to drag her hand down to touch him.

But then his will was rewarded, because she did slide her hand down his arm and onto his erection, stroking him through his trousers. Her fingers fumbled at the placket, and then his cock sprung free into her soft, warm hand.

Damn.

She gripped him hard, a pleasurable agony that brought a stifled groan to his throat. And then she began to stroke him, kissing him as she did. He could feel how her lips had curled up into a smile, and he drew back from her mouth to look at her. At her mouth, bruised and red from their kiss, at her eyes, which glinted in satisfied delight.

"Do you want me to touch you, Griff?" she said, an echo of what he'd asked a few minutes before.

He grunted in response, unable to utter a word because of how hard and fast she was stroking him. It seemed as though she knew just how to touch him, and he appreciated that she had clearly done this before. She would be an equal in their bed, and he couldn't wait to thrust into her as she begged him for more. He'd give it to her, and she would reciprocate, as she was doing now.

"Fuck, Della," he groaned, and her smile grew wider.

"That's not what we're doing, my lord," she teased. "I'm touching your cock."

God, hearing her say the words increased the pleasure that much more, and suddenly Griff realized he wanted her to say the filthiest things to him as she stroked him.

"Tell me how it feels," he asked, his voice ragged in desperation.

"Hard," she said immediately. "And like velvet. I am thinking about how it'll feel when you're inside me. If you'll fit, or if you'll have to push hard into me."

"Uhn," Griff said.

"And when you're buried inside, I'll wrap my legs around you. Tell me, Griff, how do you plan on having me?"

Every way I can.

He was so, so close, her hand gripping and stroking and sliding up and down, an inexorable rhythm that was propelling him toward his own climax.

He shouted as he came, spilling into her hand, the rush of pleasure coursing through his body, every bit of him focused on how good he felt and that she'd brought him to this.

She didn't let go, though she did loosen her grip, holding him as his cock jerked in her hand. Only when his shudders had stopped did she release him, and he groaned, dropping his head down as the feeling flowed through him.

"That was good," she said in a husky voice. "It took my mind off the odor," she added in an amused tone.

He was impressed she was able to speak. He wasn't certain he could ever make actual words again.

"Here," she said, handing him the handkerchief

she'd had pressed to her nose. He took it, and cleaned himself up, grateful he'd be returning home before being seen in public again.

They hadn't been in the cab all that long—just long enough for him to pleasure her and vice versa—and he was surprised when the cab slowed, indicating they were nearing their destination.

Actually, he was surprised he could think at all, but he wouldn't question it.

"I will meet you at the party? I believe Eleanor said she is going, and she can bring me."

"Hmph," Griff replied. Still not able to utter words. Hopefully that would change when he had to make any kind of conversation. Or not; perhaps he could just go through life muttering and grunting. As long as he got to maintain his inarticulation through frequent bouts of sexual passion with her, he would accept the inability to make words.

"Right," she said, clearly amused.

The cab stopped, and he opened the door, then leapt out to help her get out.

She took his hand, looking up at him with a sly, mischievous gaze. "We're going to have to resolve our bargain soon. I'm not certain I can wait much longer." She leaned in to whisper in his ear. "I want your body, Griff. Naked and writhing on mine."

He groaned, and she chuckled, released his hand, and turned toward the door, throwing one last naughty glance at him.

"Where to, milord?" the cabby asked.

Damn. He hoped he could speak. "Uh—the Duke of Northam's." There. That wasn't so difficult, was it?

He got back into the carriage and leaned against the seat back, closing his eyes, replaying every moment of what had just happened.

Chapter 15

*M*y goodness.

All that in just the time it took them to get from the Naval Office to her house. Della walked slowly up the stairs, hoping what she'd been doing—and had done to her—wasn't completely obvious.

Look solemn, she warned herself.

She opened the door and stepped inside, relieved that nobody was there.

"You're back!"

Except that all of them were there: Sarah, the girls, Eleanor and her child, and a few of the girls they'd rescued.

Standing looking at her.

"Am I late for something?" Della asked. She was bursting to tell Sarah of what they'd discovered at the Naval Office, but she didn't want to raise her friend's hopes if there was nothing more to learn.

"I came over to visit with Nora and Miss Emily," Eleanor said with a smile. "I thought I'd mentioned I'd bring you to this evening's party? Unless your Lord Stanbury plans to pick you up?"

"Yes, of course." Della took a deep breath. So far nobody had accused her of doing improper things in a carriage, so perhaps the day would continue well after all. "You look lovely, by the way."

Eleanor wore a deep blue gown with a darker blue velvet ribbon wrapped around her waist. The hem of her gown was edged in scalloped lace, and Della could see the toes of her blue velvet slippers peeking out from under the gown.

"Thank you." Eleanor glanced at the clock in the corner of the hallway. "We haven't much time to get you looking lovely," she said, walking toward Della, then halting suddenly, an odd expression on her face. "Where have you been?" she asked, wrinkling her nose.

"I've been—uh," Della began.

"Because you smell like a stable," Eleanor continued.

A rush of relief went through Della at her sister's words. "Yes, I do. I'll need a bath," she said, directing her words toward the cluster of maids.

A few of them scurried off toward the kitchen, and then she knelt down, gesturing to Nora to come closer.

"Have you had fun today, love?" she asked.

Her daughter gave a solemn nod. "Emily and Aunt Eleanor and I played. Because my cousin is too little to play yet," she added in a scornful tone. As though it were the baby's fault he was so young.

"That sounds wonderful." And it did. This was why she had returned after all. Not for everything she'd found and was doing with Lord Skilled with His Fingers; that was an unexpected bonus, but this was the real reason she was here, suffering possible ignominy and disdain as well as complete dismissal by her parents.

Family was more important than anything, she'd long since realized. And family meant people who were related to you by blood, and people related to you by bond. She needed to remember that, even when in the throes of passion.

She gathered Nora into her arms for a hug, feeling her eyes start to prickle.

"You have to let me go, me and Emily are going to play," Nora said in an exasperated voice.

"Of course," Della said, meeting Sarah's amused gaze. A gaze that said that the daughter was very similar to the mother.

She wouldn't do anything to jeopardize her family. She had to do everything she could to protect them, and to make them complete again by finding Sarah's husband.

Tomorrow, she promised herself. *Tomorrow we'll go to the address and see if he's still there.*

Meanwhile, she had a party to get ready for and a pretend betrothed to pretend to be betrothed to.

"LADY DELLA HOWLETT," the butler announced.

The room hushed, as Della was accustomed to. She took a step forward, then hesitated when she saw them directly in front of her. Their backs turned to her—had they just turned around or was it coincidental?—and she felt a panicked moment of wanting to scurry out the door until she realized that was just what would please them.

"Lady Eleanor Raybourn," he continued.

Eleanor took hold of her arm and gave it a reassuring squeeze.

"We can leave now if you want," she whispered. "You don't have to do this."

Della lifted her chin. Their backs were still to her. Deliberate, then. They had to have heard Eleanor's name being announced, even if they had somehow missed hers. They would have turned around to greet their daughter if they hadn't wanted to shun their other daughter.

"It's fine. Lord Stanbury will be here soon." Not that she wanted to hide behind him—even though she did—but then she would have a purpose in being here beyond being visibly ostracized by her parents.

"Let's get some punch," Eleanor said, walking down the few steps to the ballroom. A few people were nearby, glancing between the duke and duchess and them, clearly anticipating the evening's best gossip.

Della kept her gaze focused on the corner table where the punch bowl rested. She wouldn't even give them the satisfaction of a look, much less an acknowledgment. But since they were likely thinking the same thing, her determined non-looking at them would probably be overlooked.

"Eleanor."

Della flinched at hearing her mother's voice after so long. Eleanor froze, her hold on Della's arm tightening.

"Good evening, Mother," Eleanor said, turning just barely away from Della.

Della couldn't help but look at them. Her mother's mouth was pressed into a thin line, while her expression made it look as though she was on the verge of speaking, but couldn't find the words.

Unusual for her mother, who could usually find words—often the entirely wrong ones—at any given moment.

Della tried to keep herself quiet also, but she found the words spilling out of her mouth before she realized it.

"Good evening, Mother. Father." She nodded at each of them in turn, watching as her father's face began to turn a dark red.

"Let's get some punch," Eleanor said, tugging on Della's arm. Della shook her off, turning to face her parents directly.

"We can at least be civil to one another," she said, raising her voice so the people nearby could hear. She wouldn't have anyone say she was unkind or that she had avoided the confrontation.

The duchess glanced from her husband to Della and back again, her urge to speak clearly warring with her urge to keep her husband from exploding in public. "Is it true you are engaged to Viscount Stanbury?"

Della hated to hide behind the false engagement as a way to mend things with her parents, but she did have to admit it was a lot better than having them pointedly snub her when they saw her out.

"Yes."

"The heir to the Duke of Northam?" her father said, sounding skeptical.

"The very same," Della replied, taking petty satisfaction in how both her parents were clearly weighing what response would give them the best social standing.

"That is lovely news! I am so happy you are back in London, you must come to tea some afternoon."

Della pulled her mouth into a semblance of a smile. "Thank you. Nora would love that."

Her mother's eyes widened, and she glanced nervously back at the duke, who looked as though he were on the verge of saying no, but then he gave a brief nod. "We won't keep you from getting something to drink," he said in a clear dismissal.

"Please send our best to your betrothed," the

duchess added. "Perhaps he would like to come to tea as well?"

It was obvious that her parents would have continued to snub her if she had been just herself, not the recent betrothed of the heir to the Duke of Northam. It aggravated her, being so dependent on him for her good name, but then again, it would all change once their engagement was known to be broken.

So she had that to look forward to.

Ugh.

"Della?" Eleanor said.

"Yes, of course. Punch."

They walked quickly, Eleanor leaning in to speak in a low voice. "Are you all right? Should we leave?"

"No. I am thirsty, and Lord Stanbury should be here any minute now."

"You are so brave, Della," Eleanor replied in an admiring tone.

"Brave or foolhardy, I'm not certain," Della said ruefully.

SEEING LORD DID Not Appear At The Party Last Night wasn't necessarily why she decided to take Nora, Sarah, and Emily to the duke's house for a visit. She had sent a note earlier that day, and had received a prompt reply saying today would be ideal, and that the duke was eagerly anticipating meeting Nora as well as Mrs. Wattings and Emily.

That Lord Stanbury hadn't been there the night before and she was livid about it played only a small part in her decision to go to the duke's house. A furious part, but a small part nonetheless.

They'd hailed a hackney outside their house, which thrilled Nora and Emily, who hadn't taken a carriage yet since arriving in London. And seldom when they had been living in the country—they all walked, since they couldn't afford and didn't see a need to keep a horse.

"Does the duke have a dog?" Nora demanded again. Right, she had forgotten about Nora's canine obsession.

"I don't know. We'll find out," Della said. She hoped there was a dog somewhere about so that Nora wouldn't loudly complain to the duke about his obvious lack.

"Look out there," Emily said in a quiet voice. She was far less exuberant than Nora, and definitely better behaved. Della wished she could blame Nora's exuberant enthusiasm on anybody but herself, but she could not. Nora was like her at that age—fearless, determined, and outspoken.

Rather like you are now, she heard a voice say in her head. The voice sounded an awful lot like Griffith, and he sounded amused. She grinned at the thought.

Damn it. She didn't want to think kindly about him now, not when she was still angry with him.

And she could not develop any more complicated feelings for him beyond desire. That was a risk she could not take.

"Mama, look," Nora said, pointing out the window. "Look how fancy."

Della glanced out the window, her breath catching as she saw what Nora was pointing at.

Her parents' carriage, resplendent with the family crest, pulled by a perfectly matched team of horses. She turned away, meeting Sarah's sympathetic gaze.

"It's pretty," Emily said.

"It is. Why isn't ours like that?" Nora demanded.

"We're in a hackney cab," Sarah explained. "That is a private carriage for a family."

"We're a family," Nora retorted. "Why don't we have one?"

Dear Lord, Della thought. *Just once I wish Nora were a little less like me.*

"Look over there," Sarah said, pointing out the other side. "Do you see the man with the big cart? I wonder what he's selling."

The girls immediately pivoted their attention out the other window, allowing Della to catch her breath. Sarah gave her knee a discreet pat.

"Apples!" Nora said, first as always.

"Dolls," Emily guessed.

"I think it's oatmeal," Della said. Nora loathed oatmeal.

"But how would he keep it?" Emily asked.

She had an analytical mind and was constantly asking questions. Unlike Nora, who merely demanded answers.

Yes, just like me, Della thought before any voice could pop up in her head to remind her of that fact.

The carriage turned, and then slowed, finally coming to a stop in front of the duke's house.

"Ooh," Emily said.

"One person lives there?" Nora asked.

"The duke lives there, but he has staff there too. And Lord Stanbury, he's been to our house before."

"There's enough room for a dog," Nora pronounced as Della opened the hackney door.

She got out, then helped the girls and Sarah descend. The four of them walked up the stairs to the mansion, a footman standing at attention at the door. Then the door swung open and the butler emerged. His expression was somber, but he definitely had a tiny smile when he looked at the girls.

"Might I tell the duke who is calling?" the butler asked.

"Lady Della, Mrs. Wattings, and Nora Howlett and Emily Wattings," Della replied. "The duke is expecting us."

"Excellent. If you will step inside, I will see if the duke is at home."

The four of them crowded into the hallway,

only the hallway was so enormous they could have each been in one corner and had to yell to one another.

Della hadn't noticed before, but this house was even larger than her parents'. She wondered if they knew that, and if it irked them. She hoped it did.

It was petty, but it made her feel better.

"Please come this way," the butler said, gesturing for them to follow him. They walked down the hall toward where Della had seen the duke before, Nora and Emily talking in whispers, although Nora's voice was clearly audible. Something involving a dog, of course.

"The ladies are here, Your Grace," the butler said as he ushered them into the room.

The duke was in his chair, a throw on his legs, a warm smile on his face. Della couldn't help but smile back.

"Thank you for visiting, and for bringing your—"

"Family," Della supplied.

"Of course. Family." He held his hand out toward the girls. "I am the Duke of Northam. And you are?"

"Nora Howlett," Nora replied, taking his hand and shaking it vigorously.

"Emily Wattings," Emily said, dipping into a curtsey as Nora kept shaking the duke's hand.

"A pleasure to meet you both. Tea?" the duke

said, addressing the butler. "And ask Cook if there are biscuits for my friends here."

"This is Mrs. Wattings," Della said, drawing Sarah forward. Sarah curtseyed also, and the duke nodded to her, then gestured for them to be seated.

"I do apologize for not getting up, but you see—" the duke said, indicating his chair.

"Are you sick?"

Della winced at Nora's question.

"I am not feeling as well as I could be, but I am feeling much better now that you are all visiting me," he replied. "Do you like London? You've just arrived, haven't you?" He addressed his question to the girls, since he already knew the answer.

"We came with my aunt Ida," Nora said. "In a carriage, and it was crowded."

Sarah smothered a laugh with her hand as Della met the duke's gaze and offered him a wan smile. He grinned back, and she nodded to him in thanks.

"What do you like about London, Miss Emily?" the duke asked.

Emily looked instinctively at Nora, who was usually the one who answered questions. Nora nudged her in the shoulder.

"I like all the people who live with us," Emily said in her soft voice. "Mama and Miss Della and Nora and Becky and all the other girls."

"You live with an awful lot of people, then?" the duke replied.

"Mmm-hmm," Emily murmured.

"I like ices and walking in the park," Nora announced.

"Excellent things to like, Miss Nora," the duke replied.

"Do you have a dog?" Nora asked.

Della was surprised at her daughter's forbearance—it had taken her at least five minutes to ask the most pressing question in her mind.

"I do not," the duke said. "But I believe there is a dog who lives in the stables, you could go see the horses and find him, if you want."

Both girls were off the sofa before he finished speaking. Della got up also, but the door opened to reveal the butler holding a tray.

"Once you've set that down, can you take the ladies to the stables?"

The butler nodded as he placed the tea things on the table in front of the sofa.

"Come, ladies," he said, sounding as though he were escorting the queen rather than two young girls.

"Can I serve, Your Grace?" Della asked.

The rest of the visit went well. Sarah and the duke discovered they had a mutual love of maths, so the duke brought out some of his accounting and the two of them pored over it as Della tried not to yawn. And stew about Griffith not showing up the night before.

When they went at last, the duke took pains to invite Sarah to visit again. Della was pleased that the duke was as thoughtful and kind as she'd suspected.

GRIFFITH TENSED IN anticipation of seeing her. He had missed the party the night before, and he was expecting she would be angry.

She was glorious when she was angry.

He knocked at the door, which she flung open, a glare on her face.

"Where were you?"

He shrugged, knowing that would annoy her even more. "I was busy."

Her eyes narrowed, and she stepped toward him, raising her finger to point at his chest. "I went with my sister, and saw my parents, which was entirely unpleasant."

Her parents. And he hadn't been with her for it. Damn it. Although she probably would have swatted away anything he might have done to help.

But she was still speaking. "And the entire evening people were giving me these looks as though my betrothed had finally discovered who I really was. And then a few of the gentlemen offered to comfort me—"

"They did?" Griff interrupted.

She rolled her eyes. "That is not the point of the conversation. The point is that you said you would be there, and you were not. I left after a few hours of pitying looks and whispered asides.

"But I did discover the name of the man who was so rude to me. It turns out, according to my sister Olivia, that Lord Balcham is in debt to her husband. And his debt is due." She shook her head. "But that is beside the point. Where were you?" she demanded again.

"I am sorry, but there was something I had to do." Her expression grew more irritated, if that were possible. He cleared his throat, relishing the anticipation of it. "Could you ask Mrs. Wattings to come down? I have something to show her."

Della looked as though she were going to argue, and then her expression cleared and her eyes widened. "Oh! Is it? Sarah!" she said, turning her head to call up the stairs.

She returned her gaze to him, and he wanted to preen at the look she was giving him now. Not that he didn't want to preen anytime she regarded him; he did, especially since he knew she both appreciated and deplored it. But now it was so much more deserved.

"What is it?" Sarah began to walk down the stairs, carrying an armful of linens. "I was just rearranging the linen closet. The girls have been using some of the best sheets for their forts." She sounded rueful, but not dismissive.

What would it have been like for him if he'd had a mother like Mrs. Wattings? Or Della? A mother whose first thought was for her child, not regarding said offspring as an inconvenience?

"Lord Stanbury has something for you," Della replied. She looked at Griff and spoke in a low tone. "This had better be what I think it is."

He grinned at her ferocity. "It is, I promise." He walked forward to Mrs. Wattings, taking the heap of linens from her arms and placing it on one of the chairs arranged along the side of the room. "If I may?" he asked, holding his arm out.

She took it while giving him a bemused smile, and he suppressed his own, not wanting to spoil the surprise too early. Even though it was obvious Della knew what he'd done.

"If you'll just step this way," he said, walking Mrs. Wattings to the door. He reached forward ahead of her and opened it, flinging it wide with a dramatic flourish.

And there, standing on the steps, was Wattings.

He felt Mrs. Wattings stiffen, and then she was running out the door and into Mr. Wattings's arms, nearly knocking both of them over in the process. And he heard her sob, and saw Wattings's face, and felt a bone-deep satisfaction at what he'd accomplished.

"Oh my goodness." Della had stepped to his side, taking his hand in hers. Almost as though it were unconscious. And that shouldn't have pleased him as much as it did—but it did. "This is what you were doing last night."

He squeezed her hand. "It was. I was on my way home when I thought that I should just visit the address to see if we would be disappointed tomorrow. I was walking up the street when I saw him. I don't know which one of us was more surprised."

She chuckled. "Likely it was him, since you at least knew you were looking for him."

"Fair point," he replied.

Meanwhile, Mr. and Mrs. Wattings were walking back into the house, his arm wrapped around her shoulders as she stared up at him as if she were unable to believe her eyes.

"Oh! Emily!" Della exclaimed, dropping his hand and dashing up the stairs.

Mrs. Wattings walked up to him, tears streaming down her face as she enfolded him in a hug. He patted her gently on the back, meeting Wattings's gaze over her shoulder.

"Thank you, my lord," she said, her voice choked. "I didn't think it would be possible. I didn't want to hope."

The raw emotion in her voice made him ache for her, of how she must have smothered her pain to present a good front for her daughter. Della knew what her friend was suffering, of course, but Griff had never seen it; instead, he'd seen a kind woman who seemed to genuinely care about others' well-being.

He heard footsteps above and turned to see Mrs. Wattings's daughter pelt down the stairs, her eyes wide, Della following close behind. Mrs. Wattings released him from the hug as she watched her daughter's progress.

"There he is, Emily. Your father," Della said quietly.

"Papa!" the girl screeched, leaping up into Wattings's arms. Her father held her tight, and Griff heard the man stifle a sob in his throat.

Truth be told, he was remarkably close to sobbing as well. He hadn't cried in years. He couldn't remember the last time he'd cried, actually.

But now he could feel his eyes prickle and his chest tighten.

"My girl," Wattings said, patting his daughter's head. "My girl."

Mrs. Wattings wrapped her arms around both of them, and he averted his gaze, shifting his stance so as not to intrude on the moment.

Della came to stand beside him, mirroring his position so that they were both definitely not staring at the reunited family.

"You found him," she said, her voice holding an astonished tone. "I wasn't certain we would—"

"You doubt me?" he interrupted.

He could hear her roll her eyes. "No, of course

not, you arrogant man. If he was out there, I had no doubt but that you could find him. I just doubted that he could be found. And yet here he is."

"Here he is," Griff repeated in satisfaction.

The Wattingses, still holding on to one another, began to walk up the stairs, Mrs. Wattings glancing back at them with a tear-stained face.

It felt good to have done something like this. No, more than that; it felt marvelous. It felt as though he could conquer the world.

Of course, he felt like that normally, so perhaps it wasn't that remarkable.

But there was a tinge of something he'd never felt before—a feeling that he'd accomplished something that would bring about a powerful change for the three members of the Wattings family.

"Did he say why he'd left London before?" Della asked. "About why he didn't try to find Sarah?"

Griff had been dreading this question, just as he knew it was inevitable.

"It seems as though Mrs. Wattings's parents told Wattings that Sarah had gone to America with another man."

She froze, then inhaled sharply. "Dear Lord. Poor Sarah. That her parents could—" She shook her head. "I wish I couldn't believe it, but of course I do." Of course she believed it, given how her own parents had treated her. Denying themselves the opportunity to meet Nora because of their stubbornness.

The thought made him furious. "I would never do anything without your permission, but let me know if I can do anything to help. Either with Mrs. Wattings's family, or—or your own."

She bit her lip, and he could see her eyes getting moist. His fierce Della, close to tears?

His throat closed over, and he wished he could punch someone.

"Thank you," she said at last.

Two words were inadequate for the gratitude she felt. He had done what he had promised. Not only that, but he had respected her need to be independent. *I would never do anything without your permission.*

That was far more seductive than any compliment she had ever received.

"Am I forgiven?" he asked, an amused tone in his voice. "For not escorting you to the party?"

She snorted. "Of course. Although I have to say, your presence makes going to those events far easier. My parents, for example, were able to acknowledge me since they had heard the news of our engagement." She couldn't help her rueful tone. "Except for Lord Balcham, whose effrontery nearly got him clocked in the nose by a lordly behemoth."

He flung his head back and laughed, a complete, hearty laugh that made her laugh too.

"Behemoth, is it?" he said at last. "You'll have to share that one with Mrs. Wattings."

"My behemoth," Della replied.

He nodded in confirmation.

"So now that we don't have to skulk around the docks anymore, what will we do with our time?" He accompanied his words with a knowing wink.

"Honestly, is that the only thing you can think about?"

He nodded again. "I have to say when I am in your presence, yes."

"Well, then," she said, drawing closer to him and tilting her face up to his. "For once I am in perfect agreement with you."

His lids lowered, his gaze on her mouth. "Then I believe we should leave your house and find our way to a place where we can explore our shared desires."

The way he said it—*shared desires*—made her shudder in anticipation.

"Becky!" she called, and the girl scurried downstairs.

"Yes, my lady?" She cast an admiring glance toward Lord Stanbury. *He's mine*, Della wanted to say. Even though he wasn't.

But he would be. For a time, at least. She couldn't afford more than that.

"Can you check in with Mrs. Wattings and ask if she wants you to sit with Emily? I have to go out, and Mrs. Wattings—" Well, she wouldn't talk about what it was likely Sarah and Mr. Wattings were going to do later on this evening. "Mrs. Wattings might want Emily to be taken care of."

Becky's expression revealed her puzzlement at being asked to do something she did usually, but Della wanted to ensure Sarah had some time to herself.

"Yes, my lady. And I'll see after Miss Nora also."

"Thank you," Della said as Becky walked up the stairs.

"We can go now, if you like," Della murmured to Lord Stanbury.

"At last," he growled. And then he took her arm and pulled her to the door, making her laugh at his obvious haste.

Finally. Finally she was going to get to explore all of him. As he would be able to do to her.

Chapter 16

$\mathcal{G}$riffith's whole body practically vibrated with need. Needing to get her alone and naked, needing to discover what would make her cry out, needing to touch her everywhere.

Thankfully, he'd already scouted a place they could go, or he'd be in an even worse feeling of frustration. He hailed a hackney, yanked the door open and assisted Della inside, before vaulting in after her.

She grinned at him, and he found himself smiling back. He didn't think he had ever smiled so much with a woman he was also sexually engaged with; usually, the smiles were for the moments after, when he was boneless and satisfied.

He had no doubt but that she would leave him that way, and smiling, but to find himself so pleased even before things had begun—well, that was unusual.

"Where are we going?" she said in a low voice, placing her hand on his thigh.

He put his hand over hers, squeezing her fingers. "Some place where we can be alone for a while. Some place where there are no duke's daughters besides yourself, no missing sailors, no best friends who are fiercely guarding their friend."

"Has Sarah done that to you?" she asked, surprised.

He shook his head. "Not yet, but if I were to misbehave, she would make it very clear to me. You have a good friend in her."

She nodded. "I do. And what about you? Who are your friends?"

"Clark and Hyland, two of my crew. Frederick."

"I have my sisters and Sarah, you have your sailors and your cousin."

"And the many people clamoring to meet me now that I am the heir to a dukedom."

She fluttered her eyelids at him. "Surely your outsized sense of self-worth would argue with that. I mean, it is you we are discussing. Lord Handsome of the Exuberant Expression."

He guffawed at her words and she joined in. He had never laughed so much with anybody ever, much less with a woman he was planning on getting naked and sweaty with.

"I suppose I do have a healthy opinion of myself," he replied. "But really, when you look like me, how could you not?"

She exploded into giggles, and he found himself smiling at her, relishing how she didn't care if she was being exuberant herself. That she probably wanted to be as outrageous as possible so she could remain true to herself.

DELLA GAVE A few final chuckles, then glanced out the window. "Where are we? I don't recognize this area."

Griffith squeezed her hand and nodded toward the outside. "It's a few miles outside of London. I found a small inn that is quite clean where we can stay the night." He frowned, and Della felt her breath hitch. Unless he didn't want to spend the night with her?

"Unless you need to return earlier to see your daughter?"

Della let out a sigh of relief. "Becky will have Nora well in hand. I imagine the girls will want to ask Mr. Wattings all about the sea, and your boat—"

"Ship," he corrected as he helped her out of the carriage.

"Ship," she echoed, rolling her eyes at him. "Anyway, if there is any concern, Sarah will understand what has happened, particularly since she saw us together, and she knew—"

"She knew?" he interrupted in a surprised tone. "Is that something you often speak of?"

She glared at him. "It is not something that usually arises in conversation, my lord. 'I plan on taking a lover, could you make certain my daughter is taken care of?'" She shook her head. "But Sarah and I share everything."

"Oh," he replied in a subdued tone. "I did not mean to imply—"

"That I am a woman of loose morals?" she said sharply. "You are the only one I have even considered in that manner since Mr. Baxter left."

"I apologize." He spoke in a quietly sincere tone of voice. They walked toward the front of the inn. "I didn't mean that. I was more stuck on the idea that you and your friend would be so open with one another."

"Oh. Yes, we are," Della said.

"If anything," he continued, "it is a relief to find you are a woman of experience." He swung the door open.

She lifted her eyebrow toward him. She had yet to meet a man who didn't care about a lady's past.

"No, truly!" he said in response to her expression. "Imagine if I had to be the leader in that situation like so many others. For once, I'd like to be doing something and have the other person know just as well what should be done."

She couldn't help but laugh. "So you're saying that because you're the captain of a ship, and now a duke's heir, that you want to be relieved of responsibility in bed?"

"Well, I still want to be able to ask for what I

want," he replied with a knowing look. "But it is far more pleasurable if the person knows how to fulfill my needs."

Della couldn't resist the self-satisfied smile that appeared on her face. "I do, my lord. I promise."

"This way," he said, guiding her through the inn. She had barely gotten a look at it before he was bringing her up the stairs and down the hall toward where she presumed their bedroom was.

Their bedroom. She was actually going to do this, finally. After thinking about it for so long, nearly backing out of it when he had shown himself to be an arrogant ass, then changing her mind when she realized he was an arrogant ass, but he was an arrogant ass who could realize he was wrong.

Plus he seemed, at least for the moment, to be *her* arrogant ass.

He unlocked the door and guided her inside, his hand at the small of her back.

The room was small but tidy, dominated by an enormous bed that appeared to be big enough even for him.

She turned to him. "Did you choose this room based solely on that?" she asked, gesturing to the bed.

He raised one rakish eyebrow. "Of course. What other criteria would I have?"

"Excellent," she said, going to sit on it.

He walked to stand in front of her, his hands

on his hips. She drew her gaze up and down his body, biting her lip as she contemplated his size.

"Well? Do you like what you see?" he said in a confident voice.

"You know I do." She nodded toward him. "Take your clothes off."

He immediately began to shrug out of his jacket, then tossed it onto the floor.

She brought her hands to her back to begin her buttons, but stopped at the sound of his voice.

"I want to take care of that," he said in a husky growl.

"Oh," she sighed, leaning back on her elbows. "Well, then, proceed."

He undid his cravat, then yanked his shirt from his trousers, brought it over his head, and dropped it on top of the jacket that lay on the floor.

My goodness, his chest was impressive, she thought to herself. Her mouth got dry.

He had a dark dusting of hair on his upper body, the hair trailing down the middle to where it disappeared into his trousers. His stomach muscles were delineated, so much so that she could nearly count them. His arms were equally impressive, corded with muscle.

He bent over to undo his boots, and she glimpsed something on his back.

She stared, then hopped off the bed and stepped around him to see.

"Oh my lord," she breathed. "You have a tattoo."

"I do," he replied, glancing over his shoulder at her. "Do you like it?"

Did she like it. What kind of question was that? Of course she liked it.

It was a ship, one that covered his entire back. She put her hands on his shoulders—goodness, they were strong—and then skimmed her fingers down his back, marveling at the detail.

"This is gorgeous," she said. "How did you decide what to get?"

"A full-rigged ship like that one means the person has sailed around Cape Horn."

"I don't even know where Cape Horn is," she admitted.

"It's at the bottom of South America. Very treacherous passage there."

"Oh," she said, tracing her fingers on the sails.

He turned, wrapping her in his arms. "While I appreciate that you are touching me, and admiring my masculine beauty, I would far rather we were together on that bed over there. You can take a look at my ink when you've rendered me speechless."

She grinned up at him. "I know another way to make you speechless," she said, raising her mouth to his.

THEY WERE KISSING again. Only this time it was both more intense and more leisurely—knowing what was going to happen, but also knowing they had time. He explored her mouth with his tongue, and she did the same, her hands clutching his arms, sliding up and down their expanse.

He slid his hand from her waist to grab her sweet arse, holding its curve in his palm and squeezing. He felt her shudder, and squeezed harder, then let go to caress the round globe.

She placed her hands on his waist, tucking her thumbs into his waistband, his cock standing at rigid attention at the close proximity of her hand.

Please, please, slide that palm down, he begged inside his head. Mostly because he couldn't speak since her tongue was in his mouth.

Only she did better than that—she began to undo the placket of his trousers, shoved the fabric aside and began to push his trousers down his legs.

His cock arched forward into her belly, covered by his smallclothes. He needed to get everything off as soon as possible.

Breaking the kiss, he quickly pushed his trousers entirely down and stepped out of them, then put his fingers at the waistband of his smallclothes. He met her gaze and arched one brow as if in question.

She bit her lip, her head giving a vigorous nod.

He drew them off also, and then he was entirely naked.

She stepped back, her lip still in her teeth, her gaze assessing him.

He resisted the urge to preen.

His cock was pointed straight at her, and his hand went to his shaft.

She shook her head, and he froze.

"No," she said in a low, husky voice. "I want to touch you." And she lowered herself to her knees and put her hands at his waist, then licked the tip of his cock before glancing up at him with a sly smile.

Holy hell.

"Della—" he begged, and she kept her gaze locked with his as she opened her mouth to take him inside.

He held himself still, waiting for her next move. She wrapped her fingers around the base of his cock as she began to slide her mouth up and down his shaft. Licking and sucking with a focused vigor he very much appreciated.

Her grip was tight, as he liked, and she was making soft noises of appreciation in the back of her throat.

He didn't know if he could speak, or would ever be able to speak again.

He was close. So close to spending, to thrusting deep into her mouth and climaxing.

And then she raised her head, making him groan in disappointment.

She laughed, using his body to stand. "I want

your cock inside me, Lord Handsome," she said, pushing him toward the bed. He fell onto his back as she followed, clambering on top of him.

Her mouth was red and swollen, and her hair was coming down in soft tendrils.

He had never seen a more beautiful sight in his life.

Except she wasn't naked.

He got up onto his knees, and then with one swift movement got in back of her, his fingers going to the buttons of her gown. She made a noise of frustration, and he grinned.

"Patience, my lady Fuckable," he murmured, lowering his mouth onto her shoulder and nipping the soft skin there. "I will give you my cock if you can give me your sweet pussy."

"Mmm," she agreed, twisting as he lowered the fabric of her gown down her shoulders. She hoisted her arse into the air and yanked the gown all the way off her body, then tossed it onto the floor as he had his garments.

She wore a corset and her shift, and his fingers fumbled at the laces, his cock brushing against the soft fabric of her shift as she wiggled impatiently. She looked over her shoulder at him, her dark hair falling around her face. "I hope you've got better competency in the bed than you do undressing me, my lord," she teased.

"I'll show you competency, woman," he said,

yanking her corset off and then dragging her shift up over her head as she knelt on the bed.

And then she was delightfully, blissfully naked. He moved her so she was on her back, her laughing face looking up at him.

"Very competent," she replied with a wink. "So where were we?"

"Right fucking here," he replied.

"Excellent." Her hands stroked his side, and then her fingers clasped his erection.

Her expression shifted. "Only—darn it, I forgot to get—" And her fingers fluttered around his shaft.

"Right. As did I." If his hands weren't full already, he'd have slapped his forehead. He had totally forgotten about ensuring there were no accidents. "We'll make it work."

She nodded. "I trust you," she said, guiding him inside.

Which, luckily enough, was where he wanted it also.

It HAD BEEN so long, she thought to herself. But this—this was well worth the wait. His body was as large and delicious as she had imagined, rigid muscles defining his body, his broad chest narrowing to his hips, then lowering to the dark thatch of hair around his cock.

And his cock was gorgeous, even though she

didn't think the appendage was normally found particularly beautiful. It was large, as she'd anticipated, and thick, with smooth skin that was like velvet to the touch. Iron encased in velvet, which was a deliciously intoxicating feeling.

He was so big she had found it awkward to slide her lips over him, but the sounds he made and the way he jerked in her mouth as she ran her mouth up and down him were well worth any discomfort.

And now he was inside her, at last. He had drawn himself up on his arms, likely so as not to crush her, but she had to admit she craved the feeling of all that muscled weight lying on top of her. Pushing into her, ravaging her as she searched for her release.

She grabbed his arse, not surprised to find it as hard and muscled as the rest of him. And just above was that glorious tattoo, something unexpected and slightly dangerous. Just like him.

He growled as she squeezed, so of course she squeezed harder. He gazed down at her, then began to shift, pushing in even farther, making her hurt, but in an exquisitely painful way.

She tightened around him, making him groan.

"What do you want, Della?"

He was clearly eager to thrust, she could tell by his breath and how he was holding himself inside her, but still he took the time to ask what she wanted, making her emotions blossom in her chest, even though she was frantic for him to just do whatever he wanted to do to her.

Two contrary thoughts, of course, but that was who she was, wasn't it? On one hand a woman who had her own opinions about everything, thank you very much, and on the other a woman who wanted to have this specific man exert his mastery over her.

But she hadn't answered him yet, had she? She ran her hands up his back to cup his neck, drawing his mouth down to hers. She spoke just as their lips were about to touch. "I want you to ravish me until I see stars, Lord Handsome."

He smiled, a smile filled with anticipation and hunger, and she felt her insides shiver at what that smile promised. And then he began to move, sliding his cock and then pushing back in an inexorable rhythm. His hand went between them, touching her there, and she arched her back, writhing at the nearly overwhelming combination of all the places he was touching her—her mouth, her nub, her pussy.

His thrusts moved her up the bed, and she reached down to grab his arse again, pulling her body into his when he pushed inside.

The friction was incredible, and she could feel the mounting pleasure, coiling around her body as it built to a crescendo.

And then it hit its peak, and she screamed, throwing her head back as the waves of passion rolled through her, her whole body rigid under him. He was still moving, moving faster now, so fierce and furious she was completely helpless under the onslaught.

And then he withdrew, groaning as she felt his body spasm above her, his eyes closed, his expression grimaced. His hand on his beautiful cock, spending onto her stomach.

She had never seen anything so beautiful before.

He collapsed onto her, his body slick with sweat, and she wrapped him in an embrace, nuzzling his ear as the waves of pleasure subsided.

"Mmm," she said in a low murmur, "that was excellent."

They were sticky and sweaty and exhausted, and she had never been more content in her life.

His mouth was kissing her neck, and she could feel it when he smiled. "It was, wasn't it?"

He sounded entirely self-satisfied, and for once she couldn't fault him for his arrogance. It was a truly spectacular bout of lovemaking.

"Let's rest a bit and then do it again," he said, tucking his face into her shoulder, his hand stroking her hip.

"Again?" she said in surprise. She hadn't realized—but then again, he was remarkable in so many ways.

"Of course again." He licked her neck. "I want to taste you, Della."

Her eyes widened as she realized what he was saying. She hadn't ever done that before. Or, more correctly, hadn't ever had that done to her before.

And here she thought she knew everything about it.

She couldn't wait to see what he had to teach her.

"DID MY COMPETENCY please you, my lady?" He couldn't keep the smug tone from his voice. Nor did she likely want him to; she had made her satisfaction with him abundantly and loudly clear.

So loud, in fact, he was grateful it was the middle of the day and likely fewer patrons at the inn he'd taken her to. He wouldn't want to expose her to the embarrassment of a noise complaint.

He was lying on his side, his hand resting idly on her breast, thumbing her nipple as he gazed his fill at her nakedness. She didn't seem to be bothered by his appraisal; she was returning it, in fact, having spent a quarter of an hour resting on his backside tracing his tattoo with her fingers.

If he had known she would be so enamored of it he would have considered getting a tattoo on his cock. Although she hadn't lost interest in that either, so perhaps it wasn't necessary.

She laughed, smacking him on the arm. "My lord Arrogance," she said in a possessive tone of voice.

"I am yours, my lady."

He didn't intend for his words to sound so serious, but there they were, emerging as though he were committing to something.

She frowned, and he felt his breath hitch.

"Thank you for finding Mr. Wattings," she said at last. His chest eased.

"Do we still have a bargain?" he asked.

She gazed up at him, a smirk on her lips. "Which bargain do you mean? The one where I keep you company to hold the ladies off, or the one where we agree to explore our mutual attraction?"

"The former. I leave the latter entirely up to you." Only he hoped she wouldn't end it too soon—not before he'd gotten enough of her, which he was beginning to wonder if that would ever happen.

There was something so alluring about her, about the combination of sensual freedom and bold conversation wrapped up in the most desirable package he'd ever seen. She was so similar to him—both of them were strongly opinionated, independent, and refused to do what they were supposed to do. But she was also a good mother, an excellent friend, a vibrant companion, and wasn't afraid to stand up to him.

Very few people countered his opinions. Only Clark and to some extent Hyland had ever successfully argued with him about anything. Frederick had tried to talk him out of running off to sea so long ago, but had eventually succumbed to his arguments, even helping him out with money for the journey.

But she would likely attempt to stare him down and refuse to budge an inch. And he, intrigued as he was, would likely agree to anything she wanted, as long as she continued to spend time with him. Either in bed or out, although he definitely preferred the former.

"What are you thinking about?" she asked suddenly, making him start.

You.

Only he couldn't and wouldn't tell her that—he wouldn't want to scare her off. Nor did he want to admit it, even to himself.

Even though he had just done that.

She was turning him upside down.

THE FEELING STARTED slowly, but once it started, it built until she knew she couldn't lie there any longer.

"You're getting up?" he asked.

She nodded, her back turned to him, leaning over to pick her corset and shift off the floor. "I should get back."

He slid his palm on her back, and she shivered. His touch almost—almost relieved the panic, but not quite.

"But you can stay here if you want. I can get home on my own."

She heard his body move, and then he was curled around her, his front to her back, the hair on his chest tickling her skin. "I don't want to stay here. Not without you. I'll get dressed, I can have you back in half an hour."

He kissed the top of her head and then got off the bed. She busied herself with putting her shift on, then her corset, and then got up to hunt for where she'd flung her dress.

He was just adjusting his smallclothes, and her breath caught as she saw him. It wasn't fair he was so spectacularly gorgeous all the way through, from his handsome, compelling face to his strongly built body to his beautiful penis.

"What are you staring at?" he asked, his tone making it perfectly clear he knew the answer, and was more than happy for it.

"Nothing," she murmured, averting her gaze.

"What is it? What happened?"

She saw his feet approach her, and then she looked up, up into his face, his expression changed from sexually satisfied to concerned.

"It's nothing."

HE PLACED HIS fingers on her chin, staring into her eyes. "It's not nothing. But you'll tell me when you're ready." It wasn't a request. But he'd left the decision up to her as to when she would share it. Perhaps it would be soon, perhaps it would be never. But it would be up to her.

She nodded. "Yes."

It shouldn't have irked him that she had closed up so soon after sex.

Never mind. It should; he would be bothered no matter who it was. He didn't like it when Clark didn't share where he went after their nights out drinking. He would say the same about Hyland, only Hyland shared everything, so that didn't come up.

But her—usually so open about her feelings, so clear about what she wanted. Not to open up about what she was feeling now made him wonder just what it was she was hiding. But he couldn't just demand she tell him, as he would with Clark. His relationship with her was far more nuanced. He knew he had never had this kind of particular connection with anyone before, and frankly, he felt out of his depth.

But that didn't make him feel lost. On the contrary, he wanted to discover just what it was that made this, and her, so different.

But only if she allowed it. And he found he very much wished she would allow it. Nearly as much as he wanted to be allowed back into her body, and very soon.

"CAPTAIN!"

Griffith had arrived home to discover his valet-secretary or secretary-valet and Hyland were both out of the house. The butler, whatever his name was, informed him that his men had walked over a few streets to a nearby pub. Griffith thought he might as well go see what they were up to, since he had no desire to sit inside and wonder what she might be thinking.

Or recalling how she felt, or how she screamed. Not if he didn't want to hasten back over to her house so he could do it all again.

So here he was, in some nondescript pub that was empty save for Clark, Hyland, and a few assorted men who seemed as though they were upper servants from some of the nearby houses.

In other words, no lords here except for Griffith, thank God.

"Captain!" Clark shouted again as Griffith walked toward the table.

Judging by Clark's tone of voice and the number of glasses in front of him, he and Hyland had been drinking for a while.

Griffith beckoned to the barmaid as he walked.

He grabbed a chair and turned it around to straddle it. Clark and Hyland grinned at him as though they knew what he had been up to.

How could they?

Then again, he wasn't very subtle. So perhaps they could tell just by his face.

"You found Wattings!" Clark said, hoisting his glass up. Hyland followed suit, and Griff looked around for the barmaid, who was thankfully approaching with his tankard of ale.

He took it from her with a smile, then held his glass up before taking a long draught.

"I did." *And I pleasured Lady Della.*

"Good work, Captain," Hyland said, clapping Griff on the back. "You can do anything you set your mind to."

Griffith acknowledged Hyland's compliment with a nod, finishing the ale with another long swallow while gesturing to the barmaid for another.

"Was your lady pleased?"

Griffith felt his mouth curl into a smug grin, only to realize Hyland wasn't talking about sexual pleasure. Plus she wasn't his lady. Most definitely not. If she were, she would have confided in him.

He really wished that didn't bother him so much.

"Lady Della was pleased, yes," he said in a short tone of voice.

"Ah, but what about you?" Clark said, using his glass to point at Griffith. "You don't sound pleased." He leaned forward. "Have you and the lady agreed to part ways since your bargain is complete?"

Griffith froze. Their bargain was technically finished, wasn't it? They hadn't discussed it. He didn't want it to be over. He definitely didn't want to stop spending time with her, even if Society was less daunting than it had been before. Even though it was still fairly daunting.

"I think the captain has gone and fallen in love with her. That's what I think," Hyland said, draining his glass.

He sounded as though he'd had as much to drink as Clark had. Griff would have to try to catch up.

"No, he hasn't," Clark replied. He tried to raise one eyebrow, but just ended up looking like he'd gotten something in his eye. "If he had, he wouldn't be here with us. He'd be stomping outside of her house declaring his love. Making some grand gesture that would prove to her that he was the best and only person she should be with."

Griffith blinked as Clark spoke. He wanted to agree with his valet-secretary. Secretary-valet. Whatever. That he hadn't fallen in love with her, that he didn't want to be with her for the rest of his life.

Only he couldn't. He strongly suspected—and this was likely a first—that he agreed with Hyland.

Damn it. He had gone and fallen in love with her, hadn't he?

He could have chosen a better time to realize it than now. In a pub with his former crew members, downing mediocre ale like it was water.

The thing was, what was he going to do?

He knew she didn't want to marry him. Mostly because she'd said that on multiple occasions.

How could he convince her?

"Captain?"

Hyland nudged his shoulder.

"What?"

"Clark here was asking if you had something you had to do tonight. Or if we could just stay here all day and pretend you're not a nob and we're not sailors without a ship."

Griffith waved at the barmaid, gesturing to his friends so she would know to bring over three more ales.

"We've got time. And I've got something you two can help me with."

Chapter 17

$\mathcal{D}$ella let herself into the house, smiling as Nora pelted into her, wrapping herself around Della's legs.

"You're back! Mama, Emily's father is here, and everybody is crying, but they're not sad."

Della bent down and hugged Nora, feeling her eyes prickle also. "Yes, sweetheart. Emily's father is back, and we weren't certain we would see him again, but now he's here."

"Where is my father? Is he coming back too?"

Della froze. She should have expected the question—it was natural, given how much Nora and Emily shared. That one father was returned surely meant another would be returned as well?

Only she wasn't ready for the conversation. But Nora deserved an answer.

"Let's have some tea and talk about it," Della replied, nodding to one of the girls, who'd emerged from the kitchen, likely when she heard the door open. "In my sitting room, please," she added. The girl nodded in reply, then ducked back into the kitchen as Della rose, taking Nora's hand in hers.

"Will Emily's father live with us too?" Nora asked.

Della blinked. She hadn't thought about what would happen after she found Sarah's husband. Just that she was desperate to do so, and would do whatever she could to make it happen.

Including spending time with the largest, most handsomest man of your acquaintance, a sly voice in her head reminded her. What a hardship.

Hmph, Della wanted to reply. There was no guarantee that the person she'd make such a bargain with would be so large and handsome. It was just a bonus to the arrangement.

Nora ran ahead and opened the door, holding it so Della could enter, shutting it carefully after them. Della went to sit on the sofa, disturbing one of the kittens who blinked at them sleepily. Nora cooed and drew the kitten onto her lap as she sat down, crossing her ankles.

Della felt her throat tighten as she regarded Nora. So small and so in need of protecting still, but also showing signs of independence.

I wonder where she gets that from?

Now the voice sounded remarkably like Lord Handsome's.

Della put her arm around Nora's shoulder and drew her closer. The kitten stretched on Nora's lap, her tiny claws digging into Nora's gown.

Nora just giggled, petting the kitten between its ears.

"We are all so happy that Emily's father has returned. And you asked a question about your father." How could she put this? She never wanted to lie to her daughter, but she also didn't want to tell her anything her daughter wasn't yet mature enough to understand.

"Your father and I were so pleased when we discovered we were going to have you." That, at least, was true. Mostly because Mr. Baxter saw Della's pregnancy as a means to leverage money from her parents, even though Della herself was adamantly against that. Just one of the many things on which they disagreed. "But when you arrived, we realized we were better apart." This was so hard to explain. But Nora deserved the truth, or at least as much of it as Della could tell her.

"So my father left us?" Nora's voice sounded quavery, and Della's heart hurt.

Yes. He did. "He loved you so much"—which was an outright lie, but this was a lie Della could live with—"but he knew it would make all of us unhappy if he stayed."

"Oh." Nora seemed to be digesting that, and Della held her breath that her very curious daughter wouldn't ask more questions.

"So is he coming back? Like Emily's father?"

Della squeezed Nora's shoulders. "If he does,

I know he will be so proud to see you, and see what a smart, strong girl you are."

The door opened, thankfully, to admit the girl holding the tea service. She glanced questioningly at Della, who nodded for her to put it down on the table in front of the sofa.

"And biscuits!" Nora exclaimed, dislodging the kitten, who gave a disgruntled meow and scurried under the sofa. She picked a biscuit up and put most of it into her mouth, crumbs dropping onto her lap.

Della was not going to chastise her for sloppy eating. Not now, not when the arrival of the biscuits had derailed her daughter from continuing her line of questioning.

She had no doubt but that Nora would return to her questions, but for now the biscuit had saved the day.

She served herself some tea, taking a long sip as she thought about Mr. Baxter. Something she normally did not allow herself to do.

What would she do if he did return? Not that he would, not unless he sensed there was money to be had. And since her parents showed no signs of relenting in their ostracism of her, there was no possibility of that. But what if he did return? Would she want Nora to meet him?

She shook her head at herself as she finished the tea. This was all theoretical, since she had no idea where Nora's father was. It wasn't like her to ponder things that were very unlikely to happen—she was far more likely to consider the things that could happen—her losing her heart to Lord Handsome, or Sarah and her family moving away, or any number of terrible things.

GRIFFITH HADN'T BEEN able to come up with any kind of plan, even though he, Clark, and Hyland had spent hours discussing it. Along with ingesting several rounds of ale.

It was the morning after, and his head bore the ill effects of . . . everything. He was in the dining room staring resentfully at a plate filled with scrambled eggs, a steaming cup of tea to his right.

He did not want to ingest anything at the moment. Well, except for her. And even that would take him a moment to do.

He'd had to admit to Clark and Hyland how he felt about her, which caused at least half an hour of ribaldry (would he get the opportunity to share the word with her?), but then they had set their respective minds to the problem and had come up with—nothing.

Clark had offered to dress up as a highwayman and waylay them, but Griffith had rejected that because he couldn't guarantee she wouldn't just take his gun and shoot Clark herself.

Same for Hyland's idea—to serenade her outside her bedroom window. First of all, Griffith couldn't sing, and she might just shoot him on that basis alone. Second, it wasn't as though he thought she would agree to be with him on the basis of public humiliation. Because if that were true, she would have just allowed him to punch that blackguard at the party and risk public ostracism.

"My lord?" The butler stood at the door holding a silver salver.

Perhaps that was the answer he was waiting for?

"Yes, come in," Griffith said.

The butler nodded, then deposited a letter on the table, next to the still-full cup of tea, its lack of steam aligned with how Griffith was feeling.

He pushed the plate away to pick up the envelope, noting the heavy weight of the letter, indicating it came from someone who could afford to spend for good stationery.

He didn't recognize the seal on the envelope, but that wasn't surprising. He wasn't certain he would recognize Frederick's own seal, even though it would eventually be his.

He slid his finger under the seal to undo the envelope, withdrawing an equally luxurious piece of paper.

My lord:

Please visit me at your earliest convenience.

Yours,
The Duke of Marymount

He stared at it as though it would reveal more information, even though, of course, all that was there was all that was there.

Why was Della's father asking to see him? Did she know?

Of course she didn't. As far as he knew, the only time she had seen her parents had been at the event two nights earlier, when he had been occupied with finding Wattings, and hadn't been able to go to the party himself.

She hadn't mentioned anything beyond it being difficult to see them.

Or was this why she had grown suddenly distant? Had she been distracted enough by their passion to forget, only to recall soon thereafter?

Or was he thinking too much that it all had to do with him?

Well. That was a lowering thought, and not one he had ever had before.

Perhaps her distance had nothing to do with him, and everything to do with her own personal issue.

What did it mean if not everything was about him?

"The duke is expecting you." The butler took his hat and coat, handed them off to a waiting footman, then gestured down the hall. "This way, please."

Griffith followed, glancing around at the duke's

house. Was this where she had grown up? Or had she been in the country until it was time for her to enter Society?

There was so much he didn't know about her, and he now wanted to know it all. Now that he knew he loved her. He wanted to immerse himself in her, learn who she was and what she wanted.

And who she wanted. Hopefully, that would be him.

"Lord Stanbury to see you, Your Grace."

Griffith walked into the room where the duke waited for him.

"Thank you for coming," the duke said, even though his tone was not at all grateful. More as though it was entirely expected he would, and that it was a courtesy that the duke had welcomed him in so quickly.

Or perhaps he was assuming.

"It is a good thing I did not have much scheduled today," the duke continued, gesturing to a chair in front of a desk that was likely designed to look as intimidating as possible.

"Well, you did send a note," Griffith replied, allowing a wry tone into his voice.

"Hmph, yes." The duke walked around to his side of the desk, seating himself with a few grunts and groans. There was nothing to indicate the duke actually *worked* at the desk—no papers, no pens, nothing but a bronze bust of a past gentleman grimacing in Griffith's direction.

"That is my grandfather," the duke said proudly. "He had two sons. No daughters." The last part he said bitterly, as though resenting his ancestor for his good fortune.

Griffith did not want to spend time discussing the duke's forbears, given that he didn't have too high an opinion of the current Duke of Marymount, much less an opinion on some long dead relative.

"I presume your daughter Lady Della is why you have asked for my presence?" Might as well go right to the heart of the matter.

The duke shifted, and his lips thinned. "Yes. Della. We—that is, my wife and I—saw her a few evenings ago. You and she are betrothed?"

"Yes."

"And I understand you are the heir to the Duke of Northam? I do not know the gentleman myself, but I believe him to be ill?"

Griffith's chest tightened. "Yes." He spoke in a curt tone.

"So you are the proper person to deal with this letter I have just received." The duke opened his top right-hand drawer and withdrew a piece of paper, which he slid across the desk to Griffith.

Your Grace,

I am in London, and am hopeful of reuniting with your daughter Della. She and I have a child

*together, and I cannot shirk my responsibilities
as a father any longer.*

*Unless you wish to protect Della and her
daughter and provide me with funds.*

*I am staying at the Bear's Arms waiting your
reply. If I do not hear from you by the end of this
week, I will assume you welcome my return to
your daughter's family.*

*Sincerely,
Mr. George Baxter*

Griffith read the letter, then read it again, feeling the ire well up inside him. How dare he? How dare he casually mention returning to Nora's life, to Della's life, as though they would want him back? But that he was willing to forego being a responsible parent if the duke paid him enough?

Wait.

"You haven't paid him," Griffith said, placing the letter back on the desk.

The duke shook his head. "No. I wish we could, but when she left, my daughter made her own decision. I will not be responsible for any situation that might arise because of that decision."

Griffith felt his eyes widen. The man was ruthless. Although not so ruthless he didn't go to someone else—namely Griffith—for help dealing with this "situation."

"Is that why you asked me to come? To resolve this 'situation'?"

The duke inclined his head.

"Because you refuse to?"

Another nod. This one more pronounced.

How had Della—his bright, vibrant, passionate Della—grown up in this household with this father? How strong must she be not to have let his implacable dukeness infect her?

Or had it, and her fiery reaction to any attempt to control her had come from growing up with this man?

No wonder she was so determined to control her own life.

Griffith snatched the letter from the desk, crumpled it in his fist and shoved it in his pocket.

"I'll deal with it," he said grimly.

The duke gave a brief nod, then picked up a bell and rang it. The door opened immediately, and the butler stepped inside.

"Lord Stanbury is on his way out," the duke said.

Not even an offer of tea, Griffith thought, disdainfully amused. Not that he wanted to take tea—or even a stronger beverage—with this entirely unpleasant person.

"I look forward to seeing you at the wedding," the duke said in a stiff tone of voice.

Griffith entertained the notion of telling the

duke he wouldn't be invited, since he strongly suspected Della wouldn't want them there, but he also knew he shouldn't and wouldn't interfere with her and her family.

"I'll deal with it," he said again, striding out the door.

Chapter 18

So . . ." Sarah began, fixing the tea as she and Della liked it, "how was it?"

Della couldn't pretend to misunderstand. "It was wonderful." She barely recognized her own gushing tone.

They were in the small sitting room, each holding one kitten. The sun was making one last valiant effort before nightfall, and the room was cast in a warm, golden glow.

Sarah raised one dark eyebrow. "That good?"

Della bit her lip. "Mmm. Only—"

"What?" Sarah prompted, when Della stopped speaking.

"Only it felt too close. Too intimate as soon as it was done."

Sarah folded her arms over her chest and rested her back on the sofa, a knowing smile on her face.

"What?" Della asked challengingly. Fearful she knew what her friend was going to say, and unable to deny it.

Sarah shrugged, looking sly. "You have feelings for him." She reached forward to take Della's hand. "I believe you might have fallen in love with him." The last part she said in a dramatic whisper, punctuating her words by leaning forward to speak directly into Della's face.

"No, I haven't." Only her response didn't sound sincere, and both of them knew that.

Sarah shrugged. "Deny it all you want. You like him, don't you?"

Della shifted uncomfortably. "There's a vast difference between liking someone and—and that other thing."

"Falling in love with them?" Sarah supplied in a disingenuous voice.

"Yes. That." Della focused her gaze on the kitten, since she didn't want to look her friend in the eye. "He is pleasant. He is certainly pleasant to look at, and what we did was"—and she paused, searching for the word—"spectacular, but that doesn't mean I've fallen in love with him."

"Do you think about him when you're not with him?"

Always.

"Uh—"

"And do you feel comforted in his presence? But uncomfortable in an enjoyably pricklish way?"

Yes.

"Uh—"

"And when you think about him being with

someone else, or you being with someone else, how does that make you feel?"

Like I'd like to murder someone.

"Being possessive doesn't mean I'm in love, it just means I don't like to share," Della retorted, unable to keep herself from arguing even though she suspected Sarah was entirely correct. As usual.

"So you tell me. What means you're in love?" Sarah asked in a soft voice. She still held Della's hand, and she squeezed it as she spoke.

Della bit her lip as she considered it. "Feeling as though your life is less complete without the other person. Even when you're angry with them, knowing that you wouldn't be completely happy without them." A good thing for her to recognize, given how angry he often made her.

"Respecting their opinion, even when you know they're wrong. Knowing they have your best interest at heart. Trusting them to do what is best for you, no matter what."

Sarah's lips stretched into a huge smile, and she arched one eyebrow toward Della. "Anything you want to tell me? Or better yet, tell him?"

Della yanked her hand from her friend's grasp, tossing both arms up in the air. "Fine. You want me to admit it? I am in love with Captain Enormous, Viscount Whatshisname of the Broad Shoulders." She emitted a disgruntled noise.

"But we've agreed not to make this thing we have permanent at all. In fact, it would be bad for him especially given his situation."

Her casual words were the absolute opposite of how she felt inside. Something she knew Sarah already understood without being told.

It terrified her, being in love. Allowing herself to feel that vulnerability again, when she'd sworn never to.

"What is his situation? Being the heir to a centuries-old title? It certainly sounds like it would be completely dangerous for him to actually marry the woman to whom he's betrothed." Sarah spoke in a dryly sarcastic tone.

"We're not actually betrothed, you know that!" Della said. If they were—if they had a future together—she wouldn't know what to do with herself, or her anger at her parents.

Was she holding on to those feelings unnecessarily?

A quick review told her no, she was not; her parents had barely acknowledged her, and that only after she'd had some respectability restored with her fake betrothal.

If it were real, you could be welcomed back into the family, a voice whispered inside her head. *Nora could have a relationship with her grandparents, and you wouldn't have to worry about unpleasant gentlemen saying terrible things to you.*

But that would be unfair to him, to use him merely to regain her respectability.

Even though she wouldn't be doing that at all; she'd be doing it because she loved him.

But he didn't know that.

Which just meant she should tell him. And then see what he said.

"Why are you smiling like that?" Sarah asked in a suspicious tone.

So Della told her.

"You shouldn't go on your own," Clark argued, even though he'd been saying the same thing for the half an hour it had taken them to get Griffith dressed properly for a rendezvous with his lover's former—whatever he was. Just that Griffith wanted to punch first, try to define who this Mr. Baxter was later.

They were in Griffith's bedroom, a room that had initially seemed far too opulent for him, but now seemed as though it was just about the right size.

It was early evening, and Griffith had returned home from the duke's house determined to take care of things sooner rather than later. So he'd summoned Clark and the two of them had retreated to the bedroom, where they had discussed the letter and what to do.

Although they had not come to any kind of agreement.

"I should come with you, at least to the tavern," Clark continued.

Griffith snorted. "It's not as though I can't handle myself. The blackguard just wants money." He shrugged. "I have money, I will give it to him, and send him on his way. He won't dare to return, not after I've spoken to him."

"That's why you shouldn't go on your own," Clark replied mildly. "I am not concerned for your safety, but for the safety of the blackguard. What if he says something you don't like? I know you. You're as likely to knock him down as to hear him out."

"Nice turn of phrase," Griffith said with a grin. "But I promise, I won't be punching anybody." Not that she would know about it, but she would not like it if she ever heard he had punched someone on her behalf. He knew that because she had told him just as much.

He wished she could tell him why she closed up so quickly after sex. He knew it wasn't a problem with the sex itself; her cries of pleasure told him that much.

But he wanted her to trust him with her mind as well as her body.

He'd never had that thought about a woman he'd been in a relationship with before. And it wasn't as though his heart hadn't been nearly caught on occasion; he'd come close to falling in love, but just hadn't.

Until he had. Suddenly, headlong, ridiculously in love.

Now that he knew what it was, he couldn't stop thinking about it. Like a starving person looking forward to their next meal.

He wanted to devour her.

"Griffith?" Clark's voice recalled him to the present. Right. He had to go deal with this Mr. Baxter, then figure out how to tell her he loved her without scaring her off entirely.

Because he knew her, because she was so much like him—at the first sign of something potentially disturbing, he was likely to run. And it was clear from her actions that she was the same. She had run off when her family's plans had countered what she wanted for herself. As had he. And neither one of them had thought the future out, at least as far as he could tell. Because if she had thought it out, she would be happily married to this Mr. Baxter and not currently involved with him.

Thank God she hadn't thought it out.

"Right," he said at last. "I should go."

"You're certain—?"

"No, I don't want you to come. Stay here and make sure Hyland doesn't get in trouble."

"That's a full-time job," Clark rejoined.

Griffith grinned, then picked up the stack of bills he'd gotten from Fred and headed out the door and down the stairs.

"BAXTER?" THE WOMAN behind the bar glared at Griffith. "If you see him, he owes me money for his lodging. I'm not running a charity house here, you know."

Griffith glanced around the pub, which showed no sign of being charitable at all. "I can see that," he replied, noting the worn tables, the sticky shiny floors, and the broken chairs that were stacked at one end of the room.

"You are sent by the duke?"

Griffith turned at the sound of the man's voice.

"Here he is. Baxter, you owe me money," the woman said, slapping her hand down on the bar. "I'll take it now before you meet with your nob."

A nob now, am I? Griffith thought. And just a few weeks ago he had blended right in.

"Ask him for it," Baxter said, nodding toward Griffith. "Unless you want me to go somewhere else for it?" he added, a spiteful look on his face.

Griffith exhaled as he reached into his pocket for the funds. *Do not punch him out*, a voice that sounded like Clark's said in his head. *At least not until you have determined he will no longer be a threat to Della*, another voice added.

The last voice sounded like his own.

"That'll do," the woman said as Griffith dropped a bill on the table. "You'll owe more next week," she warned.

"I'll be leaving soon enough, and then you'll miss my money," Baxter replied. The innkeeper snorted. Baxter turned to Griffith, ignoring the woman entirely. Who, it had to be said, was doing the same to him. "Shall we repair to my room? It is exceedingly dirty," he said pointedly, "but it affords some privacy."

"Please," Griffith replied, gesturing for Baxter to lead them.

They walked up a narrow, dirty staircase. Griffith nearly shuddered at the mounds of dust and dirt in the corners of each stair. He really had become a nob, hadn't he? Past Griffith wouldn't have noticed the dirt. He just would have noticed if the ale was fresh or not, and would have drunk it no matter what the answer was.

They emerged at the top of the stairs to an equally narrow hallway, although it was so dark Griffith couldn't see if it was as filthy. A blessing in literal disguise, perhaps?

"Here," Baxter said, withdrawing a key from his pocket. He twisted the key in the lock, then thrust the door open and stepped inside, Griffith following after.

"You can sit there if you want." Baxter gestured to a chair that had clothing piled up on it, while more clothing was scattered on the floor. He picked up the heap of clothes from the chair and dumped it onto the bed, then yanked a small stool from beside the bed and sat down on it, his knees raised at an awkward angle.

Griffith sat, hearing the strain of the chair and

hoping it wasn't well on its way to joining its compatriots in the corner.

"What did the duke say?" Baxter repeated.

Griffith appraised the man. What had she seen in him anyway? He was taller than average, and had all his features, but that was about the most he could say about him. His eyes were sharp, darting around the room as though waiting for trouble to spring up at any moment. Griffith had seen men look like that before, mostly when they had been on the run from something and had taken to the sea as a last resort.

He'd seen the same look in his own eyes when he'd first run off to sea. Which meant that this Baxter had little to lose.

"He didn't say anything, which is why I am here. I am acting for the duke."

Baxter's eyes narrowed. "Acting for the duke? What do you mean?" He struggled to get to his feet, which was awkward, given how low the stool was. He gave up and sat back down, but his glare remained unrelenting, focused on Griffith.

Griffith didn't care. He'd been on the receiving end of equally irate glares through his years of rising up through the naval ranks. One rotten scoundrel being angry with him was just about par for the course.

"That isn't the point. How much do you want?"

Might as well get right to it. He didn't want

to stay in this filthy tavern for a moment longer than was necessary. He had a lady to woo, and a dukedom to prepare for.

"You know that I could ruin her just by revealing my presence in town."

It wasn't an answer. It was, however, a threat. Griffith was considering just how much trouble he'd be in with her if he did punch Baxter.

Likely too much, he thought with regret.

"That's why I am here. We don't want your daughter, the one you purport to care for, to know that you were here and yet you didn't make an effort to see her."

Baxter's lip curled. "It's not even a sure bet she is my daughter."

Griffith was up and at Baxter's throat before the last word was out of his mouth. He wrapped his hand around the man's neck as he lifted the man up off the stool, suspending him in air. Baxter's eyes were wide, his breathing ragged, and Griffith just stared at him for a few moments before lowering him back down. "You won't say anything like that again."

That was a threat. And Baxter knew it.

"Fine," he said, still gasping for air. "But the price went up. Now that I know you care about her."

Griffith wished he were in a good enough mood to roll his eyes at the man's idiocy—of course he cared about her, or why else would he be here? He had already made it clear he wasn't the duke's emissary, and he was clearly a gentleman.

He would have to ask Della at some point just what she saw in this idiot.

And, if she ever felt the same way about him— which he hoped she would—he might have to question her judgment. Though not enough to refuse her attentions.

But first he had to deal with her former idiot.

"What do you want?" Griffith pointed an accusatory finger at Baxter. "But this is it. I won't have you coming back for more. Whatever your price is, name it now. If you try to come back for more," he said, shrugging, "I can't promise it won't negatively affect you."

Hopefully the idiot wasn't so stupid he didn't understand what Griffith meant.

"You won't see me ever again once you pay me," Baxter said. "I know how your kind operates. You could just as easily pay to have me removed as give me money."

"I'd just do it myself, save the cost of paying someone," Griffith remarked in a mild tone. He was pleased to see Baxter turn pale. His size was still good for something. "So how much?"

Baxter named a figure that was high, but not so high that Griffith couldn't pay it. "I don't have that much on me," he said, pulling out the money he'd brought with him. "You can have this now and I'll get you the rest later."

"On account?" Baxter snorted. "How do I know you won't just leave me high and dry?"

"Because," Griffith said slowly so the man could understand, "if I don't, you'll enact your threat and make your presence known."

Baxter's expression cleared. "Right. I knew that."

Griffith shook his head as he rose. He tossed the money on the bureau next to the door and glanced back at Baxter. "I'll come back tomorrow."

Baxter folded his arms over his chest. Which might've looked impressive if he weren't effectively sitting on the floor. "I'll come to you. Don't want you forgetting to come find me."

Fine. Whatever. "You'll find me at the Duke of Northam's residence in town. My name is Stanbury," Griffith said.

Baxter's eyes widened. "Another duke? How is it possible that Della is connected with two dukes? There are only about half a dozen in England, what are the chances?"

And what were the chances that Griffith's Della—smart, fierce, fiery, independent Della—would have run off with this bag of beans masquerading as a gentleman?

She must have been very desperate.

Which meant that he should ensure she was never in a desperate situation again, so she wouldn't make another foolish decision like this one.

Like marry you?

That would take some persuading, he knew that.

One thing at a time.

He didn't bother answering Baxter's question. It was none of the man's business, Griffith's money was going to make certain of that, and he didn't want Baxter to know any more than he already did about her.

"I'll need a day to get the rest of it," Griffith said as he opened the door.

"A day, but no mo—" The rest of Baxter's words were lost as Griffith stomped down the hall. The man would come see him tomorrow, if he knew what was good for him.

Otherwise he might just lose patience and take Baxter to the docks, where a man could get lost. Or pressed into Her Majesty's service, although Griffith wouldn't want to do a bad turn like that to Queen Victoria, no matter what she might think of his improper procedure.

Chapter 19

$\mathcal{D}$o you have a plan?" Sarah asked, smoothing Della's gown.

Della stood in front of the glass in her bedroom, twisting so she could see how the gown looked.

It was a deep sapphire blue, a rich, lush color that required a particular type of assertive confidence to wear. And Della knew she had that. Or more precisely, that she would need it for what she was going to do.

She was going to tell him. She had no idea how—

"No, I don't," she replied. She shrugged, making Sarah purse her lips as she adjusted the sleeves.

"This is gorgeous," her friend said. "You do look lovely. But then again, you always do."

Della met Sarah's gaze in the glass. "Thank you." She took a deep breath. "I wish I weren't so nervous."

Sarah tilted her head, wrinkling her brow. "Do

you know, I don't believe I've ever seen you nervous. I've seen you angry, concerned, excited, and worried, but never nervous."

Della gave a wan smile. "I guess that is because I have never been in love?" she said, feeling the rightness of the words.

"Have you told him about Mr. Baxter?" Sarah asked.

Della opened her mouth to say yes, and then realized she hadn't. Not truly. Not that there was much to tell. And she knew he wouldn't judge her for her actions, he'd already made that clear. But she wanted to tell him everything, she wanted to bare her soul to the man she loved.

She wanted to trust him.

"I haven't. But I will," she said, hearing the vow in her voice.

"Well," Sarah said, giving Della one last appraisal. "You are as beautiful as you are going to get. You should head to the ball. Where is it this evening?"

Della shrugged. "I'm not certain. Griff—Lord Stanbury is coming to fetch me in half an hour or so."

"And you'll tell him? Tell him everything?"

Della bit her lip. "Yes."

Sarah enfolded Della in a hug, making Della feel warm and comforted. She wasn't normally a hugging person, but Sarah and Nora had both made it very clear that that was how they expressed their love, and she was willing to accept it. *See?* she wanted to say to him. *I can be accommodating.*

HE ARRIVED PROMPTLY this evening; not making her wonder if he was going to be off doing some remarkable deed that she would have to thank him for while simultaneously being furious he hadn't turned up after he had promised.

He looked different this evening. Or perhaps that was because she was feeling differently about him? Now that she was on the cusp of confessing everything?

"You look lovely, my lady," he said, taking her hand and putting it to his lips. The stubble above his mouth grazed her hand, and she shuddered as she thought about where else it could tickle her.

"Thank you, my lord," she replied, curtseying. Apparently they were to be excessively formal this evening. Perhaps it was to ensure they actually arrived at the ball and didn't end up frolicking in the carriage on the way over?

But she couldn't ask him, since that would give him ideas, and she wouldn't get the opportunity to tell him anything since she would be just as enthusiastic about the suggestion as he was.

The mental rigmarole one had to endure when one was concerned that one would be able to share thoughts while also wishing one were absolutely not speaking because their mouths were otherwise engaged. Being in love was so *complicated*.

"Mrs. Wattings, I trust you are well?" he said to Sarah, who had just come down the stairs.

"You know I am, my lord," Sarah replied, a grateful expression on her face. "Thanks entirely to you."

"And Wattings, no doubt," he said with a warm smile.

A blush stained Sarah's cheeks, and Della suppressed a grin.

"Shall we be going?" he asked.

"Yes, thank you." Della strode over to where her cloak hung on the hook and was about to take it down when his large hand covered hers.

"Allow me," he said, removing the cloak and holding it out for her. She slid her arms through the sleeves, closing her eyes for just a moment as he wrapped it securely around her.

This could be her life. This security, this comfort, this trust.

She just had to tell him how she felt. And hope that he felt the same.

GRIFFITH WISHED SHE didn't look so damned beautiful. It made not telling her how he felt even harder. Literally.

But he wanted to resolve the Baxter issue before he told her anything so that there was no possibility of that situation intruding on her happiness, or their future.

But still.

This evening she was wearing a blue evening gown that was cut low enough for him to see the swell of her bosom. The sleeves of the gown were so slight as to make calling them sleeves seem presumptuous—they were tiny wisps of fabric just clinging to her shoulders. Her gown darted in at her waist, then flared out at her hips. The hips he had caressed when they'd been in bed together.

Why weren't they in bed together now?

Oh right. Because they had a party to attend and a former lover to pay off and emotions to be revealed. And there was the lingering niggle of doubt in his head following her reaction when they had been intimate before—she had shut down so thoroughly he didn't know if it would have been possible to reach her.

When the Baxter matter was settled, he would talk to her. He was proud of himself for having the patience to wait—the Griffith before he met her would have just blundered into speaking his mind without considering the consequences—and he wished he could tell her how patient he was being in regard to her. But then that would negate the whole point of waiting to speak to her until things were resolved.

It was far more complicated to be a person in love than it was to be only absorbed with oneself. There were so many more things to consider.

But that was the point. He wanted to consider her as well as himself. He hoped she would allow him to focus on her, to consider her wants and needs and desires.

As he hoped she would want to consider his.

He just had to be patient.

The coach began to move, and she turned to him, her expression somehow different than he'd ever seen before.

"What is it?" he asked.

She bit her lip and took a deep breath. "I want to tell you about—about my life before."

"Before what?" he replied quickly, then realizing that that was a ludicrous question.

Her expression revealed she thought the same thing. They had that in common.

"When I left London. And how I left London. Before," she said again, and he could tell she was restraining herself from rolling her eyes at him.

Perhaps she did care for him after all.

He slid his arm along the back of the carriage seat, draping his hand on her shoulder. Resisting the urge to curl her up into his arms and dip his fingers into the front of her gown.

"Tell me. I'm listening."

He felt her take a deep breath as the carriage continued to rumble over the cobblestones, the movement sliding their bodies together. Her hip was warm against his side.

"I am the second oldest of us. There are five of us, and all of us are"—and here she paused as though searching for the word—"distinctive. I always thought it was my role in the family to follow Eleanor's lead, and support my younger sisters. I behaved properly, I did what I was supposed to, and then when it was time for my debut, I expected I would receive my reward for proper behavior." Another pause. "I entered Society with so much naivete. I thought that I would burst onto the scene, that some handsome young gentleman would love me, and that I would end up happily married and taken care of for the rest of my life."

That might still happen, he wanted to say. But he also wanted to let her tell her story, not interrupt with how he could solve everything.

She made a derisive noise. "That did not happen. I entered Society, and was immediately besieged by gentlemen who wanted to marry the Duke of Marymount's daughter. They didn't want to know me, Della. They wanted the prestige of my father's reputation, not to mention my dowry. I tried to find someone—anyone—who would listen to me and want to hear my opinion on anything, even something so minor as whether I preferred champagne to white wine, but there wasn't anybody."

He wanted to punch someone at hearing how forlorn she sounded. Although to be fair, he usually wanted to punch someone when it came to wrongs committed against her.

This was true love, wasn't it?

Lord Stanbury, how did you realize you were madly in love with Lady Della?

Well, I wanted to use my fists against anyone who hurt her. I wanted to let her speak her mind. I delayed doing what I wanted to do because I thought it would be best for her if I did so.

And I wanted to pleasure her for the rest of our lives.

But she was still speaking. He had to pay attention. That was what true love was.

"Mr. Baxter gave my sisters and I dance lessons." She shook her head slowly. "He wasn't even that good a dancer, to be honest. But he knew the steps, and more importantly, how to flatter my mother so she thought we were remarkably lucky to have obtained him as an instructor."

Griffith's fists tightened.

"I received a few proposals, but not from anyone my parents deemed worthy of my hand. Thank goodness," she added in a relieved tone of voice. "At the same time, I felt so lonely. I didn't want to tell my younger sisters how terrible it all was—I knew they were looking forward to making their own debuts, and I didn't want to taint their experience. Perhaps it was just me. I didn't know what Eleanor thought."

The carriage hit a bump, and they slammed into one another, him tightening his hold on her shoulder. She glanced up into his face and gave him a smile. Then her expression drew serious again, and she looked away, out the opposite window of the carriage. Even though Griffith could tell she wasn't actually registering what she was seeing out there.

"Mr. Baxter sensed something was wrong. Or perhaps he was just waiting for his opportunity to ensnare me, I don't know. But during our lessons he was . . . curious about me. What I liked, who I saw, how I felt. I know it was likely just a ruse to get me to trust him, or at least I know that now, but at the time I felt so seen. As though someone in the world understood me, Della, and not just a random duke's daughter whose best value was in her lineage, not in herself."

This is what Society does to people, Griffith thought. *Tells them they are only worth something because of what they are, not—who they are.*

Not that that made sense.

But it was the same reason he had run away, and he was opening his mouth to tell her that when he snapped it closed again.

Right. She didn't need him to chime in with his own experience. She needed him to listen. He had to be patient.

"I don't blame him for taking advantage of our situation."

Even though Griffith did.

"And when it became clear that he had feelings for me, feelings that I believed he couldn't admit because of our respective positions, I spoke and told him how I felt."

It stung that she hadn't told Griffith how she felt about him yet. Although she had asked if he wanted to have an affair, so perhaps he shouldn't feel too badly. Was that why she was so skittish about sharing herself with him? Because of Baxter?

Griffith wished he had the freedom to treat her former lover as he wished, but that wouldn't be the right thing for him to do. Not if he cared for her. Or, more accurately, not *since* he cared for her.

No, he would pay the blackguard off and then confess his love to her with a clear conscience.

"And so we decided to run away together. I bundled all my jewelry up, just like the heroines in the novels do when they are escaping, and snuck out of the house after a particularly late party. We were together for only a few weeks before I realized he was not who I thought he was.

I believe he was equally disenchanted with me," she said wryly. "But by then I knew I was carrying Nora, and I thought we would both just have to suffer one another for the sake of the child. Luckily, he made the decision by deserting us soon after Nora was born."

Now she didn't sound heartsick, and he tried not to feel pleased that she so clearly did not miss Nora's father.

"But why am I telling you this? It is likely you already know all the sordid details."

I don't, Griffith nearly said. *I was waiting for you to tell me.*

But she was still speaking.

"I wanted to tell you because I wanted you to know that this is different." She placed her hand on his leg and squeezed. "This is different," she said in a softer voice. "I know my own mind, so much more than before. So while it might seem as though I am repeating my mistake, I can assure you I am not."

What was she saying?

"What I am saying," she said, as though she could read his mind, "is that I have—I have feelings for you." She cleared her throat, and he stroked her arm, reminding himself to have patience.

"I believe I might have fallen in love with you." The way she spoke made it sound as though it was an accident. As though she hadn't meant to, but it had happened nonetheless. Like eating an additional biscuit at tea when you were already full, or forgetting to greet someone you'd met on only a handful of occasions.

But this was love. Much more than a sweet or a mistake.

"Well?" She sounded impatient, and he resisted the urge to grin. His impatient Della, when he was being nothing but patient.

"Thank you," he said at last, squeezing her shoulder.

"Thank you" was such a paltry response.

He could do better. He would do better. "And I have to say that I—" At which point the carriage slowed, and he glanced out the window, a dawning sense of horror filling him as he saw they'd arrived.

The door swung open before he could continue, and then the footman was assisting her out of the carriage, and he was following her, his fingers still warm from her skin.

She glanced back at him, a wry look on her face, and he felt a huge sense of relief that she wasn't currently in tears at his not responding better nor was she angry at him.

Of course a woman like Della would not burst into tears. Although he wouldn't put it past her to be angry, so he should be grateful for that.

"We will speak later," he said in a low tone as they walked up the stairs to the house. The door was flung open and lights blazed out, a whirl of dancers and silver trays and rushing servants indicating it was already a very full event. "Or we could just go home," he added hopefully.

She gave him a reproachful look. "We promised we would attend. What would Society say if they heard the heir to the Duke of Northam had done something so disgraceful as to not attend a party he had accepted an invitation to? Society would reject you."

"I doubt that." He didn't bother to hide his arrogance—she was already acquainted with that, and since she loved him—*she loved him!*—he didn't have to disguise who he was.

Not that he ever had disguised anything, not with her. If anything, he felt as though her love would give him permission to be even more himself than before, albeit one that was as concerned with another person as himself.

Which seemed a lot like arithmetic, and he was not fond of arithmetic.

"And besides, my sisters will be here this evening."

That was a much better reason to attend than any nonsense about offending Society. He had begun all this determined to navigate Society on his own terms, if he was going to have to navigate it at all. Especially since it seemed he would no longer be allowed to navigate the seas as the captain of his ship.

This was his course now, but he was determined to set it himself. With her at his side.

"Fine, then. We'll stay."

The Griffith of a few weeks ago would be aghast at his change of heart, but his heart had changed. And she was the reason.

He should probably say something. "And I love you too."

Chapter 20

$\mathcal{D}$ella wasn't nervous anymore. She was . . . *hopeful*. She hadn't been hopeful in so long, she barely recognized it, but there it was.

She knew he felt the same way, even before he said it. She'd known it, to a certain extent, since they'd been naked together in bed, but now his entire demeanor indicated he cared.

She wanted to laugh aloud at how frustrated he'd sounded when he'd said "Fine." She shared his frustration—she would very much like to get naked together in bed with him again, especially now that their emotions were more out in the open—but she also wanted her sisters to see her with him, and to behave as properly as she could so that Society would accept that they were together.

Not that he'd proposed yet, but she presumed that would happen eventually. Hopefully the proposal wouldn't interfere with more naked-in-bed times, since she was eager to continue that probably more than she was eager to become a wife.

But the only way to ensure she could be with him forever was to marry him, so she supposed she would have to do it.

And all those hopes and dreams of being in love with someone who respected her and honored her ability to make her own decisions would come true. And Nora would have a father, and she would have a partner who was truly a partner, and not a husbandly tyrant.

"Good evening, Della."

Della stiffened as she recognized her father's voice. She lifted her chin as she turned to him, feeling that same heartsick stab at seeing his face. They'd never been close—he'd always been too busy reading the paper or running to the hounds to spend time with his daughters—but they had at least been cordially fond of one another.

Until she'd run off with Mr. Baxter, at which point both her parents had renounced her entirely.

Her mother stood beside the duke, a facile smile on her face. Her mother was a silly woman, a fact Della could have overlooked if the duchess had not also been so determined for Della to do what she and the duke wanted—not what Della wanted for herself.

You have to marry someone who will bring honor to our family, the duchess had said. As though that was the only reason to marry. To acquire more respectability, as though respectability could be achieved in an infinite amount.

But to the duchess she supposed it could. Once it was clear the duke would only ever have five daughters, with no heir to receive the title, the duchess became nearly maniacal in her wish to see each of her daughters marry well.

"Good evening, Della," the duchess said, nodding.

"Good evening." Della couldn't help how brusque she sounded. Being cut out of your parents' lives because you had made a terrible mistake had a way of doing that to a person.

"Lord Stanbury." Her father's tone was warmer speaking to Griffith.

Of course. He was a man, and he was not a disgraceful daughter.

"Good evening, Your Grace. Your Grace," Griffith said, nodding first to her mother and then to her father. He sounded odd.

But then again, of course he would. She had just confessed her love to him in a carriage, and then they had arrived at this party.

She shouldn't feel concerned.

"You've taken care of that scoundrel?" her father continued. His gaze darted between her and Griffith.

She felt Griffith freeze beside her, and she turned to look at him. And then felt her spine tingling. And not in a pleasant way.

"Who did you take care of?" she asked, each word sounding clipped.

Griffith met her gaze, and she knew who it was.

"Mr. Baxter," she said on an exhale. He didn't have to confirm it, she could see it in his eyes.

Damn it.

"He will be an excellent husband, Della." The duchess spoke in a condescending tone. "He's already providing for you, and you haven't even gotten married yet. I am so glad someone has seen fit to overlook some of—" And then her mother paused.

"Overlook that I ran off and had a child with my dancing instructor?" Della tried to keep her voice calm. Mostly because she knew it would infuriate her parents. And because she *was* infuriated, but didn't want to reveal just how infuriated. And hurt. And disappointed.

But not in her parents; she had already reconciled herself to never having a relationship with them again. But how could he have done it? Whatever it was he had done?

He had kept it from her, and he knew that was the one thing she would not countenance.

"Shh," the duchess said, glancing around them. "You don't want anyone to hear."

"Can we discuss this later?" Griffith had taken her arm, and she shook him off.

"No, we cannot." She flung her head up and

stared him in the face, all that hurt and anger whirling through her body.

She saw him swallow, and she knew he was hurting also. But his feelings couldn't and wouldn't overshadow hers; he had to know, or at least she hoped he knew, what she would think about him charging in to handle things without telling her. "We'll discuss this now," she said, taking his arm. "If you'll excuse us?" Della said to the duke and duchess, dragging him away, then releasing her hold on him as soon as they were out of earshot.

"We were sitting in that carriage for a full thirty minutes," she said in a low, furious voice. "You had plenty of opportunity to tell me." She stepped forward so she was only a few inches away from him. And he still looked so handsome, damn it.

She shouldn't be noticing that, not when she was so irate.

"I was going to," he replied, meeting her gaze. His eyes were intensely focused on her face. "But I wanted to wait—"

"Until I'd made a fool of myself?" Della interrupted. "Until I'd told you all about my past and that I love you?"

He closed his eyes as though in pain. *Welcome to the club, Lord Autocratic.*

"I'm sorry," he said at last. He sounded sincere. "So am I."

Della spun on her heel and strode out the door,

her sisters gathering in a phalanx behind her as she went.

"GODDAMN IT." GRIFFITH watched as Della walked away from him, her back rigid, her sisters falling into formation behind her in their own battalion of furious feminine anger.

"My daughter is very impetuous." Della's mother had arrived at his side, and it took everything not to bark at her to go away. Not only would it be rude, which Griffith couldn't care less about, but it would be useless. Della was angry with him.

You only wanted to help.

But you know how she feels about anyone making decisions for her.

Why hadn't he thought about what *she* would want? Because he'd seen the opportunity to ride in on his financial white horse, paying Baxter enough to go away, and thinking she would never find out.

What kind of idiot was he?

The best kind, a voice in his head replied.

But you just wanted to do what would help, another voice added.

True, yes, but he hadn't considered beyond the help—not how she would feel about the help, nor the way it was tendered.

He'd just considered himself.

And now he was here by himself. No, wait—it

was even worse. Her mother was here, still giving him an interrogative look, as though she was waiting for a reply. What had she said? That Della was impetuous?

"Your Grace, if you will forgive the disagreement, I don't believe Lady Della is impetuous. I believe she knows her own mind. Thoroughly." He didn't wait for her response, but just bowed and walked out of the ballroom, vowing to do whatever he had to in order to make it right.

Even if she regretted telling him she loved him.

"ARE YOU GOING to tell us now?" Olivia demanded.

All five of the sisters were crammed into a hackney cab, Della not wanting to wait for anyone's private carriage. She had told them, pointedly, that they could just go home and not bother about her, but none of them had listened to her.

Which was why she was currently smushed between Eleanor and Olivia, with Pearl and Ida on the seat opposite. All four of them keeping their eyes on her, as though she might explode or something.

Which was a possibility.

"You are going to have to tell us sooner or later," Ida pointed out. Pearl nodded in agreement.

"Why were you all there anyway?" Della asked, glancing at her sisters. "I've barely seen you, Pearl, and I thought you were busy being a new bride, Ida."

Ida folded her hands in her lap, a prim expression on her face. "I have time for my sister. Especially since I went and located you." She looked around at the remaining three sisters as though reminding them it was her who had managed the impossible.

Her sisters just stared back at her, and Della had to stifle a laugh.

"You are trying to avoid telling us," Eleanor said. Not incorrectly.

"You've fallen in love with him. Lord Stanbury," Olivia announced.

Della rolled her eyes as Ida glared at Olivia.

"Of course she has, but something has obviously happened," Ida said disdainfully. "So what was it? You know that whatever it is, we support you."

Della leaned forward and took Ida's hand in hers, squeezing it as she smiled at her youngest sister. "I know. Thank you. And thank you for finding me." Even though at the time she hadn't wanted to be found.

"Well?" Olivia demanded impatiently.

"Well," Della began. "I will explain, but I want to wait until we are at my house. I don't want to have to say it all over again to Sarah."

The sisters were silent for the ride home, although Della could feel how Olivia was practically vibrating from wanting to speak.

They got home, Olivia paying the hackney, and then all five of them walked into the house. Neither Pearl nor Ida had visited before, so the two of them were glancing all around, likely noting the mismatched furniture and the clutter of toys and garments in the hallway.

Sarah emerged from the back of the hallway, probably having come from the kitchen. She looked as though she was about to speak, then saw Della's face and her expression grew fierce.

"Do any of you have to do with this?" she asked the sisters at large.

"No, they're here to help," Della explained, quickly, before Sarah started challenging each and every one of them to ensure they weren't the cause of Della's distress.

Her friend truly was the best.

"Let's go into the dining room, that's the only space big enough for all of us."

Mr. Wattings walked down the staircase from the upper floor, clearly having just woken up. His eyes widened at seeing all the sisters in the foyer. And looked as though he were considering just turning around and going back upstairs.

"Can I help with anything?" He addressed his question to his wife.

Sarah looked at Della. "Can he?"

Della shrugged. "He might as well come. He knows Lord Stanbury, and I wouldn't want him to be caught unawares by anything Lord Stanbury might say."

"Lord Stanbury now, is it?" Sarah said. "And said so very formally." She stepped up behind Della and removed her cloak from her shoulders. "Let me hang this up and ring for tea."

"Dear Lord, I know it's bad when you admit that tea is needed," Della replied, trying to draw a smile from Sarah.

Sarah just glared at her, as though she knew full well what she was doing.

But at least it had distracted Della from the pain of having him do something behind her back. The first time he'd tried to manage things for her she'd made it absolutely clear she would not tolerate it. But then he had gone and managed to do it again. "Manage. *Man-age*," she murmured to herself, laughing ruefully at the pun. If it were called *womanage* she didn't think so many men would believe it was their right to do it.

They all filed into the dining room after Sarah had directed one of the girls to fetch tea.

Della sat first, and her sisters and Sarah took chairs all around her, Mr. Wattings seated the farthest from her.

"Well," she began.

"Well," Eleanor echoed in an encouraging tone after a few moments.

"I suppose you want to know why I am so . . . agitated," Della said, glancing at each of the faces in turn.

Sarah reached over and took Della's hand. "You know you don't have to tell us."

"Yes, she does," Olivia contradicted.

"For once, I agree with Olivia," Ida added in a dry tone. "If we don't know what is happening with you, we cannot help. And I believe it is important to share one's true feelings with one's siblings."

"Oh, like how you told us all how you felt about your husband?" Olivia rolled her eyes at Ida.

Ida waved her hand dismissively. "I did eventually. But I am not the point here. Focus, Olivia."

Della felt a tiny warmth kindling the cold anger that was roiling inside her. It would be all right, as long as she had her family: Nora, Sarah, her sisters, and now Mr. Wattings.

"Well," Della began again. "It seems Mr. Baxter is back in town. And that Lord Stanbury has seen fit to deal with him directly without informing me."

Chapter 21

Well, you've really mucked it up now."

Griffith glared at Frederick, who merely raised one eyebrow, a mild expression on his face.

"I've got to agree with Duke here," Hyland said before downing the rest of the brown liquid in his glass.

"Your Grace, you heathen," Frederick said, but his tone was amused.

"Yes, you really did," Clark agreed, pouring more alcohol into everyone's glasses. Griffith shook his head no when it came to his turn.

The last thing he needed was to be drunk when it came time to talk to her. Which, since he was more than finished with being patient, since that had gotten him nowhere, would be in the time it took to go to her house, get let in— probably an easy task since clearly she had no butler—and apologize profusely.

"Do you know what you're going to say? You are going to talk to her, aren't you?" Frederick asked, taking a sip from his glass.

Griffith frowned at his cousin. "Should you be drinking? I mean, aren't you—you know?"

"Dying?" Frederick supplied. He grinned at Griffith. "Well, no, as it happens. I am sorry to disappoint you, but it seems I have a weak constitution, but as long as I take care of myself and drink some ghastly concoctions the new doctors have prescribed, I will be here a long time. I know you were looking forward to being duke too."

Griffith was leaping out of his chair as soon as Frederick said "no," and was hoisting him up, clasping him in a huge hug.

"I knew it was a good idea to have you see more doctors," he said.

"Don't squeeze me too hard," Frederick said, his voice muffled. "Weak constitution, remember?"

"Put him down, Griff," Hyland demanded.

Griffith complied, setting Frederick down as gently as he could.

"This means you could return to sea, you know," Frederick said.

Griffith stared at Frederick as his words swirled in his head.

Return to sea? Be the captain of his own ship again? Not have to attend parties and wear clothing that would tear if he moved a muscle?

The thought was alluring, and certainly what he had dreamt of when he'd first returned home.

"Return to sea. You hear that, Captain?" Clark said. It was as if Griffith was hearing the words through a fog.

Griffith felt as though his heart was being squeezed.

But—

But—

But then there wouldn't be her.

Life at sea was unsettled. Life could literally capsize in an instant, and he knew that she would never subject her daughter to that.

And he didn't want it anymore either.

He wanted to be settled.

He wanted to have vigorous, frequent sex with her in a bed that was properly sized and immobile, unless they were the ones moving it. He wanted to get to know her sisters, and her best friend. He wanted to argue with her, and have her call him Lord Handsome and then watch her stand up for herself.

Most of all, he wanted *her*.

"He's a goner," Hyland commented, shaking his head as though disappointed. But he had a grin on his face that contradicted his demeanor.

"Damn it," Griffith said. "I am."

"So you'll be staying here, then?" Frederick asked.

"If I can get her to agree to it," Griffith replied in a gruff voice.

Clark waved his concern away. "You can persuade anyone of anything. You got me and Hyland here to stop arguing, that was a miracle."

"Especially since all Clark is good for is reading maps and issuing orders," Hyland said.

"Whereas all you're good for is scurrying up ropes and causing trouble," Clark replied.

"Let me solve one dispute at a time," Griffith said, holding his hands up in supplication. "First let me go resolve things with my lady, and then we can return to which of you louts is the worst. And then I'll have to tell the crew." He looked at Frederick. "You have some jobs that need filling, don't you?"

Frederick nodded. "Now that I'll be here to oversee the work? You have my word there will be enough positions."

"Thank you," Griffith said, exhaling.

"Good luck, cousin," Frederick said as he raised his glass. "Bring me back a duchess-to-be."

Griffith nodded. "I'm going to try my damnedest."

Olivia, bless her impetuous heart, thought that Lord Stanbury had only done what was necessary in the moment.

Eleanor wished he had consulted with her first, which was a mild version of how Della felt.

Ida sniffed in disdain at hearing how he hadn't bothered to tell her at all, and had, in fact, heard her out without disclosing his own information.

Whereas Sarah just held her hand and shot her concerned looks.

Pearl and Mr. Wattings were both quietly sympathetic, but Della couldn't blame them, given how many words both Olivia and Ida had spoken.

"The door," Sarah said, tilting her head to listen.

"Drat, and I don't think anybody is out there," Della said, rising from the table.

"They're all getting your tea," Sarah replied pointedly.

"Hush, you." Della shot her friend a grin as she walked out toward the front door. Her family was here for her, and even if her heart was completely and thoroughly broken—plus she'd confessed she loved him, and she wished she didn't feel so humiliated about that right now—at least they were all there and supporting her.

While also arguing about the best way to support her. Which was the way of all the best families, she supposed.

She flung the door open, gasping as she saw him, his size nearly filling the frame of the door.

"Evening, my lady." He swept his hat off his head and held it in front of himself.

He looked nervous.

He should look nervous.

Because she was still angry.

And she was now angry at herself for not anticipating he might show up on her doorstep.

"Who is it—oh!" Sarah exclaimed as she strode across the hall.

"Captain, if the lady says you are to go . . ." Mr. Wattings began as he followed his wife.

Her sisters came out too, standing behind her as though preparing for battle. She hoped Ida's face wasn't too fearsome, not that it would scare him away.

"Della, do you want—?" Olivia said.

Della held her hand up. "Hold on. You do all know I can take care of myself? That is the whole point, isn't it?"

She heard their murmurs of assent.

"Will you speak with me, my lady?" he asked.

He still looked nervous. Though, to his credit, he didn't look more nervous now, even after all of her family was ranged in back of her.

"I will."

Olivia uttered a squawk of protest that was quickly stifled, likely by Ida's glower.

She turned to them. "I can handle this by myself. You should all go."

The sisters filed out the front door, Ida tossing Lord Stanbury one more derisive look, Olivia trying to whisper in Della's ear until she waved her sister away. Sarah and Mr. Wattings disappeared down the back stairs.

And he was still standing at the door, to one

side so he could allow the remaining duke's daughters to exit.

"Come in, then," she said, not waiting to see if he would follow before returning to the dining room.

Of course she felt him at her back—all that huge, glorious, muscled warmth that still made her a bit gooey inside, even though she was still mad at him.

She held the door open as he entered, then shut it firmly behind them as she gestured to a chair.

"Sit."

He didn't argue. He likely didn't dare.

Something must be wrong with her that she thoroughly enjoyed that.

She remained standing, folding her arms over her chest. Tapping her foot.

"Well?" she asked at last.

He still looked nervous.

Although there was something in his gaze, something predatory, that made her shudder in a delicious way.

Oh dear. Perhaps she didn't have the upper hand after all.

"I am sorry," he said at last. "I did the wrong thing. I didn't respect your wishes. I wanted to help so desperately that I ignored how strongly you felt, and I did what I thought was best. I didn't ask you. I just—did."

She nodded, but didn't say anything.

"And," he continued, closing his eyes as if in concentration, "I have to admit that the idea of me helping you was so compelling I didn't even stop to think about how you would feel." He opened his eyes. "Your father is even worse than you'd intimated. I wanted to protect you from having to deal with him and from ever having to see that Baxter." He spat the name out, making Della wish she felt like smiling.

But she didn't. She was still angry.

"You're so fiercely independent, Della. I thought that if there was a way to relieve some of what you carry around every day it would be an honor. I was an idiot—"

"You were," she interrupted.

"But I hoped that you might be . . ." And he paused, and she could see him wince as the word came to him.

"Grateful?" she supplied.

He closed his eyes again, and swallowed.

"Yes."

A moment as she processed what he'd said, and how she felt, and what she wanted to do now.

She wanted to forgive him. But she wanted something else too.

"Thank you for that," she said in a quiet voice. His eyes opened, and he looked relieved. Until her next words. "You might be sorry," she continued, raising her chin, "but do you understand?"

He began to nod, then caught himself, taking a

deep breath. "Explain it to me," he said. "Please," he added, after a moment.

It was the "please" that made her heart soften, just a little.

Well, that plus how ridiculously large and handsome he was. And how clearly he was suffering.

There was definitely something wrong with her.

But something she wanted to explore.

"Take your jacket off," she demanded.

He looked puzzled for a moment, but then did as she asked, placing the jacket on the dining room table.

It wasn't enough.

"Undo your cravat."

He did, his fingers working swiftly to undo the fabric, tossing it on top of his coat.

His throat was bare, and she could see his strong neck. Her teeth practically ached to bite him.

"Put your hands on your thighs."

He complied, and she wished his alacrity at obeying her didn't make her so tingly. But she couldn't lie to herself, could she?

It absolutely did.

She walked toward him, keeping her gaze on his face. He looked up at her, immobile, as though knowing he shouldn't move.

She reached him, then bent down to spread his knees apart. "Keep your hands there," she ordered.

He nodded, and she glanced down to confirm

he hadn't moved. Well. She also saw something else—just how aroused he was.

It seemed as though he might be enjoying this also.

She stepped between his legs, placing her hands on his shoulders to support herself. Then she swung one leg over one of his, then the other, so she was splayed out on his lap.

"Hands there," she reminded him as she felt his body start to shift as though to embrace her.

"Whatever you want," he replied, his voice a harsh rasp. She felt his erection against her, hard and urgent, and unable to ignore.

She slid her hands around his neck, pulling her body up against his. Placing that part of her that burned against his cock.

Oh. That felt good.

His jaw was clamped, and she could feel how he was keeping himself still—for her. Because that was what she wanted.

It felt delicious.

She leaned forward to place her mouth against his neck, sliding her right hand over his shoulder and down onto his chest. His firm, glorious chest.

"Can I touch you?" he asked in a ragged whisper.

"No," she replied, shaking her head. She dragged her teeth over the strong cords of his neck, feeling him shudder.

"You're going to let me do whatever I want to you," she continued. "Is that understood?"

"Yes."

Oh. The feeling that consumed her when he said "yes" so simply, so earnestly. As though he knew what it meant to her.

She hoped he knew what it meant to her. If he didn't after everything, then he wasn't who she believed herself to be in love with.

She rocked herself against him as she sucked his neck, her fingers undoing the few buttons of his shirt. She slid her hand down and tugged it from the waistband, yanking it up until it couldn't go any farther because it was trapped by his arms.

"Raise your hands," she commanded, and he did, allowing her to slide the shirt off his body.

He was breathing heavily, as was she. His gaze intent upon her face as though focused entirely on her.

The way she wanted it.

"Put your hands back on your thighs," she continued.

She flung the shirt behind her, where it presumably landed on the carpet. She moistened her lips as she looked at him—at his heavily muscled chest, at the strain in his arms as he resisted the urge to touch her.

She lowered her lips to his nipple, drew it into her mouth and sucked gently. She heard his quick intake of breath, and could feel how his cock twitched. She smiled against his skin.

Her left hand found his other nipple, and she

rubbed it gently, sliding the pad of her finger over it, feeling the coarse hairs on his chest tickle her palm.

He was solidly, hugely masculine, and he was entirely under her control.

It felt intoxicating.

"Are you trying to drive me mad?" he asked, his voice a low growl.

She shifted so her sex was pressed more against his cock, and then drew back, then forward in a slow rhythm.

She gave one final flick of her tongue to his nipple, then drew back, holding on to both his arms as she met his gaze.

"Perhaps. I am proving a point."

His mouth twitched into a slight smile, and she saw his eyes glint mischievously. Good.

"Then by all means, prove away. I look forward to you reaching your . . . conclusion," he said with a sly grin.

"Mmm," she said, before sliding back into him. His hard cock gave just the right amount of pressure on her, and she let out a soft moan, making his eyes narrow.

"Please, Della, let me touch you," he pleaded.

She shook her head, still working herself on him. "No. Not without my permission."

"I'll do whatever you want, Della. Just let me touch you," he said.

"No."

He let out a frustrated noise, and she bit her lip to keep from laughing. But he did as she wanted, keeping his hands clamped on his thighs as she pressed herself against him, finding the rhythm that was speeding her toward her orgasm.

And then— "Ahhh," she cried out as she came, flinging her head back as she held on to his shoulders.

"Goddamn it, Della, but you are so glorious," he said after the waves of pleasure had subsided. "Please tell me you forgive me."

She got off his legs, shaking her skirts out, unable to keep from staring at his broad chest and the erection that was tenting his trousers.

He was so glorious too.

"I know you said you were sorry, but I wanted to make sure you truly understood. That while there are things that are good—very good," she said, raking her gaze over him, "if it's not under your control, if you're told what to do, then it doesn't matter how good the thing is. It's still not yours. Someone else owns it. Not you."

He didn't say anything for a moment, and then he nodded. "I understand. I promise never to wrest control away from you ever again." And then he gave a wolfish grin. "But if you wanted to hear what I would do to you if you let me move my hands," he said, glancing down at his legs, "then I would be more than happy to comply. As in all things with you, Della."

It was a vow and a promise. And she believed him.

"I forgive you," she said at last, and then he smiled, a warm, wondrous smile that made her insides melt. As though he'd been worried the entire time that she wouldn't—that she'd do what she wanted to him, and then just leave.

I FORGIVE YOU.

"Thank you," he replied. It was taking all of his will not to leap up out of the chair and take her in his arms. But he knew just how important it was to her, and so he was willing to cede control.

Plus the way she'd demonstrated her needs was so very delightful.

If agonizing. His whole body burned where she'd touched him—his chest, his neck, his shoulders, and, of course his cock, which throbbed, unfulfilled, in his trousers.

"What do you want to do?" she asked in a sultry tone of voice.

Dear Lord, thank God you asked.

"If I may?" he said, glancing down at his hands.

"Yes. You can do whatever you want."

Permission. Permission to touch her, to tell her what he was thinking, to fuck her so hard they both saw stars.

"First I want this gown off. You're far too dressed for my taste."

He rose as he spoke, stalking toward her with

a definite purpose. She spun so her back was to him, and his fingers went to the tiny buttons at the back of her gown, undoing each one as swiftly as he could.

He heard her chuckle, and then she shifted back so her arse was nestled in his groin.

"You'll be the death of me, woman," he growled.

She glanced back at him, a mischievous look on her face. "Surely a little death will be welcome?"

"You shouldn't know that term, you're a lady," he admonished mockingly.

She rolled her eyes. "I'm no lady, just as you're no gentleman. We're man and woman, and what we do and say to one another is between us."

That was truly what she wanted, wasn't it? To be equal partners. Not having to rely on one another for anything, but knowing they could depend on one another for everything.

He wanted the same thing.

Should he propose now? While her gown was half off, his upper half was entirely bare, and she had just brought herself off against his cock?

It would be unorthodox, to be sure, but their whole relationship was distinctly different, so perhaps he should.

The thought receded when she reached behind herself to rub his erection. "Mmm," she said, wiggling in closer.

He'd propose later. Now he just wanted to bury himself inside her.

He undid the last button and tugged her sleeves off her arms, then pushed the fabric of her gown so it pooled at her feet. She stepped out of the circle of fabric, wearing her corset and shift. He undid the laces, then practically tore that off her, then yanked her shift up over her head so all she was wearing were her shoes and stockings.

She bent to undo them, but he put a hand at the small of her back. "Wait. I want you to keep those on," he said.

The stockings were pale pink, with darker pink ribbons at the top. Her shoes were ridiculously delicate slippers, achingly soft and feminine.

"And you?" she said, pointing her chin toward his trousers.

"Do you want to help?" he asked, placing his hands at his waistband.

"Indeed I do," she said, stepping forward to him. Her breasts were inches away from his chest. They were beautiful, like the rest of her, her pink nipples matching the color of her stockings.

Her fingers went to the placket of his trousers and she began to undo the buttons as he held his breath.

And then his cock sprang free and he gasped as she slid her hand into his smallclothes to clasp her fingers around him. He shoved his trousers down, then bent down to wrap his arm around her knees and hoisted her up against his chest, then strode over to the dining room table. He lowered her gently onto the wooden surface, then climbed up on top of her.

Her eyes were laughing, and he grinned in response.

He'd never imagined he would be having so much fun during sex. But this was her, and everything she did was exuberant and delightful.

He slid down her body and placed his mouth on her, feeling her shudder as his tongue flicked her nub.

"Oh," she sighed, and her hands went to bury themselves in his hair. She held him firmly in place—not that he was planning on going anywhere—and he licked and sucked her, adjusting the rhythm as he gauged her response.

Her thighs were clamped around him, and then she was crying out again as he brought her to climax, his fingers and tongue and teeth working her to ecstasy.

His cock was so hard it was painful. But it was worth the wait to taste her.

"Oh," she sighed again, then uttered a soft laugh. "You did promise, didn't you?"

"Are you satisfied?" he asked.

"Mmm-hmm. But you're not." She slid her hand between them and wrapped her fingers around his shaft, drawing him toward her entrance. "I want you to fuck me, Captain Enormous," she said as she put him inside.

"Gladly, Lady Adventurous," he replied.

And then finally he was inside her, her warm, soft heat surrounding him. She grabbed his arse, holding him to her as he began to thrust.

He didn't know how long he could last. Not when she was biting her lip, her head thrown back, her breasts jiggling against his chest. Her fingers digging into his buttocks, her passage tight.

He kept moving, faster and faster, his orgasm building until he couldn't hold out any longer, and he withdrew, spilling on her stomach, his hand gripping his shaft as he exploded.

"Mmm," she murmured when his cock had finally stopped jerking. "That was lovely."

He collapsed beside her on the table, not caring that the hard wood was likely bruising both of their bodies. He could handle it if she could, and he already knew she could handle anything.

His Della. His love.

Chapter 22

*D*ella didn't want this moment to end, although she had to admit it wasn't entirely comfortable lying on a dining room table.

In fact, not comfortable at all.

She shifted, propping herself up on her hand to look at him. He gazed back at her, a deep warmth in his eyes.

And she panicked, which she shouldn't have. She knew that. Still— "Wait," she said, placing her hand over his mouth when he was opening it to speak. "Wait until later. I need to take care of a few things first." She grabbed the table cloth and cleaned herself off.

His expression made it look as though he would argue, but eventually he nodded, and she removed her hand as she drew herself up to get off the table. She cast one last regretful look at him, spread out like a banquet just for her, then picked up her shift and put it on, then her corset, and then shook out her gown and stepped into it.

"Can you do me up?" she asked, turning her back to him.

"I'd rather not," he replied, but she heard him move and begin to do up the buttons.

"I promise we'll talk later about all this, but I don't want to until I know—"

"Until you know what? Isn't it enough to know that I lo—?"

"Shh," she said, giving him a reproachful look. "Don't distract me with your powers of persuasion, which are mighty. First you need to tell me where I will find Mr. Baxter. And I promise, I will come see you in a few hours."

He told her without hesitation. Just that; not insisting he go with her, or urge her not to do anything reckless. She'd do what she wanted to do, and he respected that.

He wouldn't try to stop her. He knew her. He understood her, even if he didn't understand what she had to do before deciding everything.

"Sarah?" Della called outside her friend's room.

The door opened, and Sarah poked her head out, a knowing look on her face as she surveyed Della's state of attire.

"I gather you accepted his apology?" Sarah said in a dry tone of voice.

Della rolled her eyes at her friend. "Yes, you know I did. You knew I would. I can't believe I've fallen in love with him, but there you go."

"And Mr. Baxter?"

Della's mouth tightened into a thin line. "I am going to see him and deal with him myself. And then, if you wish, we can go see your parents. You deserve an explanation as to why they lied to Henry."

Sarah's expression darkened. "Thank you, but that's not necessary. You've done enough. I need to do this on my own. Well, on my and Henry's own. Besides," she continued in a lighter tone, "I think you'll have your hands full with Mr. Baxter."

"If they're not wrapped around his throat," Della replied.

"And I wanted to speak with you anyway," Sarah continued. "Henry and I have had an offer from the Duke of Northam. He's asked us to come live with him. I'll be his nurse, and Henry will work in the gardens. There is a school being planned there so I can continue teaching as well, if I want. It's a generous offer."

"What about when—?" Della asked.

Sarah smiled. "He's ill, but his doctors say he's got more time now. I'm sorry you won't be a duchess soon."

"I'm not sorry at all," Della retorted. "Does Griffith know?"

Sarah nodded. "The duke told him just recently."

"He'll be so relieved," Della said. She had seen how much Griffith cared for his cousin.

"It will be a good place for Emily to live. As long as you, Nora, and Lord Stanbury promise to visit often."

Della squeezed Sarah's hands, then wrapped her friend in an impulsive hug. "I am so glad for you," she whispered.

"And I you," Sarah replied in a soft voice. "Please try not to murder anyone before you get your happily-ever-after."

Della stepped back, laughing. "I will do what I can."

"Never?" his boatswain's mate said after Griffith had spoken.

Clark and Hyland had done good work assembling as much of the crew as they could find—they were in the pub where Griffith had first seen her. When his life had changed so dramatically, even though he hadn't known it at the time.

The ale was still mediocre, but his crew didn't seem to care, especially since Griffith was paying.

"Never," Griffith confirmed. "You'll have to sail on without me, lads." He took a sip from his glass. "I'll supply references for anybody who wants one. And if you decide you don't wish to return to sea after all—if you want to follow my example— there's work to be had with the Duke of Northam."

"Huh," his master-at-arms said. "I wonder what life would be like on steady land."

"It's not half-bad, men," Hyland said. He held his mostly drunk ale in his hand, which he pointed toward Griffith. "The captain here is settling down. Mebbe it's time some of us do the same."

Griffith grinned at Hyland, who could always be counted on to support his captain, no matter what. Even if—and especially if—it meant arguing with Clark.

"Three cheers for the captain!" the coxswain said.

"Hip hip hooray! Hip hip hooray! Hip hip hooray!"

Griffith glanced around the room, at the men holding their glasses up to him, at Clark and Hyland, both of whom had smug looks on their faces.

It was time to come home. It was time to settle down. He wasn't the boy who'd run off to sea twelve years ago, nor was he the man who'd ended up the captain of his own ship.

He was ready to share his life with an equal partner. His Della. His love.

MR. BAXTER—SHE refused to even think of him by his given name—opened the door to his room, then tried to slam it on her just as quickly, but she shoved her foot in so he couldn't.

He glared at her foot, then at her face, then opened the door wider. "I suppose you'll have to come in."

"I suppose so," she replied, walking into the room.

It was untidy, his possessions scattered around like they'd been tossed by an unruly wind. He'd been that way when they'd been together as well—she was always scurrying after him, picking things up. Until she'd decided he could pick his own things up, she wasn't going to bother anymore.

"Why are you here, Della?" he asked. "I was expecting your father, or that large gentleman who came to see me."

"I'm here to see what you want. And to ensure you don't get it," she replied flatly. "I won't allow you to blackmail anybody on my behalf. I came to tell you I don't care what you say to anybody. You have no right to ask for anything after what you did."

His expression got mean, and she reminded herself he had no hold over her. Not any longer. Not ever, in fact.

It had been she who had delayed their marriage. She'd known almost as soon as she'd eloped with him that he wasn't who she wished to be with, so although he'd asked, she'd prevaricated so as not to commit. Not until she was certain.

And then she was certain—certain she didn't want to be with him.

"So if I announce I am in town and that you refuse to let me see my daughter?"

She moved so she was mere inches from his face. He stepped back, an apprehensive expression on his face. "You gave up any right to being Nora's father when you left us. You will not dare to stir up any kind of trouble." She dug in her pocket, withdrawing the bills she'd placed there before leaving the house. "You can have this. It is all you will ever get from me or anybody related to me."

He stared at the bills, his lip curling.

"Take it or don't take it, I don't care. As long as you leave London and never try to see us again."

He snatched the bills from her hand. "And if I go see your father? He'll say the same?"

"If you do, I will tell everyone our story. Do you understand? I don't care. I don't want you interfering in my family, in my life, any longer. My parents might be ashamed of what happened, and wish to shield their own reputation, but I don't care. I'll burn it all to the ground if you do anything besides leaving London."

His face grew pale, and she could see when he'd realized it was useless to argue with her. That she was going to do what she said, no matter what anybody else tried to do.

"Fine," he spat out.

She nodded at him, then turned on her heel and left the room, allowing a smirk of satisfaction to curl her mouth when she heard the door slam behind her.

Now she could get on with her life.

"SHE'S HERE," CLARK said as he opened the door to Griffith's bedroom.

And she was, because she was behind Clark, pushing the door open and striding in as though she belonged there.

At least that was what he was hoping—that she would belong with him.

"If you'll excuse me, my lady," Clark said with a wink in Griffith's direction. He shut the door firmly behind himself, and she drew near.

"How did it go?" he asked.

She shrugged. "He won't be a problem any longer."

Of course he wanted to know everything, but more importantly, he wanted to know what she would say when he asked her.

"Della, I—" he began.

He stopped speaking when she drew the skirts of her gown up and knelt down on the carpet, looking up at him.

"What are you doing?" he asked.

She smiled. "Asking you."

"Asking me . . . ?"

"My dearest Lord Captain Handsome Enormous Arrogant," she said in a formal tone of voice. "Would you do me the great honor of becoming my husband?"

As she spoke, she held the fake-engagement ring they'd bought together up to him. Its stones glinted in the light.

"You're proposing to me?" he asked, glancing between the ring and her face.

She nodded. "I wish to marry you. I want to spend the rest of my life with you. I won't promise to obey you—"

"Of course not."

"But I will trust, honor, and love you forever."

He put his hand out to take the ring.

"No, not until you answer," she said, pulling it back.

He got down on the rug too, wrapping her in his arms and gazing at her face. "Yes. Yes, I will marry you. I love you, Della."

"And I you."

They both looked at his hand as she slid the ring onto his pinky finger.

"Tell me again," she said.

"I love you."

"Now kiss me."

"So demanding," he said as he complied.

Epilogue

"This is it," Della said as Sarah gave one last adjustment to her veil. They stood just outside the Duke of Northam's ballroom. While the duke was feeling better, Griffith wanted his cousin to be as comfortable as possible—which meant having the ceremony close to home. Plus there weren't a lot of guests—they only wanted people who truly wished to be there, not people who saw it as a social opportunity. Or people who'd disowned her, which was why her parents were not in attendance.

"This is it," Sarah repeated, stepping back to admire her handiwork. "You look lovely."

"And nervous," Della added. She stepped up to the glass and regarded her reflection. Her cheeks shone pink, even through the lace of the veil.

But she had to admit Sarah was right; she did look lovely.

The gown was white, with roses made of white fabric at the neckline. More roses were scattered on the gown's skirt, which also had a few rows of ruffles near the hem.

Della didn't usually like anything so fussy, but today she wanted all the fuss and intricacy she'd planned to deny herself when she was set against marriage. So when the dressmaker suggested row upon row of laced sleeves? Della had agreed happily, and was pleased to be looking like, as Nora had said, *the most delicious wedding cake ever made.*

The veil was held in place by a diamond diadem, which caught the light, sending sparkled reflections into the mirror and the walls. She wore diamond earrings and a string of pearls around her neck.

The only thing that wasn't as traditional as possible was her engagement ring—Griffith still wore her ring, the one she'd proposed with, so she was wearing one of his rings.

It was much larger on her hand than on his, of course, so she had to tuck something inside to make it stay on. He'd had it made from one of the buttons from his captain's uniform for him and his closest sailors, all of whom were remaining on land to work for him or the duke. Griffith had agreed to assist Frederick with his projects, and Della had urged him to hire her rescues to help out.

It was a happy ending for all, it seemed.

"It's time," Sarah said in a soft voice. She turned to look at the other bridesmaids, all of Della's sisters, plus Nora and Emily. "Ladies? Let us go get this woman respectably married."

The bridesmaids walked forward in a sea of pinks, blues, and greens, matching favors pinned to their shoulders. Nora and Emily each carried a basket of orange blossoms, which they'd had to be reminded not to strew on the ground until the ceremony began.

"Nora and Emily, you can start," Della said.

The girls smiled, dipping their hands into the baskets and dropping blossoms on the path into the ballroom.

Della took a deep breath as her sisters walked ahead of her, Sarah at her side.

Griffith stood at the front of the room, his expression focused. His mouth curled into a secret smile of welcome as he saw her. She walked slowly to the front keeping her gaze locked on him as his was on hers.

And then she was there. Standing next to him, seeing his magnificent handsomeness through the gauzy veil, feeling how her heart was beating and knowing, with absolute certainty, that this was what she wanted to do.

"You are so beautiful," he murmured as he took her hand.

"As are you," she replied.

"I know," he said.

She suppressed a snort. She didn't think it was traditional to laugh during one's own wedding ceremony. Although they weren't a traditional couple, despite her wedding attire.

And then, finally, the clergyman pronounced them man and wife, and Griffith turned to her, lifting her veil as he gazed into her eyes.

He lowered his mouth to hers, giving her a gentle kiss that wasn't at all like the last one they'd had—that would definitely not be traditional and might shock the guests as well.

He drew back, his eyes damp with tears. She thought she might have been crying too. "I love you," he said.

"I love you," she replied, swallowing hard against all the emotion. She never thought she'd be a bride, and yet here she was.

He was hers. He would be hers forever.

And she was so happy.

Don't miss the other delightful and
sexy stories in Megan Frampton's
the Duke's Daughters series!

Lady Be Daring

Lady Be Reckless

Lady Be Bad

Available now from Avon Books!